HEARTWARMING

His Twin Baby Surprise

——

USA TODAY Bestselling Author

Patricia Forsythe

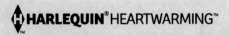

Recycling programs
for this product may
not exist in your area.

ISBN-13: 978-0-373-36835-8

His Twin Baby Surprise

Copyright © 2017 by Patricia Knoll

Printed in U.S.A.

HARLEQUIN®
™ www.Harlequin.com

"Is something wrong?" Lisa asked, but the ultrasound technician was gone.

Ben took her hand and this time, she didn't resist. "If she's not back in two minutes I'll go find her," he promised. "Along with the doctor."

"What...what do you think is wrong?"

"Probably nothing. Let's wait and see."

The technician brought the doctor back quickly. He was an older man whose white hair and smiling demeanor inspired confidence.

"Hello, Mr. and Mrs. Thomas. I'm Dr. Harber and I just want to check something here."

Neither Lisa nor Ben corrected him on their names, but watched as he moved the wand slowly across her belly. After a minute, he said, "You're probably wondering what we're seeing. It takes a little practice to distinguish it exactly." He pointed to the screen. "Right here, we have a head, and over here is another head."

Lisa's voice squeaked as she squeezed Ben's hand and asked, "I'm having a two-headed baby?"

Dr. Harber chuckled. "No, of course not. There are also four arms, four legs, and two bodies. You're having twins."

Dear Reader,

Welcome back to Reston, Oklahoma. If this is your first visit, I hope you enjoy this quirky small town and its colorful characters. *His Twin Baby Surprise* is the third book in the Oklahoma Girls miniseries and features Lisa Thomas and Ben McAdams who grew up together, but who have very different goals in life. Lisa is a hardworking, focused Realtor who wants to bring jobs and prosperity to her hometown. She leaves nothing to chance. Ben is a former professional football player who now has charities and businesses all over the world. He is charming and laid-back and has no intention of putting down roots anywhere. Their plans are derailed when they meet unexpectedly far from Reston—a meeting that will have unexpected consequences for them both.

I hope that Lisa and Ben's journey to love and accept each other is one you will love.

Happy reading!

Patricia

Patricia Forsythe is the author of many romance novels and is proud to have received her twenty-five-book pin from Harlequin. She hopes there are many more books to come. A native Arizonan, Patricia loves setting books in areas where she has spent time, like the beautiful Kiamichi Mountains of Oklahoma. She has held a number of jobs, including teaching school, working as a librarian and as a secretary, and operating a care home for developmentally disabled children. Her favorite occupation, though, is writing novels in which the characters get into challenging situations and then work their way out. Each situation and set of characters is different, so sometimes the finished book is as much of a surprise to her as it is to the readers.

This book is dedicated to my granddaughters—
Ashley, Alicia, Madison, Tamsin, Fiona and
Eleanor. May life always bring you joy.

PROLOGUE

INSIDE THE RESTON COUNTY sheriff's station, Fred Jepson was wondering about the wisdom of having eaten a whole meat pie for lunch.

Mary Alice made them down at the café and he couldn't resist them. They were huge—flaky pastry stuffed with meat and potatoes. Enough for two people, but he always ate the whole thing. Why let it go to waste? Why hurt Mary Alice's feelings? And that chocolate cake she made? It was enough to make a grown man weep. He'd had to have a piece of that.

What Fred didn't doubt was the wisdom of bringing in the McAdams boy. Ben was in the holding cell in the next room, eating the sandwich Fred had brought back for him. The cell had a cot, a sink, a toilet and nothing else. Worked out fine for the usual lawbreakers and the drunks who didn't need to be on the road on a Saturday night. A little stark and scary for a twelve-year-old, but the kid had to learn a lesson about hurting other people, about obeying the law. Better to have him here overnight now for shooting Mrs. Crabtree in the butt with a stone from his slingshot than in jail for months or years down the road for a felony.

As the sheriff, duly elected by the citizens of Reston County, he felt an obligation to set the boy on the right path.

Fred snorted. Who gave their kids a slingshot anymore? Jim and Helen were pushovers. That kid of theirs got everything he wanted just by grinning and showing his dimples.

He leaned back in his chair and loosened his belt. That was a little better. He glanced around to make sure he was alone, though he knew that all but one of his deputies was on patrol or at lunch. Deputy Earl Flake was out back, tinkering with the engine on an old cruiser, sure he could make it run again.

The office receptionist, Anita Sturm, had decided the refrigerator in the break room was disgusting and was cleaning it out. When he'd peeked in earlier, she'd been half wedged inside the freezer, scrubbing to her heart's content. Fred knew better than to get in her way when she was in a cleaning mood. He'd thoughtfully closed the door to the break room so she could work in peace and could say as many angry things as she needed to about the unsanitary habits of certain men she knew. He'd told her he'd answer the phone if it rang, but he didn't expect any calls. The town was pretty quiet at lunchtime.

He unsnapped his pants and slid down the zipper just to give his gut room to breathe for a few minutes. He'd fasten himself up again as soon as he heard someone at the outer door.

He'd gained weight in the past few months. He knew it and he was going to do something about it soon, probably tomorrow. If he had to chase down a runner, he'd be screwed. His uniform was too tight and he could barely fasten his belt, even on the last notch, but he refused to buy a larger size. He was going to lose weight and get back in shape soon.

He returned to thinking about Ben. The boy was in the sixth grade now, big for his age and eager to play football. Football was a religion in Reston. Jim McAdams, Fred's old high school rival, had been its deity during his school days. He wanted the same for his son.

Jim would have that if Ben didn't end up in juvenile detention first. The family didn't realize it, but Fred was doing them a favor by scaring some sense into their boy right now.

He was still considering that when the door to the outer office was thrown open, reverberating against the wall. Startled, Fred jerked upright. No one came in, but he craned his neck to see five kids scuffling in the dirt, fighting, clawing and kicking. Their howls echoed into the jail as they shrieked and tumbled.

Fred pushed his chair back and lumbered to his feet, forgetting about his pants as the weight of his utility belt dragged them down and they started to slip.

His horrified attention was on the kids. There was something wrong with their faces. Their features seemed to be smashed in. It was several seconds before he realized they were all wearing stockings over their heads. One kid had a pair of pantyhose over his, the legs tied up in a kind of crazy ponytail that bobbed on top of his head. Or her head. Fred couldn't tell.

"Hey, what's going on here? Stop that right now. You can't be fighting like that."

They ignored him, continuing to punch and kick as they howled and screamed, kicking up dust and knocking over a trash can. They banged up against the side of the building as they called each other names, the yelling so loud and crazy he couldn't make sense of what they were saying.

"Stop! Stop!" Fred bellowed. He started around the side of the desk, forgetting about his pants, which immediately fell to his knees, hobbling him. He tripped and went down like two hundred and fifty pounds of wet cement, face-first. Instantly the fighting outside paused and he heard footsteps running toward him.

"Sorry, Sheriff Jepson," one of them growled in an obvious effort to disguise his voice. "Just…just stay down, okay?"

"What? Stop. What are you doing?" Fred couldn't get up and he couldn't turn over because of the way his pants had twisted around his knees.

"Get the key! Get the key!" the kids were shouting in unison from where they crowded around the door.

He could hear one of them scrambling through the items on his desk, opening drawers and riffling through.

"I got it!" the kid shrieked.

Fred couldn't tell who it was—who any of them were. He groaned when one of them crouched on his back to keep him down. Blackness was closing in on him. Mary Alice's meat pie threatened to make a second appearance.

He managed to turn his head to the side enough to see one of the kids run toward the other room. He heard the rattle of the key in the lock of the holding cell. A moment later that same kid ran past with Ben in tow.

The boy was yelling, "Are you crazy? My dad woulda got me out."

The kid who was pulling him responded, "Shut up and come on. We're heading for the border. My uncle Lester's been in jail for years and Grandpa says he'll never get out."

"I'm not your uncle Lester. How come you think you're the boss of everybody?"

"I'm standing up for my friend," the kid insisted. "You gotta think about your future. You don't want to be a criminal."

"I ain't a criminal, and you didn't let me finish my sandwich."

"Oh, quit thinking about your stomach."

"I don't need you to—" Ben started to say but the other kid jerked him out the door.

Fred heard feet running away, and the one sitting on his back jumped up, freeing him. Pushing himself up onto his elbows, he cursed.

His prisoner was in the wind.

CHAPTER ONE

Twenty years later

LISA THOMAS STARED at the row of pregnancy tests—six of them—lined up on the table in front of her like crestfallen soldiers who had let their leader go down in defeat.

"They're all positive." Gemma Whitmire, one of her best friends since childhood, sat beside her. Carly Joslin, her other best friend, sat, too, and scooted her chair in closer.

They were in one of the examination rooms of the Sunshine Birthing Center, which Gemma had founded for the benefit of the women of Reston County. The walls were painted a soothing pale green, but the color did nothing to calm Lisa's distress.

Her eyes full of tears, and her lips trembling, she asked, "You don't think they could be lying?"

Gemma gave her a gentle smile, her eyes

sympathetic. "What would be their motive? They're inanimate objects. They would have no reason to lie. I've been a midwife for a long time, Lisa, so I can tell you that pregnancy tests, especially six of them done at the same time, are going to be truthful."

Panic fluttered in Lisa's throat as she looked around. "But we're in your birthing center. Don't you have a...another test I can take?"

"The ones here at the Sunshine Birthing Center aren't any different than those you bought at the pharmacy."

In desperation Lisa turned to clutch at Gemma's hands, holding them with her shaking fingers. She knew her hair was frazzled and messy because she'd been sitting and holding her head in her hands while she'd waited for the test results—which she now had. "But what if I did another—"

"Doing another test won't change the results," added Carly.

White-faced, Lisa looked at them. "Pregnant. How? How could this have happened?"

Carly raised a dark eyebrow. "Oh, I think it happened in the usual way."

"I can give you a clinical description,"

Gemma added, "but I think you know how it happened."

"I…I do know. But I'm thirty-three years old. It's not like I'm a silly teenager with her first boyfriend…and we…we used protection."

"No protection is one hundred percent reliable."

"I know that—however, I didn't think—"

"Did you suspect you were pregnant? Has anything been different?"

"I've been a little light-headed, though not really faint, for a couple of months. I thought I was just working too hard, what with the plans coming together for the resort out on the lake—"

"You always work too hard," Gemma pointed out. "And I'm not quite sure you have to be the point person on the resort project."

"Are you kidding? Do you have any idea how many jobs this will bring to Reston County? And besides, I'm not really heading it up. Mayor Morton is."

Gemma held up her hand. "I'm sorry, I shouldn't have become sidetracked. What other symptoms have you had?"

Lisa wrinkled her nose. "Things smell odd. Stronger. I had to take all the scented candles out of my home and office because they were overwhelming, and they've never bothered me before."

"Those are all symptoms of hormonal changes."

"I've felt sick every day for two weeks and I've thrown up every day, too. I thought it was some kind of flu bug or—something I ate."

"Every day for two weeks?" Carly asked. "Denial much?"

"You didn't say anything about feeling sick," Gemma put in, sending Carly a quelling look.

"My period's been off for months, but I thought maybe things change when you're in your thirties, you know?" She groaned and continued, "And they *should*. A person is supposed to have sense enough to not get unexpectedly pregnant at the age of thirty-three."

Gemma said, "Some hormonal changes are normal—"

"But a complete abandonment of common sense?" Lisa asked desperately. "I don't think so."

They all fell silent. Lisa knew they were waiting for her to deal with this the way she did most things—head down, moving forward, plans set.

She couldn't do that, though, because she'd been distracted and daydreamy for the past month. She had difficulty concentrating, and odd, random thoughts and memories had popped up like jack-in-the-boxes when she tried to focus on work. She was sure Gemma was right—it was probably hormonal.

And now shock had paralyzed her brain even more. She could barely form a coherent thought, except for one—that this didn't seem real. Or possible. "I'm going to have a baby."

"That's right," Gemma said. "In about seven months."

"So…in September?"

Lisa frowned. "So, nine months from the end of December—"

"Nine months isn't accurate. Pregnancy is actually supposed to be forty weeks, a little more or less depending on the mother—and the baby. Multiples often come earlier."

Lisa gulped as her eyes widened. "Multiples?"

"Um, sorry. I gave you too much information right there. Professional hazard." Gemma cleared her throat. "Back on track. Be forewarned, being pregnant in this Oklahoma heat and humidity won't be easy."

"Nothing about this will be easy." Lisa looked up. "And I feel sick all the time."

"That should ease up in a few weeks. We need to make an appointment for you to see Nathan. He can prescribe something to help with the morning sickness if you want. In the meantime, there are herbal supplements you can take."

Lisa nodded, then dropped her head forward. "I can't believe I'll be the first one of us to have a baby. At least you two are married."

Carly waved that away. "That just means you'll have two ready-made babysitters—until we have kids. Even then, we'll work something out."

Gemma got up and took a bottle of water from the small fridge in the examination room where she had brought Lisa to wait for the test results. She twisted off the cap and handed it to her.

Shakily, Lisa took a big drink, then held the cold plastic bottle against her cheek and closed her eyes. She had to get a grip on this, but all she wanted to do was to fold up into a ball and cry.

When Lisa opened her eyes, Gemma had

seated herself beside her once again. She and Carly were looking at her curiously.

"What?" she asked.

"We're wondering…" Gemma said. "When you're going to tell us…"

"Who the father is," Carly concluded.

Lisa pressed her lips together.

"Oh, come on, Lisa, we're your best friends. We're not going to judge you." Gemma gave her a fond smile.

Lisa looked from one to the other—Gemma, with her practical, no-nonsense approach to life, and Carly, who was strong and businesslike, but who could see a broken-down wooden chair in a junk heap and imagine it as a fun and useful porch swing.

Taking a deep breath, she released it slowly and said, "It's Ben McAdams."

"You've got to be kidding!" Carly yelped. "The Reston Rascal? Oklahoma's answer to Casanova?"

"I thought you weren't going to judge," Lisa said drily.

"Um, sorry."

Astounded, Gemma said, "I didn't even know that he was back in town, or that you two were dating, or even liked each other."

"We aren't and we don't." Lisa gazed at them miserably. "We haven't been friends since we were twelve and his parents banned me from seeing him after I—"

"Masterminded the jailbreak," Carly interrupted with a grin.

"Yeah. And that hasn't changed."

"Lisa, *obviously* something changed." Gemma smiled in sympathy. "However you don't have to tell us and—"

"*I* want to know what happened," Carly objected.

"You don't have to talk about it until you're ready," Gemma went on as if Carly hadn't spoken. She stood and began gathering the test kits for disposal.

Carly settled down and gave an encouraging nod, but Lisa, her eyes full of tears, dropped her face into her hands for a few seconds before she, too, sat back and stared at her friends.

"I feel like my head is floating somewhere off in space."

"And that will continue for a while," Gemma said. "But things will settle down. You'll get used to the idea, and soon you'll be excited about being a mother."

"I *can't* be a mother," Lisa said desperately.

"I had a terrible mother. I've still got a terrible mother. And my grandmother tried, at least when I was little, but she wasn't much of a model mother, either."

"You'll figure it out, Lisa. You're the smartest and most driven person I know." Carly gave her a hug.

The warmth of her friend's arms couldn't stop the shaking that had suddenly begun.

"I swore I'd never do this," she said fiercely. "I swore I'd never be careless and get pregnant, and leave my baby—"

"You would never leave your baby," Gemma objected.

"Lisa, you're twice as old as Maureen was when she had you and left you with her mom and dad. You've got a successful career, a home of your own, a support system. *Friends*," Carly said, emphasizing the last word as she gave her another squeeze and stepped back to look at her with an anxious expression.

Lisa took deep breaths and tried to still the quaking that came in waves from her core and moved outward. After a few moments she looked up and tried for a wan smile.

"Right now the question is how are you going to tell Ben?" Carly asked.

"I don't know, but I'd better do it soon," Lisa said. "I don't like putting off unpleasant tasks and this isn't something that can be hidden indefinitely."

"No," Gemma agreed. "And if I know you, you'll want to have every detail planned well ahead of time."

Lisa nodded even as she gave her friends a pitiful look. "I can barely form a sentence right now, much less a plan."

Gemma gripped her hand in sympathy, but Carly looked at her considerately.

"And I had plans," she went on. She knew she was rambling, but couldn't seem to stop. "The group of investors from Oklahoma City who are interested in developing a resort on Reston Lake are really making progress on the plans. Can you imagine how many jobs that would bring to this area?"

"So you keep saying."

"It will be a boost to your business, too, Carly. The resort will need fresh vegetables for their restaurants. If you get the contract, you'll have to expand your gardens, which means you and Luke will have to hire more employees. As for the rest of the county—between the construction and the running of the resort, it could bring in so much prosperity. I was going to broker the deal if I could convince the current owners to at least consider it."

Carly frowned. "You can still do all that. You're having a baby, not giving up your career."

Lisa barely heard her. "And I didn't tell you two this, but I'm thinking about running for mayor this year."

Her friends stared at her. "You're kidding," they said in unison.

"It's true. I would never try to push Harley Morton out of office, but—" she lowered her voice and nodded toward the reception area where Harley's wife worked "—Brenda wants him to retire and…well, I know I could do the job."

"Wow," Gemma said. "Just wow. I had no idea that was even on your mind. Brenda never said a thing to me."

"We were keeping it quiet." Lisa put her hands over her belly. "But now…"

"Everything's changed," Carly finished for her.

The three of them fell silent for several seconds until Carly cleared her throat. "So you got pregnant two months ago," she said slowly.

Lisa could see that her friend wasn't ready to let this go. "Obviously."

"Ben's been out of town for months. So how and where? If it was two months ago, it must have been—"

"When I was in Chicago." Lisa sighed. "At Christmastime. Right after my great-aunt Violet's funeral."

"You said you were stuck at the airport during a blizzard," Gemma added.

"I was, along with a million other people who were trying to get home. By the wildest chance, I ran into Ben. I'd last seen him in September, when he bought Riverbend Ranch and I brokered the deal. He was in Chicago for a Christmas charity event that a bunch of big-name sports figures support. It benefits cancer research. Anyway, he had a room, one of the last ones at a hotel near the airport. He invited me to share the room, and we ended up sharing one of the beds."

"Oh, honey," Carly said.

"I *never* do things like that." Lisa could feel the tears sliding down her face. "I *always* think about consequences, about how my actions will affect my future."

"Whereas Ben McAdams has never needed

to. He's always just taken chances on everything, followed the most fun path to whatever he wanted next," Gemma said.

"And that night, you were what he wanted," Carly added.

"It wasn't really like that," Lisa told them, resting her head in her palm as exhaustion swamped her. She should have known something was wrong. Besides working too much, she'd thought maybe she'd had a low-grade virus. But it wasn't. It was a baby. A baby!

Out of the corner of her eye she saw her two best friends exchange a look.

"We wondered why you were so...unlike yourself when you got back from Chicago," Carly said.

"It seemed to be more than simply your great-aunt's death," Gemma added, her face full of compassion. "You didn't say much about it, but your mother was there, wasn't she?"

"Yes." Lisa looked down at her hands, which were now clasping the water bottle. "I tried to talk to her, but she—Maureen—turned away. She seemed very shaken up over Aunt Violet, but I don't really know how she was feeling. I've only seen her half a dozen times in my life, so I don't know how she would react to anything. She barely talked to me at Grandma's and Grandpa's funerals, so—" Her voice choked off and her head dropped forward.

"Oh, that's rough," Carly said.

"Maureen didn't talk much to anyone, except the minister, and then she practically ran from the funeral home. I don't know where she went. I don't even know where she *lives*. What kind of family is this?" she asked fiercely. "I see my own mother only half a dozen times in my life and we don't have anything to *say* to each other? How is that even possible?"

"Oh, honey," Gemma said. "That's something that started before you were even born and you can't fix it with one conversation."

Lisa took another deep breath. Somehow she couldn't seem to get enough air to blow away the storm of emotions. "You're right." She paused, then said, "A little while later, I saw that the weather was closing in, so even though my flight wasn't until late that night, I said goodbye to my cousins and headed for the airport and got stuck there…or, actually, nearby."

"With Ben." Gemma reached for her hand again as Carly gathered her into another hug.

Lisa rested her head on her friend's arm and glanced up with a rueful look. "You know how he is."

"Yeah," Carly said. She and Gemma both sighed wistfully. "Charm in size twelve cowboy boots."

Lisa nodded miserably. "He was warm, sympathetic and understanding. I was happy to see someone from home, you know? I was so distraught I hardly knew which way to turn, and the thought of spending the night at the airport was more than I could handle. I know I could have called my cousins for help, but the roads were already closed and they had enough to deal with. Then I saw Ben. He took care of everything."

"Short-term responsibility has always been his strong point."

"I…I know. I needed someone to lean on right then, but it got way out of hand. I never meant for this to happen," she said yet again. "And now I'm going to have a baby."

"Which I'll be happy to deliver when the time comes, if you want me to," Gemma assured her. "The good news is that you're healthy, things look fine, and you've got some time to come to terms with this."

Lisa nodded and leaned into the hug. She had time, but not much.

CHAPTER TWO

MAUREEN THOMAS SAT in her car across the street from Reston Realty and watched the front door, trying to build up the courage to go in and talk to Lisa, the daughter she had no right to call her own.

She had returned to Reston because she'd had no choice. She'd promised her aunt Violet that she would try to make amends with her daughter. It was far too late to patch things up with her parents, or to even get answers to the questions she'd carried with her from the time she'd been old enough to wonder why her mom and dad were so different than everyone else's parents. Why their house and farm were overrun with things no one used, discards from other people that were left to rot or rust.

Before she could go back into the rabbit hole of endless questions, she pulled her mind to the present.

To anchor herself, she stared at her hands, which were scarred and callused from every minimum-wage job she'd had since she was sixteen. They were a reminder of how hard she'd fought to stay alive after she'd bound her breasts to stop the flow of milk and left her infant daughter in her parents' care. She'd sneaked away in the night, dodging the twisted metal hazards in the front yard and running down the lane, hitchhiking to Aunt Violet in Chicago.

The terror and despair she'd felt then paled in comparison to the abject fear she was experiencing now at the thought of facing Lisa.

Maureen's plan had been to stay at a motel for a couple of days, get a sense of how Lisa was, then see if they could talk. That plan had been destroyed in Wichita, Kansas, when the transmission dropped out of her car and she'd had to make a roaring, rattling entrance into a nearby garage.

The repairs had taken almost all of her spare cash, so now her plans had changed. She couldn't stay at a motel, couldn't eat at Margie's Kitchen. There was no money.

Besides, she didn't want to be seen around town, at least not until she had talked to Lisa.

She would stay out of sight and sleep in her car again if necessary. She'd done it last night, driving to an old barn off the highway that she'd remembered as abandoned. But, of course, things had changed in the thirty-three years since she'd been back. The place was now a prosperous-looking organic gardening operation.

She had driven on, searching for someplace to park for the night, and had ended up at Reston Lake. Posted signs said the park was closed, but she'd driven around them and parked behind a stand of trees, leaving before dawn to avoid detection.

Maureen hated that she was sneaking into her own hometown, skulking around to see her daughter, but she simply wasn't ready to face anyone else from her past. It would take all of her courage to talk to Lisa.

The uncomfortable truth was, if she wanted to follow Aunt Violet's last wish, she would have to ask Lisa if she could stay with her. Lisa had once had an apartment in town— she'd proudly sent pictures of her place to Aunt Violet years ago when she'd gone into real estate. Heaven knew the girl had never sent pictures of the old Thomas place. Who would want their relatives to look at photos of a landfill?

"Now she owns the office. She's an agent and a broker," Maureen said aloud, gazing out her car window as she experienced a flurry of pride in what her daughter had accomplished in spite of the lousy circumstances she'd been handed.

Maureen reached for the door handle, hesitating to see Lisa at work, fearing a humiliating rejection. Still, she'd been humiliated before and she'd survived. She was terrified that's all she would ever do simply survive.

Jerking up on the door's stiff handle, she stepped out of her old sedan. As the door clicked shut behind her, she smoothed the front of the coat that had fit her so well a few months ago but flapped around her figure now. At least it was good quality. Nothing to be ashamed of there.

As she walked up to the glass-fronted doors, she reached for the handle just as a man's hand grasped it.

"Excuse me, ma'am," he said in the local drawl she'd longed to hear again. "Let me get that for you."

Flustered, she looked up at the handsome

dark-haired man. He looked familiar, but she couldn't recall where she'd seen him. She stepped inside and he followed.

The moment passed as the secretary looked up and broke into a wide smile. "Why, Ben McAdams, as I live and breathe. I didn't know you were back in town."

"I am for now, Sandy."

Maureen recognized the secretary, too. Her name had been Sandy Westlyn, but the nameplate on her desk said Sandy Borden. Maureen used to babysit for her and her two little brothers. She'd known the Borden family, too, but it had been so long, she couldn't think of which one of the sons Sandy might have married.

Sandy managed to move her dazzled smile to take in Maureen's somewhat subdued appearance and switch to being professional. "I'll be right with you, Ben. How can I help you, ma'am?"

Maureen clenched her hands inside her coat pockets, grateful that Sandy didn't seem to recognize her. "I'd like to see Lisa Thomas, please."

"What a coincidence," Ben said affably. "That's just what I want, too."

Maureen answered with a shaky smile, then went to a chair so she could stop the trembling in her legs. And get her bearings.

"LISA, YOU'VE GOT VISITORS."

Sandy Borden's voice pulled her away from the paperwork she was compiling for a new listing. She had spent an hour rereading the resort proposal, checking facts and figures. The more she read, the more excited she became at the prosperity the resort would bring to the county. She'd finally put the report away, knowing there was much work to be done before any ground-breaking could take place.

The faraway tone of her receptionist's voice caught Lisa's attention.

Intrigued, she closed her laptop, stood and walked to her office door. "Yes? Oh." Her attention darted from her receptionist to the man at the front of the office.

Ben McAdams stood by the glass front door of Reston Realty. He tipped his hat and winked at Sandy. "So, how are you, beautiful? Haven't seen you since little Derek won the roping competition at the county fair. How is he? How's the family?"

Delighted color washed up Sandy's face.

As if she couldn't help herself, she fluffed her hair and moistened her lips. "Oh, Ben. It's great to see you. Everyone is fine. Little Derek is taller than you are now and he's going to Oklahoma University in the fall."

"Go, Sooners," Ben said, making a fist and pumping the air. "That's great. You must be proud of him."

"Cliff and I both are."

Ben tilted his head as he gave her a teasing grin. "I'm wondering, though, how he's going to get out of the house with you two hanging on to his leg crying, 'No, no, please don't go.'"

Sandy laughed. "I don't know. You're supposed to raise kids to let them be independent, but I'm sure we're not ready for that."

"I'm sure you and Cliff have raised a good man. He'll be okay."

Lisa was so shocked to see Ben in her outer office, she could barely form words. She'd been thinking about him constantly for days, but she hadn't contacted him about the baby because she couldn't decide what to say—a rarity for her since she usually met problems head-on. Was it possible that her imagination had conjured him up?

Distracted, she looked around to see that someone else had come in, as well, and had taken a seat against the wall.

She glanced at the woman, then away, but her attention shot back to her, astounded.

"Huh… H-hello," Lisa stammered.

"Hello, Lisa," Maureen said. "Can I talk to you?"

Lisa stared at her and then at Ben, who was having a great chat with Sandy, his distinctive rumbling chuckle breaking out. That happiness would disappear the minute Lisa told him the news.

She fought a ripple of hysteria as she looked from Maureen's solemn face to Ben's laughing one. Maureen, who hadn't had time for her at Aunt Violet's funeral, wanted to talk to her now. But Lisa had to talk to Ben first. She couldn't put it off.

"I'm…I'm so sorry. I can't see you—at least not now. I've got…"

"I understand," Maureen said, standing. "Maybe we can try again later."

"Yes, later," Lisa agreed, even though her excellent memory reminded her that "later" seemed to always be the time when Maureen was departing. She had to take that chance, though. When she did talk to her mother, she wanted to be able to give the conversation her full attention and she couldn't do that until she'd dealt with Ben.

Lisa scooped her cell phone out of her pants pocket. "Do you have a phone? Can you give me your number? I'll call you as soon as I'm free."

Of course, there was no guarantee that Maureen would answer if she did call.

Maureen gave a nervous little smile, supplied her number and left, the door swinging silently shut behind her. She hadn't asked for Lisa's number.

As she tried to control her reaction to the double shock of seeing both Maureen and Ben, Lisa watched Ben charm Sandy's socks off. She wouldn't have been surprised to see her receptionist's eyes suddenly turn into beating pink hearts like a love-struck cartoon character's.

It wasn't simply that he was handsome, with his rich, dark auburn hair, dark gray eyes, thick lashes and strong, square chin. It wasn't only his size. He was a big man, at least six foot four, slimmed down somewhat from his days as a linebacker in the NFL, but still muscled and strong. The thing was that Ben was genuinely interested in everyone and could focus his attention on the person he was listening to as if they were the most interesting human on earth. When he listened, he leaned in from the waist, turned his head slightly and narrowed his dark gray eyes just a little, as if he wanted to block out the rest of the world and everything in it. When he smiled, deep dimples appeared, and when he laughed, he threw back his head and didn't hold anything in.

As if all of that wasn't enough, his voice had a rolling timbre that made everyone in any gathering stop their own conversations to turn and hear what he had to say. The Oklahoma drawl that she'd heard all around her every day of her life was somehow more enthralling when it came from him.

That Southern Gentleman Charm should be labeled as a lethal weapon.

Lisa's heart fluttered anxiously. She'd been on the receiving end of that charm and look where that had gotten her.

Automatically she sucked in her stomach, although it was still perfectly flat, and reached over to the coat tree by her office door to snag the jacket that matched her slacks.

As she did that, the office door swung open and Calvin Swenson, the deliveryman, stopped in with a package. He recognized Ben and shook his hand, saying, "Man, it's good to see you, Ben. You gonna be around for a while?"

"A few months, at least, Cal. I've got some work around here."

"Let's get together, go fishing. Trout are biting out on the lake and the season ends in a few weeks."

"Let's do that," Ben answered. "Let's see if Junior Fedder can join us. I'll give you a call."

"Yeah. Have you seen him? There was a time he couldn't have fit in my boat, but he's dropped some major pounds."

"Good for him." Ben seemed genuinely pleased. "I haven't seen him in months, but I'll give him a call and let you know."

With a happy nod, Calvin left and Lisa shook her head. Everyone wanted to spend time with him. Ben charmed all living creatures. Men, women, children, dogs, cats—it didn't matter. Everyone fell under his spell.

Finally, Ben leaned over Sandy's desk and

gave her a smile that threatened to melt her into a puddle as he said, "Hey, beautiful, it's been great catching up with you, but I need to talk to Lisa."

Sandy looked concerned. "Oh, I gave her your messages. Didn't she call?"

Lisa watched as Sandy turned her head and gave her a look that suggested she had betrayed all womankind by not returning Ben's calls.

"Nah, but it's okay. I know she's the busiest Realtor in six counties and you're the best assistant, so I know she got the messages."

Sandy, mother of three and married to a good man for twenty years, fluttered her eyelashes and fluffed her hair again. "Oh, Ben, you're so sweet to say that."

"I only speak the truth."

Lisa decided it was time to step in. Steeling herself, she plastered a polite smile on her face and stepped forward as she casually fastened the three buttons down the front of her jacket. She was delighted that she had worn four-inch heels today. It put her closer to eye level with him. "Here I am, Ben. Come on into my office. What can I do for you?"

He gave Sandy another wink that made her

giggle and strode into Lisa's office. As soon as she shut the door behind him, he turned to her, swept the sides of his jacket aside to plant his hands at his waist and said, "Why have you been ducking my phone calls?"

"Oh, well…" Lisa paused, indicating that he should sit as she returned to her chair and put the width of her desk between them. "I've been very busy." She tried to sound professional as she folded her suddenly damp hands on top of her desk and asked, "Were you interested in seeing another property?"

He raised an eyebrow at her as he removed the leather jacket he wore with crisp jeans and a dark blue shirt. As he sat, he said, "No, I'm interested in finding out why you won't talk to me, why you've avoided every one of my calls since that night in Chicago." He balanced his cowboy hat on his knee as he watched her face. The laid-back charm dropped away and he became laser-focused. "Can you tell me why?"

Heat flooded her features and her gaze jerked away. She *really* didn't want to think about that night, but she knew she had to tell him the consequences of the time they'd spent together.

"I was worried about you," he went on, obviously realizing she wasn't going to answer. "I wanted to know if you'd made it home safely."

Lisa gave a nervous laugh and held out her hands. "As you can see, I got home just fine."

His lips twisted. "I *do* see that, but would it have killed you to let me know?"

"Um, well, I...I thought that..." She let her voice trail off, unable to articulate how she'd felt the next morning and for days afterward as she'd questioned her actions—the need, the abandonment of self-control—that had driven her into his arms.

He leaned forward and pitched his voice low. "Contrary to popular opinion, I'm not the love-'em-and-leave-'em type. I wouldn't do that."

Lisa's eyes widened at the fierceness of his tone. She did know that. Every woman he'd dated in Reston was still his good buddy, so it was obvious he hadn't treated any of them badly.

"I...I guess I—"

Her words stumbled to a stop. He waited, but she didn't know what she'd been going to say except, "I don't do things like—"

"Like what happened in Chicago?"

Ben looked at her thoughtfully, then said, "No, what you do is try to control every situation you're in. You've been that way since we were kids." He gave her a rueful smile. "Even before you broke me out of jail. That seemed to give you a sense of your own power."

She stared at him. She'd had no idea he'd realized that about her.

He went on, "I've barely seen you in the past fifteen years, but I know that's probably still true." He paused. When she didn't answer, he prompted her. "Isn't it?"

Lifting her chin, she gave him a steady look. "Yes, which is why I've got a successful business."

"Which is why you look a little pale." His eyes narrowed. "Do you ever get out in the sun? Take a hike? Go fishing?"

Glancing away, she didn't answer but felt color rushing into her face.

"That's better," he said approvingly. "You know, Lisa, a person can be successful and still have some fun in life. Do you ever have fun?" He gave her a sly grin. "Other than with me?"

Lisa pressed her lips together. There was absolutely no way she was going to answer that.

He waited for a second, then turned on his winning smile, the one that was so warm and convincing. "Hey, how about I take you to lunch? Have you had lunch?"

She'd barely managed to keep down her breakfast. Lunch wasn't even on her radar yet. She didn't have to answer, though, because her intercom buzzed.

"Sorry to interrupt, Lisa," Sandy said, "but Mayor Morton heard that Ben's in town and says it's urgent that he speak to him."

"Ben?" The mayor's voice boomed into the room, making both Lisa and Ben jump. "You in there? I've been trying to call you, but I guess I had the wrong number. I need to see you, and it'll take a while."

Ben gave Lisa a pained look as he called out, "Coming, Mayor Morton."

The intercom clicked off and Ben stood. "He always thinks his business is more important than anyone else's."

Lisa knew that was true, but in spite of her determination to tell Ben about the baby, at this moment she could have kissed Harley Morton full on the lips.

Ben gave her a direct look. "I'll call you later," he said. "Please answer."

He shut the door behind him, leaving Lisa to reach for the glass of water on her desk and gulp down a long drink to try to settle her stomach. She should have known he would seek her out when they were both back in Reston. She had avoided telling Ben about the baby long enough. It was time to take action. She couldn't have him coming here, flirting with Sandy, interrupting the routine—reminding Lisa of the night they'd shared.

She wouldn't tell him over the phone or at her place of business, though. She would go to his house at Riverbend Ranch later and tell him. That way, she could escape when she needed to.

BEN STOOD ON the bottom rail of the cedar fence and gazed across the pasture. Delighted, he grinned at the sight of a mare and her foal running through the dried grass, their hooves kicking up chunks of dirt as they went. Tailspin, so named because of the swirl of dark red spots that circled her rump, took her colt, Prince's Folly, from one end of the pasture to the other. At three months the colt was similarly marked, but his spots were a darker red.

Ben was fascinated by the play of muscles beneath their shiny coats, their smooth-gaited run and their tricolored manes and tails—brown to red to blond—that rippled in the wind. He didn't know if that type of mane was rare or not. He'd have to ask Jason Littletrees about it.

It was relaxing to watch the horses run, to see the mustangs adjusting to their new home. The simple pleasure of it was something he could understand.

Lisa Thomas was something he didn't understand at all. He'd gone to see her as soon as he'd returned to this place, gotten the herd moved in with Jason's help and settled a few other things. It annoyed him that she wouldn't talk to him, and he didn't like being annoyed. He liked things settled, his relationships uncomplicated, easy. Not that he and Lisa had any kind of relationship. They didn't even have a friendship.

He could blame Harley Morton for interrupting them today, but the truth was he wasn't sure he could have convinced Lisa to have lunch with him. She hadn't wanted to talk to him and she'd looked pale and distressed—really distressed—to have him in her office. He wasn't accustomed to having that effect on a woman.

"Ben."

His dad's voice broke into his thoughts. Ben had almost forgotten he was there.

"Yes?"

"Are you sure about this, son?" Jim Mc-Adams asked, grunting slightly as he pulled himself up beside Ben on the tall fence. "What is the purpose of having horses you can't race, or train to work cattle, or train for the rodeo?"

"What are you talking about, Dad? These mustangs can do all those things and more, and have been doing it for centuries." Ben looked at his father, who just shook his head. "They're not big, but they're bred for endurance and can outdistance most other breeds. I can't believe you've lived your whole life in southeastern Oklahoma and you've never heard of the Choctaw Wild Mustangs."

"I've heard of them. I just never saw any reason to own or breed them. I can't believe Jason has talked you into starting your own herd. You don't know much about horses."

"I'll learn. Besides, it's an opportunity to

help save the Oklahoma Heritage Horse." Ben liked the idea of preserving the breed for posterity. And why not? He had the money and the resources.

Jim hooked an arm around a tall fence post and rubbed his chin. "Yeah, I guess that's important, but it sounds expensive."

Ben's lips twisted ironically. "I don't doubt it for a minute, but it'll be worth it."

"To each his own, I guess. I've given up trying to keep track of all the things you want to spend your money on."

With a chuckle Ben said, "That's probably a good choice."

He watched as Jim looked around at the acreage that encompassed Riverbend Ranch, so named because the Kinnick River made a dogleg bend at the edge of the property. The grass-covered land, long since shorn of all but a few stands of trees, sloped to a stock pond then lifted to rolling hills. The acreage was big enough for the herd of thirty mustangs to run free, but the pastures were secured by solid fences. Two wooden barns were situated beside the corral, and the house stood on a rise a few hundred yards away.

Even at his most generous, the only word

Ben could think of to describe it was *ramshackle*.

The main house had been built in the nineteen twenties, added onto several times since then and been unoccupied for many years. The floors were a patchwork of wood—some maple, some pine—and none of them flush. Most had a strip of wood at the bottom of the doorway to smoothen the transition from one room to the next, but Ben had tripped a dozen times already. He'd finally learned to walk on his heels and lift his toes when going from one room to another to minimize the danger of falling.

Most of the doors had warped in the heat and humidity of past summers so that now only a few of them would close all the way. The ones that did close were hard to open, only coming free with hard jerks and a few well-placed kicks. All the electrical and plumbing needed to be updated and the place cried for paint and wallpaper. His great-grandmother would probably have felt right at home with the ancient appliances in the kitchen.

But Ben didn't care what the place looked like or how inconvenient it was. He'd never been a nester. Too many other things to do.

Once he got the herd established, he wouldn't be there much.

"I'd tear that house down if I were you. Build a smaller one," Jim said. "It's falling apart, anyway, and much too big for one person." He gave Ben a sidelong look. "Unless you plan to have a family to fill it up."

"Dad, you know that's never been in my plans." He lifted his hand and made a circular motion that encompassed the ranch. "At least I've got my own place in Reston so you know I'll be around part of the year."

Jim shook his head. "Just part of the year? Yeah, I know. Places to go, things to do. Your mother and I have long since given up any hope of being grandparents."

"I know, Dad." They'd had this conversation so many times Ben didn't even feel the need to engage in it. He simply gave his stock answer. "I know it's a disappointment to you, but that's just the way it is."

His father answered with a long-suffering sigh and went back to their original topic. "Who's gonna take care of this place when you're off on one of your projects, or chasing around the world on the next wild hare you get?"

Ben didn't take offense. He and his dad would never see eye-to-eye. "Jason Littletrees is looking for someone."

"He'll find someone. The whole Littletrees family is involved with horses one way or another."

"Yes. Hadn't seen him in years, but we ran into each other at the Choctaw Nation Labor Day Festival in Tuskahoma last fall. He was showing some mustangs there—"

"And you thought, 'Great! Here's another way to burn up some money.'"

"Dad."

Jim looked chagrined. "Sorry. Knee-jerk reaction. Well, at least Jason is trustworthy, and I guess he'll find someone who knows these mustangs."

"That's the plan."

"I was happy with registered quarter horses and, since I don't ride anymore, it doesn't matter." Jim stepped down, taking a moment to steady himself against the cedar rails.

"Is your leg bothering you?" Ben asked, forgetting about his horses for a minute. He hopped down from the fence to stand beside Jim.

"Nah, no worse than usual," Jim answered with a shrug, but he bent over to rub his left knee. "Five years since I rolled my truck on that ice patch, and it doesn't get any better. Doesn't matter. I can still do what I need to do. As long as I can keep working, I'm happy."

"I know, Dad." It saddened Ben to think of his father never taking time for a vacation, or any kind of break, but as the old man said, "To each his own."

"By the way," Jim said, "Harley Morton's been trying to get in touch with you. Did he find you?"

"Yes. I talked to him today."

"What did he want?"

Ben stifled a laugh. His dad absolutely couldn't help himself. He had to be involved in everything, know everything. "He wants me to run a football camp this summer. Apparently he's convinced Wolfchild Whitmire that they need to do this out at the Whitmires' old campground."

Jim snorted with laughter. "How many footballs do you think will go flying into their lake?"

"Probably more than the city budget can afford."

"You gonna do it?"

"If I can fit it into my schedule."

"Good. That'll keep you around for a while longer. Give you some useful work to do."

Ben only shrugged.

Jim clapped him on the shoulder. "Speaking of work, I've got things to do at home, son. I'll talk to you later." With a wave, Jim headed for his truck, then paused and glanced back. "Wild mustangs. I sure hope you know what you're doing." He climbed into the truck's cab and drove away.

Ben gazed after his dad and knew that, physically, at least, he was looking at himself in forty years. But he was determined to have a different focus in his life. His dad had raised cattle, bought and sold land, operated a construction company and a gravel-mining operation, and run a few other businesses. He'd achieved his goal of financial comfort long ago but still worked nonstop.

Ben knew his mom wanted to travel, see something of the world before old age came calling. She was only sixty but saw life passing her by because Jim wouldn't slow down long enough to have any fun. Ben had taken his mother to Europe and to Thailand. Even though she'd enjoyed the trips, she'd really wanted her husband there to share it, but Jim had insisted he had to work.

His dad was the reason Ben had long ago made the decision that work wouldn't rule his life.

Ben's goal was to enjoy life, to travel, meet new people and make friends all over the world, start businesses, fund projects. He'd done a good job of investing the money he'd made playing professional football. Now he considered his job to be to spend it wisely but in fun ways. He knew his reputation around his hometown was that he was something of a squanderer, but he didn't care. It was his life and his money. Anyone who cared to look carefully could see that he spent his money to benefit others, but he wasn't going to advertise the fact.

As he walked back to the house, he took out his phone and checked his calendar. His attention was caught by the sound of tires crunching on gravel. A dark red, sporty sedan was heading toward him. He frowned for a second as he tried to see who was driving, then grinned.

So his visit to Lisa's office had paid off. But he was surprised she'd come out to his ranch.

He watched as Lisa pulled her car to a stop and looked up to meet his eyes. Her solemn expression, the twin of the one she'd given him earlier in her office, made him pause before he walked over to open her door and hold out his hand to help her out.

She stood, somewhat unsteadily, smoothed the short, black wool jacket she wore with matching slacks, and braced herself in the door opening. Finally she looked at him. Her lips flickered in the faintest smile. "Hello, Ben."

"Hey, Lisa. Thanks for coming over. I would have called, headed back to your office. You didn't need to come all the way out here."

"It's okay. I wanted to," she said, stepping aside so that he could close the door behind her.

Something about her complete shift in attitude made his words stumble. "Um, yeah. I wanted to see if you were okay after your aunt's death…and…well, you know…everything that happened." Ben felt embarrassed heat climb his throat. "But you didn't respond."

"I know." She glanced away, apparently distraught. Her face was as pale as it had been earlier and her eyes seemed sunken. "I was hoping we could start this conversation again."

"Yes, sure, but are you okay?" he asked, reaching to take her arm.

At last she met his gaze. "Can we go inside, Ben? I have something…important to tell you."

CHAPTER THREE

"PREGNANT?" BEN STARED at her, swallowed, then stared some more. "And…it's mine?"

"Of course it is!" Lisa fought down a burst of hysteria. "You don't think I go around sleeping with—"

"Of course not. Of course not," he answered hastily, holding up his hands, palms outward. "But…we used protection."

Hearing him say exactly what she'd said to Gemma and Carly a few days ago didn't make her feel any better. "I know."

He sat forward, as if all the strength had been drained from him, and rested his forearms on his thighs. Looking down, and then up, he seemed to struggle to form a sentence.

Lisa knew this wasn't at all the conversation he'd expected to be having when he'd come to her office. She wondered if that was the last lunch invitation she'd ever receive from him.

Unable to meet his shocked gaze anymore, Lisa looked away, taking in the shabby living room she'd last entered late in September when she'd handled the sale of the ranch to him. The house looked as bad as ever, but she'd been so agitated when she'd driven up today, she hadn't even noticed if he'd done anything to improve the outbuildings or acreage, although she'd noticed a small herd of horses in the pasture.

She looked around, feeling her mind drifting from the subject at hand. This time, she didn't try to stop it as the Realtor in her assessed the positive aspects of the house.

This room had beautifully carved crown moldings that could easily be returned to their original beauty if touched up and painted, maple floors with a buildup of grime around the edges that could be cleaned with refinishing, and dingy mint-green paint on the walls. She didn't think any upgrades would happen. Ben had brought in two new-looking chairs, a sofa and a couple of floor lamps, but she had no idea if he intended to make it any more homey.

Ben looked as though he'd been working hard since he'd returned from town, if his worn, dirt-streaked jeans and blue flannel shirt were any indication. She hadn't noticed earlier, but his dark auburn hair needed a cut, or maybe it only looked disastrous because he'd been repeatedly running his hands through it, exactly as she'd done when she'd first learned of this news.

Ben cleared his throat, bringing her attention back to him. His dark gray eyes, the color of a winter storm, looked at her. "Is that why you've refused to talk to me?"

"Not at first. I was…embarrassed."

"Because you never do what you did? What *we* did? I get that. But you don't have anything to be ashamed of." When she didn't respond, he asked, "How long have you known?"

"Only a few days, but I've known something was…different for a while."

"Have you…thought about…what you're going to do?" His expression was that of a man going down for the third time, grasping at any twig of hope for a different outcome. There wasn't going to be one.

She scooted forward in her chair, sat straighter and gave him a hard look. "I'm *having* it and I'm *keeping* it."

"Of *course*. I wasn't suggesting anything

else, I swear. Listen, it's your choice." He stood and paced around the room, his boots thumping on the hardwood. "I'll do my part, of course. I'll pay child support."

She waited, wondering what he would say next. Would he want to be part of the baby's life? That wasn't what she wanted. Did most men say they wanted to help when they were handed a bombshell like this one? Other than a name on her birth certificate, she didn't know who her father was and doubted he knew of her existence.

Ben swung back to look at her. His face worked for a minute before he went on, his voice strangled. "I have to tell you, though, Lisa, I never intended to be a dad. I like kids, but I've got the life I always worked for—money to do what I like, go where I want, deals working, projects and businesses all over the world." He shook his head and frowned. "I just had this conversation with my father. I never saw myself with a family because I thought it would be unfair to a kid for me to either be gone all the time or to drag it around the world with me."

"You don't ever want anything to impinge on your freedom."

He barely seemed to think about his response. Throwing his hands wide, he asked, "Would you?"

Lisa started to answer but a wave of nausea rose in her throat. She stumbled to her feet and ran to where she recalled the downstairs bathroom was located. Desperately hoping the ancient plumbing worked, she lurched into the room and shoved the door closed behind her.

A few seconds later she had emptied the contents of her stomach into the toilet bowl and stood trembling, holding on to the washbasin as she rinsed her mouth and splashed water on her face. She spotted a roll of paper towels beneath the sink and used one to pat her face dry. Staring at her miserable reflection in the mirror, she took several deep breaths and then scooped more water into her mouth.

She could hear Ben pacing to and fro outside, which meant it was time for her to leave. She had done what she was supposed to do. After stewing about it for days, choosing exactly the right words, even writing out what she planned to say so that her sudden onslaught of brain burps wouldn't hijack her thoughts, she had told Ben he was going to be a father. Shock and surprise were what she'd expected, but she hadn't counted on his adamant statement that he'd never wanted to be a dad.

She should have guessed, though. He'd had legions of girlfriends over the years, some in Reston, others scattered around the country, maybe even the world. If he'd wanted to stay with one woman and start a family, there probably would have been at least one of them who would have been happy to accommodate him.

"Lisa?" he called from the other side of the door. "Are you okay? Can I get you anything?"

"No. I'm fine." She pulled on the knob but nothing happened. She looked to see if she'd locked it, but the old-fashioned door had only a slightly rusted bolt. She tried the knob again but the door wouldn't budge.

"I think it's stuck," Ben said in an apologetic tone. "Let me try."

The knob twisted and she heard a thump and a grunting sound. She stepped back hastily, but not fast enough. The door flew open and Ben shot through, slamming her against the edge of the sink, knocking the breath out of her in a whoosh.

Ben made a grab for her, his arms going around her shoulders to keep her on her feet as he said, "Sorry! Are you okay?" He held on to her as he looked her up and down.

"Yeh…eh…hess," she wheezed, fighting for her breath. She managed to loosen one arm and surreptitiously rub her hip where she knew she would have a bruise.

He took the hint and stepped back, his worried gaze still on her. "Sorry about that door. Every single one in the place sticks, but I guess that one's the worst. I've never closed it before."

"What?"

He shrugged. "I'm here alone. No need to shut the bathroom door."

"Oh." She lived alone, too, but always closed the door to the bathroom. In fact, she closed her bedroom door every night, too. She paused, considering it. Growing up, those were the only two doors in the house that *would* close because everywhere else was so stuffed with her hoarder grandparents' things. She frowned at Ben.

"Come on," he said, ushering her into the

hallway. "Let me get you something to drink. You want some coffee?" He looked around helplessly. "Or tea?"

"No thanks. No caffeine."

As if he couldn't help himself, he glanced down at her belly and then up. "Oh, of course. Um, I've got soft drinks. Lemon-lime soda, maybe?" Suddenly his worried expression cleared. "And crackers! I've got some saltine crackers."

Before she could respond, he helped her back to her chair and strode into the kitchen. As he rustled around, she twisted in her chair and rubbed her hip again. She could ask for an ice pack but doubted that he had one. A dripping bag of ice cubes wouldn't do her wool slacks any good, although she wasn't sure why she was worried. Her waistline would soon expand so much that she wouldn't be able to wear this beautifully tailored outfit, anyway.

A few minutes later he returned with a glass and a bowl of saltine crackers. She considered turning down the snack, but her lurching stomach told her she'd better not.

Since there was no table on which to set anything, she placed the bowl in her lap and held the soft drink in one hand. As she nibbled and sipped, Ben roamed the room and turned up the thermostat. The old-fashioned wall heater rattled and groaned to life and soon had the room at a stifling temperature.

With a sound of annoyance, he turned it off once more. "I've got to do something about that."

After an awkward silence had stretched far too long, Lisa set her empty glass on the floor, knowing any condensation from the glass wouldn't harm the already-warped boards.

Ben finally sat opposite her and cleared his throat. "I guess we should talk about…financial arrangements…for the…"

"Baby. It's called a baby."

"Yeah, yeah, of course. You'll need money for…"

As his words trailed off, Lisa watched him try to think of what an expectant mother might need. She didn't yet know much about it, but he knew even less than she did.

"Ben, I'm…I'm glad you're willing to provide financial support, but we should have a legal agreement." She studied his face, unsure how he would react to that statement.

"That makes sense, and I can pay for…for your before-baby care, too."

"It's called prenatal care. Thanks, but I don't need your help. I've got health insurance, a good hospital, a good doctor. And Gemma will help deliver the baby when it's time."

He nodded. "And the time will be…September?"

"That's right."

"I've been invited to help establish an American-style football league in India. I have to be there in August, but sometimes there are delays. I might be in town in September," he said.

Lisa dropped her head forward in surrender. Leaning down, she set the bowl beside the glass and stood. "I'm so glad you think you might be able to fit the birth of your child into your schedule, but I *don't* expect you to be there."

He surged to his feet. "I didn't mean it like that. I want to help—"

"Yes, as long as it corresponds with what you already have planned and doesn't interfere with your freedom." Turning, she stomped to the door.

"Be fair," he insisted, following her. "I don't know anything about kids."

Unwanted tears sprung into her eyes as she said, "And that's the way it's going to stay, isn't it, Ben?" She waved a hand in dismissal. "You can be whatever kind of father you want to be."

Eager to escape a situation that had gone from uncomfortable to unbearable, she grasped the doorknob. Of course, the door wouldn't open. Ben reached around and gave it a tug, but this time she was quick enough to move aside and avoid injury. She hurried out and down the steps to her car with him following.

As she slid behind the wheel, he leaned in and said, "We can talk about this later, when we've both had time to process it a little."

"You'll be hearing from my attorney," she responded, jerking the door shut.

Ben called after her, but she started the car, turned in a big circle and slammed on the gas pedal, shooting up gravel that had him scrambling backward. Blaming overactive hormones for her out-of-control emotions, she wiped away her tears, took a breath and concentrated on driving.

She had done what she was supposed to do.

Ben now knew he was going to be a father, a role he obviously didn't want. She didn't know exactly what she'd expected to happen, but this was worse than she'd imagined.

Now that she'd had time to come to terms with her impending motherhood, she felt exhilarated but also terrified. She had to remember that she had friends, a support system that would help her every step of the way. Her baby would have honorary aunts in Gemma and Carly and uncles in their husbands, Nathan Smith and Luke Sanderson—even a cousin in Carly and Luke's adopted son, Dustin. Her child wouldn't have a father. But then, Lisa had never had one, either.

Long shadows were stretching across the road as Lisa gratefully headed for home. She couldn't wait to go inside, put her feet up, eat dinner and try to come to terms with what had turned out to be an emotionally wrenching day. She'd known it would be hard telling Ben about the baby, but she hadn't expected the overwhelming disappointment she'd felt in the charming, winsome Ben McAdams.

She wanted to talk to Gemma and Carly about it, but it was dinnertime and they had family responsibilities, so the lengthy talk she would need to put this into perspective would have to wait.

As she approached her home, she glanced over in surprise to see an ancient compact car parked out front. Her stomach quivered nervously when saw the Illinois license plate. The car appeared to be stuffed with bags and boxes.

Cautiously, she parked in her carport, grateful for the automatic lights that flipped on as soon as she pulled in. Looking around as she stepped from the car, she reached into her pocket for her cell phone, prepared to call for help. She was two miles out of town, though, so she didn't think assistance would arrive as quickly as she might need it.

"Hello?" she ventured, her gaze darting around. She kept the car door open in case she had to leap in and make a fast getaway. Fortunately the carport was open at both ends and no longer obstructed by the broken-down tractor that had once barred the way.

At the sound of a hesitant step behind her, she spun around. She had her keys in her hand, the tips protruding from between her fingers—the only weapon at her disposal.

"Oh, hello," a woman's voice said as she stepped into the light.

Lisa blinked, astonished. "Maureen?"

"You said we could talk later," Maureen said with a hesitant smile, running a hand through her short, dark hair. She shrugged one shoulder in a way Lisa thought looked vaguely familiar. "Hello, Lisa."

"Um, hi. I'm sorry I didn't call you. I've had…a crazy day and…" Her voice trailed off. The drama with Ben had made her forgot about Maureen.

"It's okay. I know it must have been a shock for me to come strolling into your office that way. It's a lovely place, by the way. Very neat and clean."

"Thank you."

"I was taking a look around while I waited," Maureen said, her hands sweeping out to encompass the property. "I hope you don't mind. The place is wonderful. What did you do with all that junk Dad had piled everywhere?"

"Um, uh, sold it, donated it, tossed it…" Lisa's voice trailed off. She couldn't seem to make sense of what was happening, couldn't believe what her eyes were telling her. The mother she barely knew was standing in front of her, casually talking about how great the old homestead looked. "Were you looking for...something?"

Maureen answered with an awkward laugh. "No. It's just that I'd never seen the place without piles of old tires, wrecked cars and various abandoned tasks all jumbled together." She paused, glanced around and stuffed her hands into her pockets.

Good grief, Lisa thought. What should she say to this woman? The mother who'd left her when she was a month old?

Her curiosity overcame her trepidation. Stepping away from her car, she closed the door and said, "Would you like to come in?"

Immediately, Maureen's shoulders relaxed and relief flooded her face. "Yes, thank you."

Maureen waited while Lisa unlocked the door and held it open so she could precede her into the kitchen.

Once they were inside and Lisa had flipped on the light in the kitchen, she was able to get a better look at her mother. Maureen was examining the room, her mouth open in awe.

There was no denying who Maureen's parents were. She had Grandma Lily's dark blue eyes, which Lisa had also inherited, and her face was square-shaped like Grandpa Wesley's. Her short dark hair was touched with gray and her face was free of makeup. Lisa thought she appeared drawn and thin, but she saw her mother so infrequently, she couldn't be sure.

She attempted to see the kitchen as her mother did. It had been completely gutted, and where piles of books, boxes of odds and ends, and other detritus had once made it impossible to move without the danger of injury, the simplest of hickory cabinets, white-tiled countertops and stainless-steel appliances had been installed. A row of glass jars filled with rice, pasta and beans was the only item on the counter. A couple of antique signs advertising long-vanished brands of ice cream hung on the wall over the breakfast nook. The cozy little corner held a small wooden table and two chairs Carly had found and refurbished for her. Lace curtains on the east-facing windows let the sunshine in every morning, brightening the whole room.

Maureen pointed to the hardwood floor that gleamed a dark honey color. "Was this underneath that nasty old green tile?"

"Yes, quarter-sawn maple."

"Unbelievable." Maureen shook her head,

moved into the small dining room and marveled at the polished mahogany table and chairs. "I've never seen the top of that table in my life."

"Me, neither. I grew up thinking the natural color of the wood was nasty gray. Turns out that it was grime all along."

Maureen answered with a pained look. "I remember. It's beautiful now."

"My friend Carly Joslin refinished it for me."

And so it went throughout the remainder of the house—living room, three bedrooms and two bathrooms. As they moved through the house, Lisa cast surreptitious glances at Maureen, who now carried her coat over her arm. She thought her mother looked thinner than she had when in Chicago, and fragile, as if she'd been sick. But for all she knew, Maureen's skin always had that paleness. Lisa doubted that she'd always worn such baggy clothes, though.

They ended up back in the living room. The floors had been stripped and refinished so that the wood gleamed. The walls had been painted a restful shade of soft cream and the built-in bookcases on each side of the fireplace had new, unbroken glass in the doors. Best of all, there were only a few cherished items on the shelves and on the mantel over the fireplace, including the one good photograph she had of Lily and Wesley Thomas. It had been taken in the sixties, when they were newly married and anything seemed possible.

Maureen stopped and turned to her, tears filling her eyes, her lips trembling.

"What did you *do* with it all?" she asked. She waved a hand. "The junk, the garbage, the years of crud that was more important to them than—" Her head slumped forward and she lifted a hand to her eyes. She hunched her spine as if weighed down by crippling sorrow.

Taken aback and filled with pity at Maureen's distress, Lisa's natural instinct was to draw her mother into a hug, but the defensiveness of her shoulders made her stop. Instead she stammered out the same thing she'd said before. "Sold it, tossed it…a bunch of people helped me and—"

"How long did it take?" The words seemed to be wrenched from Maureen.

"Six months and then another two to renovate the house. I'd had an apartment of my own until they got sick and I moved back in to care for them, but when we started the cleanup, I lived with my friend Carly until it was done." She fell silent. Maureen couldn't possibly be interested in her living arrangements while Rich Richmond's construction firm had finished the renovations. Nor would she be interested in hearing of the emotional support she'd needed after losing the ones who had raised her within weeks of each other, and when she'd sorted through mountains and hills and piles of the worthless junk they had spent more than fifty years collecting.

A wave of nausea rose in her throat and she had to say, "Excuse me," and hurry to her en suite bathroom where she couldn't be heard. She threw up, rinsed her mouth and once again stood looking at her devastated face and stunned expression in the mirror.

This had been a day of shocks, and she had the horrible feeling they weren't over yet.

"The hits just keep coming," she murmured, rubbing her sore hip.

Her thoughts went to Ben and the shock he must have felt when she'd told him about the baby. The surprise of having Maureen show up made her a little more sympathetic about

Ben's reaction. But not much, she thought, pushing away from the sink and returning to the room where Maureen waited.

The older woman looked as though she had pulled herself together. She glanced up from where she'd seated herself on the sofa. "Are you all right?" she asked, her gaze swiftly taking in Lisa's appearance from head to toe.

"Yes. I'm fine." Lisa provided the automatic reassurance, although she didn't feel fine. She took a chair opposite the sofa.

Maureen looked around, her face still dazed. "It's so clean and beautiful. I can't believe all you've accomplished." She paused and then she met Lisa's gaze. "I'm sorry I didn't call first. I—" She shook her head again. "Honestly, it didn't occur to me that you still lived here. When I drove up, I thought I was in the wrong place. I didn't have to drive through head-high dead weeds or dodge a row of engine parts and a dozen old transmissions."

"And a pile of wheels and axles," Lisa added. "Grandpa started moving those to the front of the house in the year before he died. Not sure why he didn't display that particular collection sooner."

"It's impossible to know how his mind

worked." Maureen's lips tightened and she looked away, her attention going to a small brass statue of a pair of praying hands that stood on the end table. Reaching out, she ran her hand over it. Lisa had found it in the bottom of a box of papers, its surface unmarked from having been buried for half a century. The words *Lily and Violet* had been scratched on the bottom in childish carving, so it must have belonged to one of them as a child. "There was so much of it…everywhere, strangling everything."

Lisa couldn't tell if she was experiencing grief, sorrow, disgust or some other emotion. She didn't know her mother well enough to read her expressions, know her thoughts. Sadness, fueled by her tiredness and expectant-mother hormones, had tears springing into her eyes. She quickly wiped them away and stood to go to the kitchen. Forcing normalcy into her voice she said, "I've got to get something to eat. Would you like to join me?"

"Yes, please." Maureen sounded surprised at the invitation. "Do you need some help?"

"No, thanks. I've got it." Lisa waved a hand. "Look around some more if you want to."

Happy to escape and collect her thoughts,

she went into the kitchen and pulled out a chicken stew she'd made on Sunday. She poured it into a pan and, while it heated, made a salad. The whole time her mind was frantically racing, trying to figure out why her mother was there. Maureen had only visited a handful of times since she'd left at the age of sixteen. She had never spent the night.

Lisa paused in her preparations, staring down at her hands. Did Maureen expect to stay the night? Or longer? If so, why?

She set the table and called Maureen in.

"Oh, this smells wonderful," her mother said as she sat. "Did Mom teach you how to cook?"

"A few things. Mostly I taught myself."

Maureen gave her a thoughtful look. "Forgive me, Lisa, but I have to ask. You don't have to answer if you don't want to. After they…died, why did you stay here? Fix it up? You could have simply walked away." She gave a laugh. "Or set a match to the whole thing."

Lisa's lips wavered in a smile. "Don't think I didn't consider that, but arson is against the law."

She hadn't answered the question but

Maureen didn't push her. In truth, Lisa had cleaned up and refurbished the place because she was hoping it would give her some answers about why her grandparents had been the way they were. Why Maureen had left. She hadn't found any of those things and had frequently questioned her own sanity while sorting through and disposing of the mess. She didn't want to say such a thing quite yet, though.

She knew that if Maureen felt free to ask why she'd stayed, Lisa could ask why her mother had left. She didn't want to hear the answer tonight, though. She'd had enough.

Dinner conversation was awkward. Lisa knew it was because the only things they had in common were the unlivable home in which they'd grown up and the two people whose lives could best be described as dysfunctional.

As they were finishing their meal, Lisa made them each a cup of tea. Maureen took a sip, then played with the handle of the cup. She jerked in a deep breath and said, "Dinner was delicious. Thank you. I guess you want to know why I'm here."

"Yes, I'd like to know. I mean, if you want

to talk about it." Lisa lifted her hands help-lessly. "I've only seen you a few times. This past hour has been the longest conversation we've ever had."

"I know." Maureen looked down at her hands, which Lisa could see were scarred and work-worn. "Did you ever read a poem by Robert Frost that has a line in it about home being where they have to take you in when you go there?"

"Well, yes. I studied American literature. It's called 'Death of the Hired Man.'" Lisa drew in a sharp breath. "Maureen, are you *dying*?"

Horror flooded Maureen's face. "No, no. I'm sorry. I would never burden you with that. I didn't mean for it to come out like that. I'm saying this all wrong. I'm not dying, but I've been sick with an antibiotic-resistant infec-tion. Even though I had health insurance, the hospital bills and treatments wiped out most of my savings. I lost my job and my apart-ment. I had to get away from the weather in Illinois, so I thought I'd come here." Shame filled her face. "I know it's a lot to ask. You probably think I've got a lot of nerve."

"I don't know what to think," Lisa admitted. Her brain and her emotions were on overload. She desperately wanted to go to bed and pull the covers over her head. She could see that Maureen was as exhausted as she was, her eyes drooping and her face set in grim lines.

"When I drove up tonight, I planned to ask the new owners of this place if they knew where you lived, but then you came home—"

"And...you want to stay?"

"Only a little while, until I can find a job, get back on my feet." She gave Lisa a desperate look. "I promise it'll only be for a little while."

Through the swirl of her emotions, she mostly felt curious. "Why, after all these years?"

"Several reasons, but mostly unresolved history, and I decided I had to return to my hometown and quit being a coward. When I... ran away, I went to Aunt Violet in Chicago."

"Yes, Grandma told me."

"Before she died, she told me I had to come here, make things right, or I would never have peace." She tilted her head and gave another little shrug.

With a start, Lisa remembered that her grandfather had made exactly that gesture.

Lisa's heart ached. She had been dealing with her own problems all day, but she knew this woman had a much bigger one. Lisa might be expecting a baby that would change her life in ways she couldn't yet imagine, but she had security, friends and her own business. Maureen had nothing except a daughter she barely knew—and consequences for actions she'd taken thirty-three years ago.

Lisa wanted to know more, much more, about Maureen's motivations, reasons, life, but she couldn't handle one more thing tonight.

In her mind Lisa could hear Gemma and Carly warning her to be careful, that it might all be a scam, but she met Maureen's hesitant gaze and said, "Of course you can stay. You can have my old room—your old room, or the smallest bedroom, whichever one you want."

CHAPTER FOUR

IN SPITE OF the chilly wind that was swirling dead leaves around his boots, Ben stood jacketless and bareheaded by the pasture fence and stared out at his mustangs. He had enough land to support a herd twice this size, but right now this was as much as he could handle.

He was waiting for Zach, Jason Littletrees's cousin, who would teach Ben about the horses and manage the herd.

Jason had suggested Ben should learn all he could while Zach was on the Riverbend. Zach never stayed in one place too long, so when Zach moved on, Ben would know what to look for in a new ranch manager. Ben hadn't planned to hire another one. He'd hoped Zach would be a permanent fixture. However he'd called around and learned that Zach was the best at what he did, and that was what Ben wanted. He would deal with a new hire when the time came.

In the meantime he was brooding about the bombshell Lisa had dropped on him the day before. He'd had twenty-four hours to get used to the idea of being a dad, and he still couldn't wrap his mind around it. He hunched his shoulders against the cutting breeze and thought back over the conversation they'd had the day before.

Everything he'd told Lisa was true. He'd never intended to be a father or thought it would be forced on him. On the other hand, Lisa probably hadn't intended to be a mother, either, at least not right now. He knew he felt reluctant about his impending fatherhood, but he didn't know how Lisa felt about motherhood. She was adamant about keeping the baby, but he didn't know how she actually felt about it. He didn't really know her.

They'd been friends when they were kids, at least until the infamous jailbreak, after which his parents had refused to let him have anything to do with her. It still made him chuckle to remember that her plan had been for them to make their way to where the Canadian River ran through Oklahoma and follow it to Canada. The Canadian River would have taken them nowhere near Canada, but they'd had no chance to find out because his dad and Sheriff Jepson had tracked them down only a few blocks from the jail.

His punishment had been to apologize to Mrs. Crabtree, weed her garden all summer and burn the slingshot that had landed him in jail in the first place. He'd been so busy, there'd been no chance of getting into any trouble, or even seeing much of his friends until fall. He obeyed his parents' orders to avoid Lisa and it had become a habit over the years. Until last December in Chicago.

He walked along the fence line, favoring his right knee, an old football injury that stiffened up on him in the cold. What did he actually know about Lisa, the woman who was going to be the mother of his child? They had graduated from high school together and he'd gone straight to play for the Sooners. Oh, and got a business degree while he was at it.

Lisa was smart, near the top of their class, but she'd gone to the community college, taken care of her grandparents on that landfill they'd called a ranch and had become a whiz at real estate, even had her own business. He felt a spark of pride in all she'd done for herself. It was good to know their child wouldn't lack for ambition.

What would the kid lack, though? What did a baby need beyond the tangible items like food, clothing, a crib, diapers? He had no idea.

At the sound of someone pulling into his lane, he turned around to see an older pickup with shining silver paint pulling an ancient Airstream. It was coming his way.

It must be Zach.

Ben had offered to let him live in the house, but the horseman had said he would bring his own house with him. Ben knew that itinerant ranch and rodeo workers often had their own motor homes or mobile homes, but he'd never before seen one like this. It was old, but its top-of-the-line pedigree showed in the Airstream's clean lines and shining silver skin. It had either been well cared for or beautifully restored, and so had the pickup, which he could now see was a 1950s-era Ford F-1 painted silver to match the Airstream.

Ben knew the rig must get a lot of attention as it rolled down the road.

Zach deftly pulled his truck to a stop, reversed, and maneuvered his home into place beside the rambling ranch house. The shining truck and trailer only served to make Ben's place look even worse. Before he could walk over to greet his new employee, he heard another vehicle on the road and glanced back to see three more cars following Zach onto Riverbend Ranch.

Amazed, Ben saw that all three of them were classic cars, built in the days when Detroit really knew what it was doing—a 1955 turquoise-and-white Chevrolet Bel Air, a 1959 Chevrolet Impala with sparkling black paint and distinctive tail fins, and a root beer–colored 1966 Ford Mustang convertible that made Ben's heart pound. All three cars were driven by women who stepped out and walked toward Ben, hands outstretched in greeting.

They were dressed in tight jeans and snug tops that showed off their figures. Ben had been carefully taught by his mother to never ask a woman's age, but he guessed these three to be well past fifty.

"Hello. Ben, isn't it?" the petite, blonds driver of the Mustang said as she took his hand. "I'm Denise Clark, a friend of Zach's." She removed the scarf that had been protecting her hair from the wind and turned to wiggle her fingers at Zach, who was walking over to join them.

"Um, hello. I'm, uh, happy to meet you, Ms. Clark." Before Ben could say any more, Denise was elbowed aside by the other two women, who Ben could now see were twins. Denise stumbled back and gave them a dark look.

"Hi," one of them said. "I'm Ginger Afton, and this is my sister, Cinnamon Vale."

Ben nodded. Ginger and Cinnamon? Really? "Uh, welcome to Riverbend Ranch."

Zach joined them right then and introduced himself, giving Ben's hand a bone-shattering shake that reverberated up his arm and rattled his teeth.

"Glad to meet you, Ben, and glad to be back in the area where I can work with some Choctaw ponies."

"He's been in Arkansas," Denise breathed, a wistful tone in her voice. "That's where we met him. In Fayetteville. At a classic car show."

That explained the vehicles, if nothing else, Ben thought. "That's wonderful, ladies."

The three sighed in unison as Cinnamon—

or was it Ginger?—said, "Happiest day of our lives."

Nodding, Ben recalled that Fayetteville was in the northern part of the state, almost a four-hour drive away. Looking from one to the other of the women, he tried to decipher their expressions and finally decided it could only be described as love struck.

"Oh, now, you ladies are being too nice. Meeting ol' Zach couldn't have been the *best* day." His expression said he expected them to dispute that, which they did with declarations of how much they would miss him.

"We came along to make sure he arrived safely," the other twin offered. "We would be heartbroken if anything happened to him."

All three women sighed and Zach shrugged one shoulder and ducked his head modestly as he removed his cowboy hat, revealing a shock of thick, black hair touched with gray. He held his hat over his heart as he said, "My guardian angels."

Who is this guy? Ben wondered, returning his attention to Zach, who was smiling at the three women with a fond expression. The guy was fifty if he was a day, possessed of a hawk-like nose that had been broken at least once and deep-set eyes that were so black and intense it was impossible to distinguish the pupil from the iris. He had a winning smile but was missing a bicuspid on the top right side. Maybe that added to his appeal to these women.

Obviously looks weren't everything, Ben decided. Zach had some admirers.

"It's wonderful that he's got, um, friends like you ladies," Ben said in response, though he knew none was expected. He could have disappeared into thin air and none of his guests would have noticed. He wondered fleetingly why the three of them hadn't ridden together, but when he saw the snapping, side-eyed looks they were giving each other, he figured there had been danger of one of them pushing the other two out of the vehicle as they followed Zach to Reston.

The Choctaw charmer turned a smile on the ladies. It was so full of sweetness and gratitude they all seemed to blush in unison. "You girls made my stay in Fayetteville a visit straight to heaven. I hope you come back and visit me again real soon."

"I will," they said, once again passing a challenging glare between them.

"I'll hold you to that," he said, beginning to walk his three admirers to their cars.

"Now, Zachie, don't forget to call me. You've got my number," Denise said. "I put it in your phone myself. It's listed under my name and also under Sexy Lady."

Ginger and Cinnamon snorted in disdain, but Zach said, "I sure do have your number, honey. And you other two beautiful women, too."

Gallantly, he opened the driver's doors for each of them in turn, gave them a kiss on the cheek and then watched, his face full of regret, as they made the big turn in Ben's driveway and started out for Fayetteville. Zach gave them a sad wave as they each pulled out, their arms stuck out the windows, hands flapping in goodbye as they went.

Ben had to admit it. The old guy had some moves. When the last car in line pulled out of sight, Zach turned to Ben, rubbed his hands together and said, "I'd like to go down and take a look at the horses as soon as I get my trailer hooked up to power and water. I've got a hot date tonight."

He hurried to his Airstream as Ben gaped

after him. Things just got a lot more interesting at Riverbend Ranch.

"YOUR MOTHER? YOU mean Maureen, right?" Carly asked, a slice of pizza suspended in front of her mouth. Slowly she returned it to the plate and sat staring at Lisa. Gemma appeared to be equally astounded.

In spite of husbands and family responsibilities, Gemma, Carly and Lisa had vowed to continue their Girls Night In at least once a month. Fortunately this one had fallen on the night after Maureen's arrival, so Lisa had an excuse for delaying her return home. They had gathered around Carly's dining room table to enjoy their feast of pizza, salad and soft drinks. Carly's husband and son had gone to play cards with Nathan.

"That's right. Showed up yesterday, out of the blue, asked to stay." Lisa told her friends everything that had happened, including her talk with Ben.

"Oh, you *did* have a busy day." Carly returned to her slice of pizza, taking a bite and chewing thoughtfully. "How do you feel about all of that?"

Lisa took a tiny bite of pizza, although she

was afraid even that much wouldn't stay down. She couldn't face another bite of saltine crackers or anything else bland. She craved something with flavor. "I was shocked to see Maureen. I didn't get a chance to talk to her this morning before I left for the office. All I know is that she's been sick and has no place else to go. And Ben...? I'm disappointed."

"Humph," Carly snorted. "Might be time for another visit from the Stiletto Mafia."

Gemma and Lisa exchanged a look. "Maybe," Gemma said.

Carly grinned at them. "My husband tells me that he was shaking in his boots last summer when he received that visit from you two at his office in Dallas right before he came up here to work on his oil extraction process."

Gemma snickered. "It was only a friendly chat."

"Oh, come on. You gave him the distinct impression that if he hurt me, he'd end up at the bottom of Lake Texhoma modeling a pair of cement shoes." Carly glanced at Gemma. "Only, this time, you and I will be the ones protecting Lisa's back."

Lisa smiled and sipped her lemon-lime soda even as she blinked back tears at the loyalty of her friends. Their support of her was straightforward and unbending. They were the ones she could always depend on. That was good because she doubted she could depend on Ben, except perhaps financially, and she had learned long ago that Maureen would never be a part of her life.

As if she'd picked up on Lisa's thoughts, Gemma asked, "Besides needing a place to recover, did your moth—uh…Maureen say why she came to see you?"

"To make amends, but she seems…I'd say desperate but I don't know her well enough to know if it's desperation or something else."

Even if she had been sick and was out of resources, there must have been other options open for her. Lisa didn't even know if her mother would be at the house when she got there or if the place would be cleaned out of all valuables. But as she'd told Gemma, other than owning more shoes than she needed, Lisa didn't collect things. Any items lost could be replaced.

"It just seems so strange," Carly said. "You haven't seen her more than a few times in your life, and now she's moved back in."

"It's only temporary," Lisa hastened to say.

"Although I don't know how temporary. I long ago gave up any idea of having a relationship with her." Lisa shook her head. "When I was little, I constantly dreamed she'd show up and sweep me away to the fairy castle where I was sure she lived—with my dad, the magical king."

Gemma and Carly exchanged a look. "We remember," Carly said.

"It's strange having her there," Lisa went on. "Nothing like what I imagined as a little girl. Honestly, I didn't know what to imagine. When I was small, I tried to picture her in our house, but I couldn't imagine a fairy queen in full royal regalia sitting on top of the stacks of magazines that covered the sofa, or eating at the dining room table between the car parts and empty egg cartons."

"I think by the time we were twelve or so, you'd given up on her ever coming back," Gemma said.

"That's true and, really, she did me a favor. She went away and stayed away and anytime she came, she always made it clear that it was for a very short visit, a few hours at most. I suppose that was better. I only got my heart broken once instead of over and over like some kids do." She frowned.

"What?" Gemma asked.

"Saying that made me think that maybe Ben is right."

"That's a first," Carly said. "Why?"

"He never wanted a family because he's gone so much. He said it wouldn't be fair to a child."

"But now there *is* a child," Gemma pointed out. "That changes things."

"No. It's a reality for me, but not for him. My life, my goals of all I want to do in Preston, will probably change. His won't. Even if I loved him, I couldn't be with a man who will be gone so much his child would begin referring to him as 'Uncle Daddy.'"

Her friends laughed.

"I'm serious," Lisa said firmly. "My child will be in the same situation I was in—having an absent parent. I know what to say and do to help my baby deal with it—to learn not to expect anything more than financial support."

"That's sad," Carly said.

"But it's the way things are."

All three of them fell silent, deep in thought. Lisa's shoulders slumped. "What if I'm like

Maureen? What if I fail my kid? The only thing my baby will have that I didn't is that he'll know who his father is."

Both of her friends rushed to hug her. "That won't happen. You won't fail, and besides, you'll have us," Gemma said.

Lisa blinked back tears. She wanted to believe them, but she was too overwhelmed to think clearly.

That was one of the most frustrating aspects of this situation. She always had a plan in mind, and Plan B and C as backups. Being indecisive had never been a problem before.

Returning their hugs, she stood. "I've got to go. If Maureen is still at my house, I hope to get some answers."

"And I'd better save some pizza for Dustin."

Gemma frowned. "But Nathan was cooking dinner for them. He made a huge pan of lasagna."

"Believe me, Dustin will still be hungry." Carly sighed. "And so you know, if he convinced Nathan and Luke to make bets on the outcome of the card game, he may also be in possession of the deed to your house, all your good jewelry and quite possibly your retirement fund."

Gemma laughed but Lisa said, "It must be hard having a child who is smarter than all the adults in his life put together."

"You have no idea," Carly said, but Lisa heard a hint of pride in her voice.

MAUREEN SAT AT the small breakfast nook, sipping a cup of tea and watching out the window for Lisa to come home.

She asked herself, yet again, what she was expecting from this visit. She knew that Lisa would ask her that question at some point, and Maureen hoped to have an answer.

What she had told her daughter was true. After a lifetime of minimum-wage jobs, living either with Violet or in cheap apartments, she'd worked her way into better and better situations and then lost what she'd saved to illness. She hadn't inherited anything from Violet and hadn't expected to. Her grief at her aunt's death had been overwhelming, especially when she'd seen Lisa at the funeral and been unable to speak much to her.

She knew she could never make up for the past and she had no idea what kind of future she had, but she'd been at rock bottom when she'd arrived in Oklahoma, her old home, and been taken in by the daughter she had no right to claim.

She had spent the day walking over the property where she had played as a child, where her own daughter had played. Now it was free of the car parts and rusted, twisted metal that had been such a safety hazard.

There were no more acres of old tires that looked like ugly black doughnuts that filled with rainwater in the summer, perfect breeding ground for the swarms of mosquitoes that had made summer outdoor life so miserable at the Thomas homestead.

The entire place had been a hazard, with tetanus, mosquito-borne illnesses, serious cuts and other injuries waiting to happen. It was also where she had abandoned her baby, an action that still weighed her down with guilt.

Since she'd grown up and learned something about health and safety laws, she had wondered why the county hadn't forced them to clean the place up. Maybe it had been too much for even career bureaucrats to tackle.

She had marveled at the landscape revealed by the cleanup. In a few weeks, it would be enhanced by the first shoots of grass and wildflowers. Filled with a mixture of joy and surprise at what Lisa had accomplished, and regret that she'd had to do it alone, Maureen had been worn out from her trek. Still weak from her illness, she had fallen onto the guest room bed, where she had breathed deeply, drawing in scents she'd never before detected in this house—lemon furniture polish and fresh air.

Lisa pulled into the driveway but didn't come into the house for a few minutes, so Maureen went to the back door and peeked through the curtain. To her alarm, she saw that Lisa was standing in the V formed by the open car door and was bent over double, one hand to her throat, the other on her stomach.

She jerked the door open and dashed down the steps. "Lisa, what's wrong?"

"I'm okay," Lisa murmured. "Just need a minute."

"You obviously *aren't* okay," Maureen answered, taking her daughter's hand and urging her to step out so she could get an arm around her and support her into the house.

Once she had Lisa seated in the kitchen, she ran out, gathered her purse and laptop case from the car, locked the vehicle and rushed back inside.

"Do you need to go to the emergency room?" Maureen asked, putting a hand on Lisa's forehead then touching her cheeks. "You don't have a fever, but sometimes it doesn't start right away when you get sick."

"No," Lisa answered, her voice distant. She turned her face away as she repeated, "I'm okay."

"You're white as paper," Maureen declared frantically. "I'm calling an ambulance right now."

"No!" Lisa lurched to her feet, but when Maureen tried to push her back into the chair, she was shaken off. "I...I need the bathroom."

Lisa stumbled through the house with Maureen following, peppering her with questions that Lisa ignored. The bathroom door was shut firmly in Maureen's face, but she heard the sound of retching, which only raised her level of alarm.

When the toilet flushed and Lisa emerged, face still pale, her eyes tearing with illness and distress, Maureen grabbed her around the waist and helped her to her bed.

"How long have you been like this? This could be a serious case of the flu or...or some other virus or bacteria. I should know. One just like this nearly killed me. I'm calling an ambulance. If it's really bad, they may have to put you in isolation and—"

"I'm not sick!"

"You're not only sick, you're probably contagious." Fear and dread set Maureen's heart pounding. What if she caught it, too? Her immune system was still recovering. Another virus could kill her. But if her daughter needed her… "But…but don't worry. I'll take care of you." She gulped. "No matter what."

Lisa perched on the side of the bed. "No, Maureen. I'm not sick."

Caught up in the memory of her own illness, the days of fever, the painful shudders that had racked her body, the weakness that had prevented her from so much as turning herself over in bed, Maureen didn't hear her.

"I'll be with you every minute. I'll take care of you." She slipped off Lisa's high heels and set them beside the bed as she talked. "I won't even leave you alone at the hospital. I'll make them bring in a cot or something for me. I'll make sure you get the best care. You've got insurance, right? Believe me, you don't want to be without insurance

when you've got a major illness like this."
She reached to swing Lisa's feet onto the bed.

"No!"

"I'm glad you agree," Maureen said. The
more the thoughts of illness overcame her, the
faster she talked. "I know you have insurance.
You're a successful businesswoman. You'd
never be without something that important."
She tried to settle Lisa against the pillows,
but Lisa resisted.

"No! Stop," Lisa said weakly.

"Just lie down. I'm making you more comfortable."

"Maureen!" Lisa's voice rose to a shout and
Maureen looked up, blinking.

"What?"

"I'm not sick. I'm pregnant." Lisa lifted her
hand and let it fall. "It's only morning sickness, except I have it all day and sometimes
all night. I can't keep anything down."

Maureen staggered backward and plopped
into the chair Lisa had positioned beside a
reading lamp. "Pregnant?" she asked. "I'm
going to be a grandmother?"

LISA STARED AT MAUREEN, thinking that in
order to be a grandmother, didn't a person

have to be a mother first? Or at least show up every once in a while and act like one? She didn't say that, however. For all she knew, the craziness of the past ten minutes may have been Maureen's way of acting like a mother. It was too overwhelming and confusing, and she couldn't sort it out while she felt this lousy.

"I'm due in September," was all she answered.

Moving cautiously, she sat up, gave her head a moment to clear, then scooted back. Before she could prop the pillows against her back, Maureen leaped up and did it for her, taking pains to adjust them just so.

When she was finally satisfied, she said, "There," and tried to gently ease Lisa to rest her head against the headboard.

"I can do it," Lisa protested, though her voice was weak. The wave of nausea had passed.

"Well, a baby. Th-that's wonderful…" Maureen's voice trailed off as she once again sat in the bedside chair.

Lisa didn't respond, knowing from first-hand experience how hard it was to absorb this news. Once her stomach settled a little more, she swung her feet to the floor and got ready to stand.

Immediately, Maureen was beside her, taking her arm. "You need to stay in bed."

"I can't. I've got to get ready for a meeting tomorrow. Some investors from Oklahoma City are sending a representative to see property on Reston Lake. They're considering building a resort there."

"A resort?" Maureen asked. "In Reston?"

"That's right."

"Things really have changed." She seemed taken aback for a moment but then focused once again on her daughter. "For right now, you need to let me help you. Where do you need to go? Back to the bathroom? Maybe we should keep a bucket and a bedside portable toilet here."

"I'm not an invalid," Lisa protested, horrified at the idea. "My doctor says this will pass and I'll feel much better, but in the meantime he gave me something for the morning sickness. It's in my purse." She had picked up a prescription that Nathan said would help the nausea, and she was certainly ready to try it.

"I'll get it." Maureen pushed her back onto

the bed, reached down to sweep her feet up, then dashed from the room.

Dismayed, Lisa stared after her. Even though she had lived with her grandparents, they'd had their own interests—obsessions, really—her grandfather with his collections and her grandmother with her books. Lisa had been left to her own devices, which was why Gemma's and Carly's families had been so precious to her. She wasn't accustomed to having anyone fuss over her.

If Maureen stuck around, this was going to be a very long pregnancy.

CHAPTER FIVE

BEN PULLED HIS phone from his pocket and stared at the blank screen as he sat on his porch steps. He hadn't heard from Lisa in the past week. Considering the way they'd parted at his ranch, he'd decided to let her cool down.

He also hadn't heard from her attorney about arrangements regarding the baby, and he hadn't contacted his own. That gave him hope that they could work this out without getting lawyers involved. A legal agreement might be best, but he didn't want to be seen as someone who ducked his obligations.

Until they had matters settled, he wasn't going to tell anyone about the baby. He dreaded telling his parents. They would be thrilled about the child, but he knew it would be a battle to make them understand that this wouldn't change how much he would be around. As he'd told Lisa, he'd never intended to have children.

He had a number of important projects coming up, including plans for his lengthy stay in India. He had to go out of town to meet with the governing board for one of his charities, and he wanted this settled before any more time passed.

He was determined to try talking to her again. He punched in the cell phone number he had finagled out of Sandy Borden and when Lisa answered, he said, "Please don't hang up, Lisa. It's Ben, and we need to talk."

"Ben." Her voice went flat with surprise. "I didn't expect to hear from you again."

He held the phone away for a second, stared at it, then replaced it by his ear. Had she thought he was going to let this drop?

"If you want to get lawyers involved, we can do that, but I think if we meet and talk, we can work things out. Anyplace you want to meet, Lisa," he said. "Anytime. I can come to your house or your office or—"

"No. We can meet on neutral ground, at the new little park by the post office. It's a nice day and…we can sit on a bench."

"All right, but why out in the open like that?"

"Everyone is going to find out about the baby soon, anyway. It's not like it's something I'll be able to hide for much longer. Um, by the way, have you told your parents yet?"

"No. I'll tell them when you're ready for people to know. They've always wanted a grandchild but—"

"Not this way."

"Honestly, I think they'll be happy about the baby and they'll want to be involved if that's okay with you. But regarding…everything else, I don't know how they'll react."

They agreed on a time and hung up, but Ben sat for long minutes, staring across his pastures to where Zach was doctoring a gash on the front leg of one of the mares.

His thoughts raced ahead to everything he had to accomplish in the next year, obligations he'd set up months ago with the help of an occasional assistant in Tulsa. He wondered briefly if he was committing to too many things, taking on too much. He liked having many interests, though. He became restless and bored if he didn't keep busy.

Leaning forward, he rested his forearms on his knees and clasped his hands loosely. He wasn't ready to give up his busy lifestyle.

There was no reason to, at least not yet. He would do the right thing by Lisa and the baby, but he saw no reason to change his life.

Satisfied with that conclusion, he went inside and got ready to meet Lisa.

THE SMALL PARK on the northwest corner of Main and Vogle had once been the site of a crumbling brick building that had, for many years, been a grocery store, then a Laundromat, then a garage. It had devolved into an abandoned eyesore when Lisa and some other citizens had convinced the mayor and city council to let them raise funds for a park.

As Lisa sat on the bench, made of heavy recycled plastic, and waited for Ben, she smoothed the full skirt of her navy blue dress and checked to make sure her beautiful Simon Love boots were still spotless.

She was glad she had chosen this outfit today. It was comfortable but completely professional. Of course, she hadn't known she would be meeting Ben when she had dressed that morning, but she always made a point of dressing nicely and choosing exactly the right shoes from her extensive collection. Before long, her dresses wouldn't fit and her swollen feet would lap over the sides of her shoes. No doubt, she would have to wear sneakers or flats every day.

To her horror, Gemma had told her that many women ended their pregnancies with bigger feet than when they had started. The muscles and bones in the feet relaxed to accommodate a pregnant woman's gait and often didn't return to their pre-pregnancy size. That meant none of her collection of beautiful footwear would fit.

Horrible. But for now she had something more important to focus on.

She made a few nervous pleats in her skirt before lacing her fingers together and sitting quietly. It was a beautiful day, warm for early March, and she took a deep breath of fresh air to calm herself. She knew meeting with Ben was the right thing to do. A calm, rational meeting would benefit both of them, but she couldn't seem to stop fretting over the outcome.

To ease her worries she proudly surveyed the park, which she'd chosen as a meeting spot because it was down the street from her office and she felt so proud when she saw it. The park included a small track around the perimeter for people who wanted to be off the street to take their morning walk, and a toddler play area with thick rubber mats beneath the swings and slides.

When she'd become involved in the project, it had been purely as a way to clean up a neglected lot and provide a bit of needed beauty to the area. It had never occurred to her that the generically named Main Street Park would one day be where she'd bring her own child to play.

Although she still didn't feel well most days, thanks to taking Nathan's prescription for the past week, she was no longer racked by overwhelming morning sickness. She was able to think ahead about her baby's future. She was still terrified at the thought of being a mother, but she knew she had to pull herself together and focus on what needed to be settled right now. And that included Ben and whatever he had to say.

Out of the corner of her eye she saw Ben's pickup pull into the parking lot that served both the park and most of the nearby businesses. As she watched, Ben stepped out, settled his cowboy hat on his head, slammed the door and started toward her. He was dressed in a dark red shirt beneath that buttery-soft leather jacket, crisp black jeans and black cowboy boots. Even though she knew the knee he'd injured probably gave him some pain, he didn't let it show; he walked quickly, with purpose. She hoped he wasn't in such a hurry so that he could check their business off and go on to the next thing on his agenda.

Before he reached her, he was stopped by two men who wanted to shake his hand and, no doubt, indulge in a lengthy talk about football. After a minute Ben extricated himself and continued toward her.

On the street, Deputy Sheriff Wayne Fedder, Jr., known as Junior Fedder to everyone in Reston County, honked and slowed down, calling out questions about their proposed fishing trip. Ben stopped to answer him while drivers lined up behind the deputy, waiting for him to move on and not daring to show their impatience.

Arrangements finally made, Junior went on his way, the line of cars began rolling, and Ben strolled toward her, waving and responding to people who called out to him.

"On second thought, maybe this wasn't the wisest choice for a meeting place," Lisa said with a rueful shake of her head. "Your adoring public doesn't seem to want to leave you alone."

"Ah, it'll be all right," he said. "I've been gone for a while. People are surprised to see me, that's all."

And soon he would be gone again, she thought. Might as well get this matter done and dusted.

As if he'd read her thoughts he said, "I'll be away on business for several days, so I wanted to get this settled."

"Of course." That made perfect sense, Lisa thought, but it bothered her that he was so businesslike about it. She took a sheet of paper from her purse and spread it open on her lap. "I've been researching the costs of raising a child and trying to come up with what seems to be a fair calculation of shared costs. Eventually we'll probably have to sign a legal agreement, but this seemed like a good place to start."

Ben took the paper from her. "You researched it?"

"I research everything, especially if it's important to me or to one of my clients. I don't like financial surprises."

"Well, no one does," Ben said as he glanced at the spreadsheet she'd prepared. His eyes widened comically and his eyebrows shot up to the inner sweatband of his hat as he read the bottom line.

"*This* is how much it costs to raise a kid these days?"

Lisa could have sworn she saw his hand tremble as he pointed to the figures.

"Yes. Like I said, I've done a great deal of research and—"

"Oh, I believe you," he said hastily. "But… wow."

"I know," she answered in a quiet tone. "I was shocked, too." She watched as Ben's gaze started at the top of the page again and ran down to the bottom. "Sandy mentioned that as kids get bigger, their clothes get more expensive. You wouldn't believe how much Derek's sneakers cost now that he wears a size thirteen." She glanced at Ben's hand-tooled boots. "Well, maybe you would."

Ben barely seemed to be listening as he examined the figures she'd come up with.

"And that's really only an estimate," she added. "But it does factor in a college fund."

"Unless he can get a football scholarship," Ben murmured, obviously thinking of his own method of getting to the university.

"He?"

Ben glanced up. "Um, sorry. I guess it could be a girl."

Lisa gave him an amused look. "Well, apparently we've got a fifty-fifty chance."

"Ah, Ben, there you are," Harley Morton called out as he dashed across the street from the Main Street Diner. His face was red and he was sweating profusely. "I need to talk to you again." He glanced over. "Hey, Lisa…" He paused to catch his breath. "How…how are you?"

"I'm fine, Harley," she answered, then scooted over quickly to make room for him on the bench as she saw him stagger slightly. Ben made a grab for his arm. "Here, sit down. Are you okay?"

The mayor sat, but waved away her concern as he mopped his face with his jacket sleeve and said, "Fine, fine, just…fine. Little touch of indigestion, is all. Probably should have skipped the coconut cake I had for dessert."

"Um, yes." Lisa and Ben exchanged alarmed looks as more sweat popped out on Harley's forehead and he breathed hard for a few seconds.

"I'm okay." He turned to Ben with a smile that looked ghastly in his suddenly pale face. "So, Ben, I was thinking we need to rename this park in your honor. Ben McAdams Park. How does that sound?"

In one of the typically expansive moves Lisa had seen him make a thousand times, he lifted his hand to encompass the park but instead, suddenly, clutched his side.

"I don't...I don't feel so—" He slumped against Ben, his head lolling.

Horrified, Lisa made a grab for him as he fell into unconsciousness.

"Lisa, call 911," Ben said as he lifted Harley away from her and swung him around so his feet were on the bench. Bending, he checked the mayor's pulse and began pressing rhythmically on his chest.

A crowd quickly gathered, with others stepping in to take over the chest compressions from Ben. The paramedics arrived within minutes to whisk Harley to the Reston County Hospital that had reopened only months before.

Shaken, Lisa watched the ambulance pull away, carrying the unconscious mayor, the one who could be counted on to be everywhere and involved in everything.

With unsteady hands, she called Gemma at the Sunshine Birthing Center so she could alert Harley's wife. Brenda could probably meet the ambulance when it arrived. The Sunshine was right next to the hospital.

"He'll be okay, Lisa," Ben assured her when she disconnected, though he didn't sound quite convinced. "Maybe we'd better go to the hospital, see how he is."

"Yes. We might be needed."

They hurried to Ben's truck and drove the ten blocks to the hospital. Inside the waiting room, Brenda Morton sat weeping, with Gemma holding her hand.

Lisa rushed over and sat beside them.

Brenda clutched at her, saying in distress, "They think it's a heart attack. He's only fifty-five! Gemma says you were there. What happened?"

Lisa reported Harley's actions just before he collapsed.

"Of *course*, he would be taking care of town business," Brenda said, wiping her eyes with a tissue. "He can't stop, or let anything go, or delegate what needs to be done. Won't take more than the weekend off. We haven't had a real vacation since he was first elected mayor. And every day he's got some new idea that has to be taken care of today if not sooner."

"He'll be fine," Lisa said, knowing it sounded lame and looking at Gemma, who gave a tiny shrug.

"With Jay going off to college in the fall, we'll finally be empty nesters," Brenda said. "He promised he wouldn't run in the next election. That he'd take it easier, visit our kids more often."

Harley had been mayor for twelve years and had been responsible for bringing new businesses and developments into town. Lisa knew the city would be very different without him at the helm, even though she nurtured her own dream of being mayor.

"I'm sure you'll still be able to do those things, Brenda," Gemma assured her. "Let's just wait and see what Nathan and the other doctors have to say."

The Mortons' son, Jay, rushed in with his girlfriend, Sheena. Brenda immediately folded them into her arms.

Lisa and Gemma stood and moved away so the family could be together.

Right behind Jay came the deputy mayor and all three members of the city council. The four spoke briefly to Brenda and Jay, then huddled in a corner.

Lisa and Gemma exchanged an apprehensive look at the four men, which Ben must have noticed because he whispered, "What's going on?"

"The deputy mayor and the city council members can't get along for more than five minutes. They're like horses pulling in all directions of the compass. Harley always acts as mediator in order to get anything done," Lisa told him.

"Which probably only adds to his stress."

"No doubt," Gemma said. "I'm going to go see if Nathan has anything to report." She disappeared down the hallway.

Ben leaned up against the wall and crossed his feet at the ankles. He frowned as he looked at the city officials. "I wonder why they're here."

"Habit," Lisa answered, taking an empty seat next to him. "They all own businesses that could use their attention, but they each have different interests and different goals for the city. If something happens that might affect their own interests, they swoop in to make sure their voice is heard. You should have seen the battle we had two years ago over finding a buyer and reopening the Mustang Supermarket."

Ben gave her a blank stare. "I admit I don't know much about city business, but what was it they couldn't agree on?"

"Deputy Mayor Dale Barnal wanted the supermarket, but only if he could be the sole owner, when really, he hadn't shown any interest in buying and reopening the place until it looked like some out-of-town investors might be stepping up. They wanted tax breaks, which Dale didn't think they should get.

"Councilman Roland Hall wanted the Choctaw tribe to annex the property and turn it into a casino. Councilman Dalton Bunker—"

"Let me guess," Ben broke in. "Bunky wanted the building to be turned into a dance hall. I know he loves to dance."

"And has no sense of rhythm. Whenever he hears music, it's like he's possessed by some kind evil spirit of the dance, and he wants Gemma to be his partner. Bunky wanted the property to be a cabaret or nightclub, with him as the master of ceremonies."

Ben grinned. "In this conservative town? I'll bet that didn't go over well."

"No, it didn't. They finally agreed on tax incentives for the investment group to take on the supermarket project, but the group didn't want to repave the parking lot, which made no sense. The city council refused to dig up and repave it, though. There's still a dip in it that fills with enough rainwater to swamp a Volkswagen Beetle."

"Still?"

"Always. I guess they think it's part of the charm."

Ben nodded. "And the younger guy? I don't know him," he asked, nodding to the last member in the group.

"Trent Sanderson—Luke's cousin—has been in town for only a few years. He's new on the council, has some good ideas the others won't listen to because they're old and crotchety and he's young and progressive." Lisa smiled. "He had no idea what he was getting into, poor guy. I guess it's unfair to say he's pulling in the opposite direction from the others. I think he's only trying to hang on for dear life in hopes of getting them to listen to reason."

"Good luck to him."

Ben watched the youngest member of the council turn away from the others with a massive eye-roll. He stalked across the room toward Lisa, who introduced him to Ben. The two men shook hands.

Trent blew out a frustrated breath and said, "Harley could be knocking on death's door and the only thing the three of them can think of are their own interests. I've ridden bulls that were easier to control than they are."

Lisa snickered, but grew solemn when Nathan strode into the room accompanied by Gemma and one of the new doctors who had moved into the area and opened a practice, Neil O'Conner. He and Neil pulled Brenda Morton and her family aside to confer in low voices. The city councilmen strained to eavesdrop and looked disappointed when the group headed down the hall. Gemma came over to Lisa.

"It was a heart attack. Harley says he's been feeling bad for weeks but didn't want to worry anyone. Nathan and Dr. O'Conner are sending him to a cardiac unit in Tulsa. It will be a long recovery." Gemma took her phone from her pocket. "I'm going to call

Carly. She'll want to know what's going on since Jay and Sheena both work for her. I'm betting she'll ask her family in Tulsa to let the Mortons stay with them until Harley can come home."

Before she called, she gave Lisa a puzzled look and said, "In the meantime, Harley wants to talk to you. Says he won't leave here until he does. In fact, he wants to see you right after he sees his family."

"Why me?"

"I don't know, but he's adamant."

Lisa looked at Ben and Trent, who both shrugged. "Okay. I'll see what he wants."

"I'll come with you to try to keep him calm," Gemma offered.

With a nod, Lisa hurried from the room and down the hallway, Gemma rushing along with her. Before she even entered the examination room, Brenda came out, grabbed her arm and pulled her into an alcove.

"I need to talk to you before you see him," Brenda said.

"Of course. What is it?"

"Harley wants you to be acting mayor until he's well," she said.

"What?"

"You heard me." Brenda's face was frantic with worry and set with purpose. "Please, Lisa, you've got to do this." She turned to Gemma with a pleading look. "Tell her she's got to do this."

Gemma's eyes widened as her gaze met Lisa's.

"Me? That's…that's impossible. We've got a deputy mayor and three councilmen. Don't we have a city charter that says one of them takes over in case the mayor can't serve?"

"Yes, but Dale is going to be gone for months on a project to build rural schools in Guatemala. Trent's the only one with any common sense, but he doesn't know the town as well as you do."

"But Roland…and Bunky—"

"Are nuts. You know that better than anybody. You've been involved in every big undertaking in this town for years now. You've been to every public meeting the council has held and been involved in most projects. Roland and Bunky are impossible. They argue about every little decision just to hear themselves argue."

Gemma raised a hand. "Lisa can't be getting in the middle of that."

Still distraught, Brenda answered, "There's no one else. Lisa, you've got every bit as much experience as they have, and more brains." Brenda reached out and grabbed Lisa's hand. "Besides, all the council members know you don't have the same kind of political agenda they do. You only want what's best for Reston."

"Yes, but—"

"You and I have talked about you running for mayor. This is your chance."

"I wouldn't be running. I'd be—"

"Acting mayor. There is actually a provision in the charter that the mayor and city council can appoint a citizen to take over running the city in an emergency. It was put in place back during the Depression when so many people had to leave town to find work and the whole place nearly shut down. That provision was never changed, so it can be used in this case. Please, Lisa. It'll…it'll be like a trial run to see if you would even want to be mayor."

"She *doesn't* want to," Gemma said, but Brenda ignored her while Lisa gave her a trapped look.

"There's got to be someone else, Brenda," Lisa said.

"No one with your reputation for honesty and your concern for the town. Some people might object, but it'll only be temporary. If I can tell Harley you've agreed, he won't worry and he can settle down and focus on healing. It'll only be for a few weeks, and by then maybe I can convince him to retire. The stress is obviously killing him."

"So you want it to kill me instead?" Lisa's hands slid down to cover her belly as she thought about her baby. An unexpected wave of nausea rose in her throat but she swallowed hard and forced it down. Gemma saw the gesture and shook her head emphatically no.

Brenda knew nothing about Lisa's pregnancy and Lisa couldn't tell her now. Her mind was spinning at this new development.

Brenda said, "Of course I don't want it to kill you, but you know how to delegate, get help, won't try to handle every detail yourself. Harley doesn't know how to do that, and he never will. Believe me. I've been married to the man for thirty years. The only times he's been able to give up control of anything is when he's been forced to by circumstances. This is one of those times."

Lisa looked helplessly at her then at Gemma, whose expression had changed to one of worried resignation.

"Please, Lisa, so Harley can relax a little. He'll be impossible otherwise. I'm so relieved he'll be at a cardiac center in Tulsa. Otherwise he wouldn't be able to let go at all."

Lisa thought it over, attempting to weigh the pros and cons at warp speed while Brenda all but danced from one foot to the other. Gemma pressed her lips together in distress while shaking her head. The only positives were that the job would be short-term and might keep Harley from fretting so much.

"Okay," she said slowly. "I'll act as mayor until Harley is better. Don't worry about a thing."

Relief flooded Brenda's face and she began to cry. She pulled Lisa into a fierce hug as she choked out, "Thank...thank you. You'll never regret this." Turning, she rushed back into the examination room.

"Good grief," Lisa whispered in horror. "What have I done?"

"Lost your mind," Gemma suggested drily,

then smiled and gave her a hug. "I'm warning you, though, if I see even a hint that you're doing too much or getting overtired, I'll put a stop to this."

Lisa gave her a steady look. "Oh, really? And how do you plan to do that?"

"Remember I worked in some rough neighborhoods in Okie City. I know people. Tough people."

"To stop me?"

"No. To stop Bunky and Roland from hassling you. Trent will have your back. Dale will be gone, but those other two will be a pain in your behind."

Lisa laughed. "Well, I said I wanted to run for mayor. Maybe this will be a way to see if I can actually do it."

"Oh, you can do it. The question is *should* you do it. For now, I'll keep my opinions to myself—"

"That'll be the day."

"I'll go find some paper bags."

"Whatever for?"

"For the city council members to breathe into. When you tell them what's going on, they'll probably hyperventilate."

"No." APPALLED AT her news, Ben stared at Lisa. "You can't do this and no one has any right to expect you to." He glanced down and made a vague gesture. "Especially since you're—"

"I didn't tell them I'm pregnant," she broke in crisply. "And you're not going to, either."

"You should have. It would put a stop to this nonsense."

Lisa stared right back at him. He watched her face flush with anger as she said, "You have no right to tell me not to do it. You've made it very clear that you want little to do with this baby beyond the financial."

Ben frowned. He couldn't deny that. "I do have good reasons."

"They're your reasons and they don't affect what I've got to do. Now, please drive me back to my office so I can get my car."

"Okay, but you're going straight home, right? Put your feet up, do…what do pregnant women do?"

She rolled her eyes. "You mean carry on with their regular lives? That's exactly what I plan to do. So far today, I've created cost projections of how much it's going to cost to raise a child. I've had a man go into car-

diac arrest in front of me, agreed to be acting
mayor of this town for the foreseeable future
and fought two members of the city council
to a standstill.

"Tomorrow, I'm doing the final walk-
through on a property I just sold, which
means I've got to deal with two people who
I *know* are going to have buyer's remorse over
the fixer-upper they insisted they wanted, and
I've got a budget meeting at city hall, which
means I have to read the budget and see what
the heck it's all about. I'm tired, I'm hungry
and I'm cranky, so don't mess with me."

Furiously she stomped across the hospital
parking lot and stood, arms folded, eyes defiant and foot tapping, as she waited for him
to unlock his truck door for her.

Flabbergasted at her tone and demeanor,
Ben strode after her. He knew if he hit the
automatic unlock, she'd vault inside and sit
there fuming. Maybe she had a right to do
that, but he wanted to have some control over
this fiasco. He waited until he reached her
before he hit the unlock key and swept the
door open for her, taking her arm to help her
into the seat.

"Thank you," she said primly, buckling her

seat belt, placing her handbag in her lap and crossing her ankles.

Ben slid in behind the wheel but before he started the engine, he said, "I can't do anything about you being tired and cranky, but can I buy you some dinner?"

"No, thank you, I'm—"

"Going to need your strength to read over that budget. Besides, we never finished talking about financial arrangements for the baby. How about it? Quick run over to Toncaville, find a good place for dinner? I'll bring you right back. You can go home, put your feet up and read the budget until numbers start swimming in your head."

He tried to sound upbeat and convincing even as his mind scrambled for some way to persuade her not to go through with this harebrained idea of being the acting mayor. She was right. It wasn't his business, but that wouldn't stop him.

She looked at him for a second. "I'll need to stop at city hall and pick up the budget from the mayor's office, but then… Fins," she said.

"What?"

"Fins is a restaurant in Toncaville. The chef

makes the best grilled fish in the county and she buys her vegetables from Carly, so you know she's focused on quality. I've been trying to convince her to open a restaurant in Reston."

He started the engine and pulled out of the parking lot. "So you've already got a head start on this acting mayor gig, then?"

"In a manner of speaking. A good restaurant in town would draw people from all over, and once they're here, they would shop at other stores, too." She pointed to a shop. The sign over the door was fastened to an old bicycle frame painted bright red. It had the word *Upcycle* printed on it. "That's Carly's place. She restores and refurbishes all kinds of furniture and goods. Tourists eat that kind of thing up."

"Along with a meal at a good restaurant," he added, and she smiled.

After a stop at city hall, where she picked up a paper copy of the budget, they made the twenty-minute drive to the restaurant. Ben didn't even try to make conversation, just showed Lisa where to turn on a reading light so she could get a start on examining the budget. She pulled a pen from her purse and began making notes in the margins.

Ben glanced at her, amazed at how quickly she could immerse herself in something new, like the city budget, even when she was tired and hungry.

She was smart. He'd always known that. He liked the fact that she was ambitious, but her ambition was focused on making things better for other people when she should focus on herself.

Dusk was falling by the time they arrived, but the service was fast and, as promised, the food was outstanding. Three different people came up to their table and requested a selfie with him. Ben happily complied each time.

When he sat after the last one, Lisa asked, "Does that get old after a while? I mean, it seems that you can't go out, even in your own hometown, without people wanting something from you."

"Nah. These were the same people who were cheering for me when I was playing ball in high school, then college and then in the pros. This is payback. And besides, maybe when they're feeling generous, they'll give to one of the charities I support."

She smiled. "Ah, your real motive is revealed."

Ben smiled back and then spent the rest of dinner subtly trying to point out flaws in Lisa's plan to be mayor in Harley's absence.

"Ben, why do you care?" she finally asked. "You've made it clear that neither I nor this baby will interfere in your life. Why are you interfering in mine?"

Maybe he wasn't so subtle, after all. And that was an excellent question—to which he didn't have a good answer.

"Dessert?" he asked.

"Back to my office so I can pick up my car," she answered. "I've got a budget to finish reading."

Ben didn't argue, but kept quiet on the ride to Reston so she could concentrate.

"I'm going to have to request previous budgets," she murmured.

"So, more work for you?" he ventured.

"If I'm going to do this job, even temporarily, I'm going to do it right."

"I don't doubt that."

She gave him a curious look but didn't answer. When he dropped her off at her car, she didn't wait for him to open the door for her but thanked him for dinner, jumped from the truck and hurried away.

Ben watched until she was safely on her way home before he turned his truck toward Riverbend Ranch. They still didn't have anything settled about financial arrangements for the baby, and they might still have to get attorneys involved. But this afternoon had been a revelation. Lisa was deeply involved with the life of their hometown. While he, and many of the kids they'd grown up with, had made lives elsewhere, she had stayed here. He'd always assumed it was because her grandparents had been here and after they'd died she'd simply chosen to stay. He wasn't so sure about that now.

He pulled up memories of her grandparents... The way his dad had described Wesley Thomas as a hoarder and "just plain crazy" and Lily Thomas as someone who always had her head in the clouds, reading a book or simply wandering around her property.

If anyone had had a good reason for leaving town as quickly as possible, it would have been Lisa. She hadn't done that, though. In fact, she still lived in the family place, cleaned up and upgraded, from what he'd heard from

Sandy Borden. She was involved in many town projects and it seemed that her goal was to make Reston a better town. But mayor? Even temporarily, it would be a big job.

Ben still didn't understand why she would take it on when she was pregnant. Couldn't stress like this jeopardize her health or that of the baby? He understood wanting to help, but most of the help he gave was monetary, or related to a subject he knew a great deal about, like football. Even taking on the mustangs was a worthy cause, but not likely to improve the lives of a whole town. It made him a little uncomfortable to see how willing she was to put her own convenience second to what was best for the most people in Reston. Unlike him.

CHAPTER SIX

"You're just in time for dinner," Maureen called out as soon as Lisa walked in the door.

"Oh." Lisa looked around at the preparations. She smiled and sniffed the spicy aroma of the sauce that Maureen had been slowly simmering for the past hour.

"I can't wait for you to try this spaghetti sauce. It's a recipe I developed myself and you had all the ingredients in your cupboards, so it was easy to put together."

And best of all, Maureen added silently, there had been no reason for her to go into town.

Lisa shook her head regretfully. "I already ate. I'm sorry. I should have called. I had no idea you were planning to cook dinner."

"Oh!" Maureen glanced away as she struggled to hide her disappointment. "My...my fault. I should have called to tell you. It's okay. I like to cook, which is a good thing since that's what I've done the most in my life."

"Oh, really?" Lisa set her purse and briefcase on the kitchen table. "I didn't know that. I...never knew what you did for a living."

"Mostly any job I could find. Short-order cook in a few greasy spoons, food prep, finally worked my way up to sous chef in a trendy restaurant, though my only training has been hands-on."

When she saw the troubled frown Lisa was giving her, she pressed her lips together, regretting her sudden impulse to talk about herself. One thing she had learned over the years was to keep things to herself until she discovered if she could trust someone. It was far easier to focus on someone else.

She returned to the stove to stir the sauce. She turned the burner down to simmer and asked, "How are you feeling? Is the nausea better?"

"Um, yes. I had a couple of bouts today, but they weren't bad."

"Well, you have to be careful. You have to take good care of yourself."

"I am," Lisa answered. She picked up her purse and briefcase once again. "I'll leave you alone to let you enjoy your dinner. I've got some work to do."

"Work? Didn't you just get off work?"

"I've got a new job."

Maureen listened with consternation and growing concern as Lisa reported what had happened that day.

"Oh, Lisa, I'm sorry about Mayor Morton, but you can't do that job. What about the baby?"

"I received that reaction earlier today and I didn't like it then, either," Lisa said. "I know what I'm doing."

"You don't! You've got to be careful. You don't have any idea how hard it is to...to be a mother...to take care of a baby."

"And you do?"

Maureen felt the color drain from her face while Lisa's flushed with shame.

"I'm sorry, Maureen. I shouldn't have said that."

Maureen couldn't meet her eyes. "I'm trying to look out for you, look after you."

"I don't need you to. I'm an adult. I've taken care of myself since I was eighteen. Even before that, really, because—"

"Because what?" Maureen stared at the

daughter she didn't know well enough to understand.

"It doesn't matter now. I've…I've got to study the town budget, so…enjoy your dinner."

Clutching her things, Lisa hurried from the room and Maureen heard her bedroom door click shut.

Sick regret clawed at Maureen's throat. She had known it would come up. It was like the elephant in the room, the tiger under the table ready to spring out and rip apart this tenuous relationship. No, she thought. Her abandonment of her baby girl was a heavy chain that linked her to the past and connected her with her daughter, but kept her tethered like a buoy, forever bobbing in place, never moving forward.

"FOR THE LAST TIME, Bunky, we're not going to fund a dance contest on Main Street. If you want to get the Main Street merchants and the other merchants in town to sponsor a contest, we'll support it, but the city of Reston isn't going to pay for it. If you want to have one as part of the Founder's Day celebration, you can, but you'll have to get sponsors.

Again, the city won't pay for it. It's simply not in the budget." Lisa smiled in an attempt to soften her words, but Dalton Bunker gave her a huffy look and stared out the window.

"I told you that, you crazy old goat," Roland Hall insisted. "How come you don't ever listen?"

"Nothing worth listening to," Bunky answered in a sulky tone.

Lisa looked around the conference table. She had been acting mayor for a week and this was the third budget meeting they'd had, since consensus on the budget still cluded them.

To her surprise, after their initial resistance, Roland and Bunky had been accepting of her role as acting mayor, but during their first meeting, she had realized it was because they wanted to remain on the council as equals. If one of them had more authority, they wouldn't be equals anymore. She wondered if they thought their ceaseless arguments would be an insult to the dignity of the mayor's office, but didn't know why they didn't see it as an insult to their role as council members.

Dale Barnal had left town, with great fanfare, for his volunteer project in Guatemala. His departure had left her with two members who squabbled constantly and Trent Sanderson who tried to keep the peace. But even he was at the end of his patience.

"Bunky, Roland, knock it off," Trent said. "I've got a toddler at home who's more mature than you are. Now, council members, if you will behave, we can vote to accept these budget changes, which we should have done days ago when Mayor Thomas asked us to."

Lisa gave Trent an appreciative smile and called for a vote to accept the budget. Trent raised his hand right away then treated Bunky and Roland to a stern look until they each raised their hands.

"The ayes have it," Lisa announced. "Thank you all for your time."

"You're welcome, Mayor," Trent answered, giving the other two men another pointed look as he picked up his cowboy hat and settled it on his head. "Let's go," he said. "The mayor is a busy woman, lots to do, and I have a ranch to run. You two can take your disagreements outside."

Lisa knew Roland and Bunky would have preferred to stay in her office and continue sniping at each other, but she was sure that Trent could, and would, hustle them out if need be.

When they were gone, she sat for a moment and tried to recall why she'd ever thought she would like to be mayor. Accomplishing tasks that benefited the town was enjoyable. Dealing with the council was not.

So far, she had helped approve the purchase of new equipment for the volunteer fire department and delegated several tasks to city employees that Harley had always handled. That freed up a little of her time to take care of other business.

Meanwhile, Sandy Borden was keeping Reston Realty running smoothly and Lisa was deeply grateful for that since she had hardly seen the inside of her office all week. She never thought she'd be glad to see a day when the real-estate business was slow.

She hadn't seen Ben, either, although he had called a couple of times to check on her. They hadn't talked for very long and she assumed he was working with the mustangs he'd bought, or was out of town at some charity event, but at least he had given up trying to convince her not to be the acting mayor.

They had never settled the matter of financial arrangements for the baby. He had her cost projections, though, and she was sure they could come to some kind of equitable agreement. In the meantime her pregnancy had begun to show. It was as if everything fit fine one day but wouldn't even get close to buttoning the next.

Lisa stood and smoothed her loose-fitting top over her belly, stretching the fabric so that the slight mound was obvious. She wouldn't be able to hide it much longer, but she didn't plan to make a general announcement, either.

Her thoughts were interrupted by a knock and she hastily arranged her shirt as the door opened and Carly stuck her head in.

"Hi," her friend said, coming inside and shutting the door. "I haven't seen you all week. I stopped by your office and Sandy said this is where you are."

"Almost all the time," Lisa said, motioning for Carly to have a seat.

"I still can't believe you're doing this," Carly murmured.

Lisa gave her a steady look.

"On second thought, yes, I can believe it. I

just hoped you were kidding about someday running for mayor."

"Well, I didn't run for it. It ran to me. The only good thing about it is that Brenda says Harley is able to relax and he's already improving."

"Good." Carly paused. "How is all of this going so far?"

Lisa told her about the budget battle. "They were simple adjustments to the outgoing funds, but every item was a reason for Roland and Bunky to fight. And this building…" She looked around. "I had no idea it was in such bad shape."

"It's almost a hundred years old." Carly wrinkled her nose. "And it has a funky smell. I think most old buildings do if they don't have constant upkeep, and I doubt Reston has had the money for it."

"No, and Harley wouldn't have spent the money on upkeep if he'd had it. His focus has been on sowing money back into the city."

"Sounds like you." Carly smiled. "So since we were talking about upkeep and renovating—"

"We were?" Lisa smiled at her friend. Carly's livelihood came from her organic gardens, and from the furniture and accessories she unearthed at secondhand shops, yard sales and thrift stores. She was passionate about refurbishing these pieces whenever possible and about preserving the crafts of the past.

"We were about to."

"I should have known. I've discovered that having this job means my best friends show up with things for me to do. What have you got in mind?"

"At least we're not asking for handouts or favors." Carly sat forward, her expression eager. "You've heard of the world's longest yard sale that starts every year in Gadsden, Alabama, and goes all the way to Michigan?"

"Um, no, but I get the feeling I'm about to."

"Well, I think we could do that. Yard sales all the way through every town, only on a smaller scale, clear across Reston County. Every community on the highway, even off the highway, would benefit. We would have tourists from all over. We could have food trucks—selling food made with my produce if at all possible—ice cream, snow cones, souvenirs, crafts. You name it."

Lisa tilted her head as she listened carefully. "You're thinking this could happen this summer?"

"Fall, actually, and anyone who was too far off the highway could rent a space in town. Main Street Park would be the perfect place to set up booths of all kinds."

"And exactly who do you think would organize all of this? Although I think I know the answer," Lisa said, pointing to herself.

"No. Not you. You don't have time. Neither do I. I was thinking of Luke's aunt."

"Frances Sanderson?"

"Yes, she's a genius at organizing things like this, and now that the hospital is up and running again, she doesn't have to focus on fund-raising for it so much. She can charm anyone, knows how to delegate and make volunteers feel appreciated, and I think she'd enjoy the challenge."

Lisa thought it over then nodded. "I like the idea. I think it would be fun. Exhausting, but fun. I suspect you've got an ulterior motive, though."

"Nothing gets past you," Carly said with a grin. "Can you just imagine the treasures people have tucked away in their houses, sheds, barns and garages, that haven't seen the light of day in years? Decades? Things that could be recycled and rescued."

"By you."

"Or some other community-focused, recycling-minded—"

"Nut," Lisa provided with a laugh. "I'll put it on the agenda for the next city council meeting. I think if we can fit in a dance contest, Bunky will go for it and probably Roland, too."

"Good." Happily, Carly settled into her chair. "Now, tell me, how are you feeling?"

"My morning sickness is almost gone, and I feel good most of the time." She propped her elbow on the desk and her chin on her palm. "If only I could convince Maureen." She told Carly about the conversation she'd had with her mother.

Carly winced. "That must have been hard."

"It was. I didn't mean to sound harsh. I'd like to know why she'd left me behind when she took off, but I don't want to ask when she's still recovering. The problem is that, since then, she hovers over me, encouraging me to eat more, rest more, take my vitamins, wants to know when my next doctor's appointment is. It's as if she wants to prove she's a good mother but…"

"She's suffocating you."

"Yes."

"She doesn't have anything else to focus on. What does she do all day?"

"As far as I can tell, Maureen never leaves the place. She walks the property, like Grandma did, but without that dreamy wandering gait of Grandma's." Lisa lifted her hand and twisted it in a slow, figure eight. "Maureen...basically she stomps around the property like she's mad. At the same time she seems to be actively building up her strength and stamina, but also looking for something."

"You mean searching the ground?"

"No, she walks around and looks the ground over, sometimes stops to kick over rocks or move aside some plants or low-hanging branches, but it's not like she's looking for a specific thing." Lisa stopped and shook her head. "I don't know."

"Family eccentricity showing, maybe?" Carly suggested. "Besides, there's nothing to find. You had the place practically scoured of all your grandpa's collections, and let me tell you, his assortment of barbed wire was downright terrifying."

"I know. I'm just glad nobody ended up with tetanus from dealing with all that junk."

"We'd all had our shots. So what else does Maureen do?"

"When she isn't outside, she's cooking. I have to stop at the supermarket almost every day for ingredients. She always offers to pay for everything, but I know she hasn't got much money and, really, I don't mind. The only problem is, the refrigerator and freezer are jam-packed with leftovers." Lisa sighed. "She's a wonderful cook."

Carly grinned at her. "I can send Dustin and Luke over to take care of those leftovers for you. Even though I grew up with a brother, I thought it was a joke about how much boys eat. It's not. I've never seen anyone pack it away like my son and husband can. So it's not too much of a hardship. Do you know how long she's planning to stay? Or if she's going to get a job?"

"No idea. And I don't want to ask her to leave—"

"At least not until you get some answers."

Lisa shrugged. "Well, yes, but I don't need someone to take care of me. Any minute, I expect her to start recording my pulse and blood pressure."

Carly laughed. "Come on, I'll buy you some lunch."

"I can't take a lunch break. I've got too much to do." Lisa reached into a desk drawer and pulled out a paper sack. "Maureen sent me with two sandwiches, both high-calorie, an apple and two of her chocolate cookies."

Carly stood and came around the desk to haul Lisa to her feet. "You certainly can and *will* take a break. We'll eat lunch outside in the fresh air. Breathing this hundred-year-old air isn't doing you or the baby any good."

"*Now* who's hovering?"

"Not me. I just want one of those cookies."

"IT'S TIME," MAUREEN murmured to herself as she started her car and pulled onto the road heading for Reston. She had been at Lisa's for several weeks. Her initial shock at the way her daughter had cleaned up the family place and her daily rambles over the property had told her things were very different, and so much better than she could have imagined.

She felt immense pride in Lisa and all she'd accomplished, although she hadn't been brave enough to tell her that yet.

Because she had been alone for most of

her life, she found it hard to share what she was feeling and, strangely, it was even harder when she was in the same house with Lisa. The depth of her shame was too great for her to express, so instead, she took care of her. Looking after Lisa now was an honor and a privilege. She had abandoned the responsibility so long ago.

She also hoped that she would soon be able to meet Lisa's two best friends, Carly and Gemma. Maureen had known their families in her youth, but since she had been at Lisa's, recovering from her illness, Lisa's friends hadn't been around. She preferred to think of that as the reason she hadn't met her daughter's friends and not to consider that Lisa might be ashamed of her.

Maureen was feeling so much better and stronger after weeks of convalescing; she was sure she was ready to go into town and buy some toiletries for herself. It was one thing to depend on Lisa for her food, which she justified by doing all the cooking and taking care of all Lisa's other needs, but she couldn't expect her daughter to buy shampoo and toothpaste for her.

She dreaded running into anyone she used

to know, but she drove through town, taking the time to really examine the changes made since she had left so long ago. Her memories were those of a self-involved teenage girl, who hadn't really noticed very much outside her own interests. Now she could see that the town that had depended on logging, cattle ranching and farming now had other industries going on.

Along with three busy supermarkets, there were several shops that sold items of interest to tourists, hunters and fishermen who wanted to take advantage of Reston Lake. Two motels, which had been seedy and unappealing in her youth, had been spruced up and made more inviting.

From conversations she'd had with Lisa, she knew her daughter had been involved with much of the town's improvements. Although Maureen didn't quite understand why Lisa had stayed in Reston—and was now acting mayor—when she could have made a success of herself anywhere, she was proud of her girl's accomplishments.

There were a couple of fast-food restaurants and Margie's Kitchen, which Maureen remembered as delicious but often a surefire route to heartburn. A chain drugstore had been built on the corner of Main and Holmes. Maureen pulled into the parking lot and went inside.

She tugged a shopping cart from the lineup and began perusing the shelves, looking for her favorite brands. It was time to color her hair again as inch-long graying roots were showing. As she picked up a box of hair color to read the label, someone spoke from behind her.

"You've got a lot of nerve," a woman said.

Maureen glanced around, though she was sure the woman wasn't speaking to her. A short, dumpy woman about her own age stood, hands on hips, glaring at her. There was something about the look in those fierce eyes that Maureen recognized. But she couldn't place her.

"You heard me, Maureen Thomas," she said, stalking closer. "You've got a lot of nerve."

Alarmed, Maureen stepped back. "Do I know you?"

"Yeah," she said, jerking a thumb toward her own massive chest. "Dorcas Poole."

Maureen couldn't help the way her jaw dropped or stop her stunned gaze from traveling the morbidly obese figure from head to toe. "No," she said. "It can't be."

Dorcas's lips hardened and her eyes turned into piglike slits. That was an expression Maureen recalled all too well.

Dorcas had been the beauty queen of Reston High School and also its biggest bully and meanest Mean Girl. Maureen Thomas, who'd lived in a junk heap with her strange parents, had often been the target of her bullying. It was obvious things hadn't changed.

She tried to ignore Dorcas as she turned away, dropping the box of hair color into her cart and grabbing a bottle of shampoo as she rushed past, heading toward the toothpaste aisle.

Dorcas stalked along right behind her, her girth causing the shelved products to vibrate as if caught in an earthquake. "Don't try to ditch me. You've got a lot to answer for— leaving your baby like that, running away."

With a gasp, Maureen swung around. "That's none of your business."

"It's everybody's business when scum like you gets knocked up and then sneaks off, leaving her baby for her parents to raise."

"You didn't care anything about my parents. You didn't even know them. And I doubt you know Lisa, either."

"I know she's done good for herself, no thanks to you." Dorcas planted her hands on her enormous hips, completely blocking the aisle. Behind her, another woman started to walk their way but, spotting Dorcas's aggressive stance, whipped her cart around.

Maureen was so stunned, it took her a few seconds to form words. When she did, they burst out as if from a volcano. "And I'm sure Lisa's success is no thanks to you, either, Dorcas. I have no doubt you were as mean, spiteful and judgmental toward her as you've always been to me—and everyone else, for that matter."

"I tell people what they need to hear."

"No, you bully people to feel better about yourself. You always have."

Dorcas's face turned purple with rage. She started toward Maureen, who turned her cart to block the aisle, and fled. As she hurried from the store, tears started into her eyes. She should have stayed out of sight. Dorcas wasn't the only one in town who would hate and judge her for what she'd done. No matter that so many years had passed, so many lives had changed. She would always be the stupid girl who'd gotten pregnant and then abandoned her baby. The worst part? That was how Maureen saw herself.

"LONG, SLOW GRAZING, Ben, that's what they need," Zach Littletrees said as he and Ben moved among the herd. A few of the horses gave them curious looks, but mostly ignored them. "You might want to experiment, plant different varieties to see what's best for 'em. 'Course, they're used to being wild, eating and running, so they're not going to be expecting much attention from you."

"That's good," Ben answered. "I didn't intend to be a farmer."

"You want them to thrive, don't you?"

"Well, of course. But I've always planned to get a good manager to keep an eye on things, since I'll be gone a lot."

Zach shrugged. "Yeah, Jason told me that and I gotta say good luck. You might find someone responsible enough to take good care of your place while you're gone, but you'll have to pay for it. The best managers already have jobs and the ranch owners who need one are usually happy to pay for them."

Ben nodded and rubbed his chin. It was turning out that there was a lot more to this business of raising wild mustangs than he'd thought. He'd had some vague idea that if they were wild, they wouldn't require much care. However, when a person was trying to help preserve a strain of horses, attention had to focus on health and bloodlines.

Zach changed the subject. "Occasionally you'll come across a horse that's smarter than you are," he said, moving his toothpick from one side of his mouth to the other. "In that case, you have to learn from them rather than the other way around."

"Oh? How so?" Ben frowned.

He usually took notes when Zach spoke, but this time he hadn't been planning on a lesson. Yet one little question was all he'd needed to ask and Zach was off and running, talking about horses he'd trained all over the Western and Midwestern states, and waxing poetic about the ones he'd loved the most.

"Now, Little Lupita was the smartest mare I ever saw. She was a mimic. She would watch me and try anything I did. Caught her trying to climb over the corral fence one time because she saw me do it."

Ben got a kick out of listening. Zach's stories were fascinating. Zach was proud of his Choctaw heritage and had plenty to say about it, but he had two favorite subjects—horses and women.

Since he'd been at Riverbend Ranch, Zach had checked every horse in Ben's small herd, done some doctoring and begun to make notes on which ones would make the best cow ponies and which mares should be bred. He got an amazing amount of work accomplished, considering he was out late every night and had a whirlwind social life. He never seemed to suffer any ill effects from it, though, and was always ready to go in the morning.

"That sweet girl right there—" Zach pointed to Tailspin, mother of Prince's Folly "—reminds me of Little Lupita. Got the same type of markings but she's a darker brown."

Zach had brought Ben out to begin showing him how to care for the herd. A few good rains and warm days meant spring grass was coming up and the horses were happily grazing the hillsides. It hadn't taken Zach long to realize Ben knew almost nothing about raising the animals he'd bought. Although they'd always had horses when he was grow-ing up, and he'd learned to ride when he was young, they had been his father's hobby. Ben had always been more interested in sports than in horsemanship. Besides, the big quar-ter horses and thoroughbreds his father had owned weren't like the Choctaw Mustangs. These horses were compact but strong.

"Well, boss," Zach said, turning to walk back to the new four-wheeled vehicle Ben had purchased for ranch use, "I'm ready to quit for the day. Got a new lady friend in town who's promised to make me some dinner. I'm hoping she cooks as good as she looks." He winked and clicked his tongue.

Ben slid in behind the wheel and started the engine. "Zach, you've got more girlfriends in more places than anyone I've ever met."

"Well, thank you, Ben. I admit that I like the ladies."

"You never saw the need to settle down?"

"Sure did. Got married three times and it was a mistake every time. I'm not skippin' down the aisle again in this life. As long as I've got me a job and a home—" he jerked his thumb toward the neat little Airstream "—and I've got good friends who like to have fun, I'm happy. And that's what life's about, right? Being happy?"

Ben gave him a quick, sidelong look. Well, maybe there was more to it than that.

"Do you have any kids, Zach?"

"One daughter. She lives in Atoka. She grew up there, raised by her mother, my first wife. I see her a couple of times a year. She's married. Got one—no, two little boys."

Ben frowned. Of course, Zach had been working in the north end of Arkansas for many months, so maybe he hadn't had time to go see his family. Still, Atoka was less than an hour away.

Ben planned to be gone a lot and he didn't want to interfere with how Lisa raised their child, but he hoped he saw the kid more than twice a year.

"Anytime you want to take a couple of days off and go see her, Zach, feel free to do that. I mean, family is important."

Zach gave him a look that didn't encourage any further comment on the subject.

Ben tried to think of a change of topic. "Did you like working in Arkansas?" He knew there were some things Zach had liked since three of them had followed him to the Riverbend to make sure he arrived safely.

"Yes. Yes, I did. Nice people. 'Course I did have a slight disagreement with one gentleman."

"Oh, about what?"

"His wife. Apparently she didn't take her marriage vows as seriously as he did and she'd neglected to inform me he might take exception to her dating another man." Zach shook his head. "Mind you, that's the kind of thing you usually find out *before* the first date."

"What happened?"

"Well, she and I were in her living room and things were gettin' interesting when he came in the front door swinging an Arkansas toothpick."

Ben was familiar with the deadly knife. "What did you do?"

"I told the lady good-night and went out the back door." Zach scratched his ear. "'Course, I'd left my boots behind, but the husband was nice enough to return them to me. Found 'em on my doorstep, cut to ribbons."

Ben stared at him. "You left her with her husband swinging a knife?"

"Did I mention she was a professional wrestler? She'd already taken the knife away from him by the time I made it outside, but I guess she gave it back so he could take care of my boots. She called me, said they were going to marriage counseling."

"I should hope so." Ben didn't like this new glimpse into the other man's life. "You lead an interesting life, Zach."

"Yup, and that's the way I like it. Always something to do. New places to go and new people to meet."

"Sounds like fun," Ben said, then thought, *Sounds like me.*

When they reached the house, Zach hopped out to get ready for his date, but he turned back.

"Say, you probably know the lady who's cooking me dinner tonight. Name's Millie Hardy."

"The secretary at the high school?"

"Yeah. She's not married, is she?"

Ben thought about the much-married Millie and shook his head. "Not this year."

Zach grinned, showing the gap in his teeth. "Good to hear." With a wave, he hurried home.

Still mulling over Zach's eventful life, Ben

parked the four-wheeler, closed the barn and went inside. He had promised his mom he would come over for dinner, and she wouldn't like it if he was late, although she would just chalk it up to him getting involved in something and forgetting to call her. However, she'd promised to use the last of the peaches she'd canned last summer to make him a cobbler and he knew he might have to arm wrestle his dad for it.

Later, as he drove into town, Ben's thoughts turned to Lisa. He hadn't seen her in a couple of days, but he'd heard that Harley was doing well at the cardiac center. If he was feeling better, that meant he wasn't fretting over what was happening in Reston, which Ben took to mean Lisa was doing a good job. He'd like to know how the budget meeting had gone, but she had made it clear that she didn't want him meddling in what he considered to be a crazy-making exercise in futility. It was true that he hadn't been in town much, but what he knew about the members of the city council told him Lisa's dealings with them would be far from easy.

On the other hand, she was right that it wasn't his business. She was an adult, a savvy businesswoman who successfully managed everything in her life, from what he could tell.

Still, when he reached Reston, he didn't go straight through town to get to his parents' place, but turned onto the side street where the city hall and county courthouse stood, along with the jail. He slowed his truck to a crawl as he rode by and frowned when he saw that the only vehicle still parked in front of the building was Lisa's sedan. The only light shining in the building was on the second floor right—the mayor's office.

She was deadly serious about this job she had taken on. If she decided she liked it, would she want to run for mayor, serve a full term? It was entirely possible because, as he'd already noticed, she was devoted to this town.

Ben pulled into the space beside Lisa's car and sat with his motor idling, his wrists perched on top of the steering wheel. He didn't like the idea that she was all alone in the building.

Although he knew she wouldn't thank him for it, he decided to at least do a quick check of the front door, make sure it was securely locked in case some nutcase staged a jail break. He grinned, remembering how she'd broken him out of jail all those years ago.

Ben turned off the engine and stepped out of the truck. Everything was quiet on the street, which saw little activity except when there was a meeting at city hall or a hearing at the county courthouse—or if a bunch of rowdies needed to be locked up.

He climbed the twenty steps to the front door, smiling at the memory of Coach Allen making the football team run through town, up and down every set of stairs he could find, including these.

Ben grabbed both door handles and pulled. Finding them locked, he muttered, "Good," then leaned forward and cupped his hands around his eyes to see into the foyer. A staircase rose to the second floor, where city offices were.

All appeared to be quiet until he saw movement at the top of the stairs. Suddenly he could see Lisa, running back and forth and waving her arms in the air.

CHAPTER SEVEN

"LISA! LISA, OPEN the door!" Ben pounded on the glass doors, waved his hands in sweeping arcs and shouted, but she continued to dash to and fro, flailing her arms. He could also hear her yelling, although he couldn't make out the words.

Determined to help her, he turned and looked around. The windows were too high off the ground for him to try to climb in, so he dashed down the stairs and ran around back. If he couldn't find a way in, he'd go to the sheriff's office for help.

At the rear entrance he saw that the window in the top half of the door was glass. Hoping it wasn't thick safety glass, he pried a brick from the flower bed border and smashed in the window. That immediately set off an alarm, but he ignored it, knowing it would bring help but fearing they might be too late for Lisa. He used the brick to break out the remainder of the glass and reached in to unlock the dead bolt and open the door.

Crunching over broken glass, he darted through the dimly lit downstairs hallway to the back stairs. Taking them two at a time, he ignored the twist of pain in his knee and arrived at the top just as Lisa made another run across the landing.

Since her arms were in the air, and her head was down, she didn't see him until he reached out to snag her around the waist and pull her to safety.

Lisa shrieked and ducked away, but Ben, who had spent many years taking down running men and catching flying objects, had a firm grip around her waist. At that moment his thigh muscles clenched in sharp spasm and the two of them tumbled to the floor. A sickening thump told him he hadn't managed to catch Lisa's full weight.

The alarm suddenly fell silent, the lights came on and thunderous steps pounded up the front staircase.

"Okay, buddy," Junior Fedder said from the top of the staircase. "Move away from the lady and let me see your hands."

"Junior, ih-hih…it's…muh-hee," Ben wheezed,

trying to catch his breath while gutting out the pain shooting from his leg and gingerly move Lisa, who was a dead weight. She also seemed to be struggling for breath.

"Ben?" Junior rushed over to them, followed by another deputy. "What are you doing?"

Before he could answer, Lisa groaned and reached up to grab her elbow, then touched her head. "Oh, what happened?"

When she removed her hand, blood streaked across her palm.

"Lisa, are you all right?" Ben asked.

"Ben, what did you do to her?"

"I was trying to save her! Call the paramedics. She's got a head injury."

Another deputy, followed by Sheriff Held, pounded up the steps to join them.

"What's going on?" the sheriff asked.

"I'm still trying to determine that, sir, but Mayor Thomas is injured." Junior unhooked his radio.

But before he could make the call, Lisa reached out to stop him. "Mayor Thomas is just fine, thank you very much, considering she just got tackled by a two-hundred-pound linebacker," she said, sitting up all the way. "I don't have a head injury. I've got an elbow injury. See?" She held up her arm where a bright rug burn oozed blood.

Sheriff Held drew his breath in with a sympathetic hiss of pain as he reached down and gingerly helped her to her feet. "You okay other than that?"

"I'm fine, no thanks to Mr. McAdams, here. Ben, what in the world did you think you were doing?"

Because he couldn't trust his leg muscles to hold him and not spasm, Ben stayed where he was. Looking up at her, he said, "I thought you needed help. I looked in the front doors and saw you running back and forth across the landing, waving your arms and yelling. What were *you* doing?"

Lisa glanced away as she smoothed her hair and then straightened the hem of her shirt. "I was working in the office, minding my own business, when two bats flew in out of nowhere."

"Why didn't you call for help?" Junior asked. "We're right next door."

"Have I ever been the kind of woman who needs to be rescued from a couple of bats? I tried to get them to fly out, but they seemed to fly straight at me and…I may…have overreacted a little bit. And the shrieking alarm only made the bats crazier." She looked up. "Although they seem to be gone now."

"Yeah, it's not general knowledge, but we've had bats in this building for years," the sheriff said, leaning back to peer up at the ceiling. "Can't seem to get rid of them."

"Well, I didn't know that. I wish someone had told me." Lisa shook her head in annoyance. "I can't believe that in this town where everyone knows everything, that's been kept quiet."

Disgruntled, Ben said, "I thought you were under attack...or...or something. I broke the window in the back door. I didn't know it would set off the downstairs alarm." Avoiding her furious look, Ben stood and leaned against the stair railing, gritting his teeth against the pain that gripped his knee and made his thigh muscles seize. Pinpricks of light danced in front of his eyes. He shut them to hold the tears of pain back.

"Ben." Lisa rushed to his side and grabbed his arm to support him. "You're the one who needs the paramedics."

"Nah. You do." His head lolled. "You're the one who's pregnant."

IF SHE COULD have tipped Ben McAdams over the railing at that moment, she would have done so happily and then danced down the stairs and out the door to jail. Instead she gripped his arm to keep him upright even as she gave him an outraged look.

The silence that filled the two-story foyer was as deafening as the sound of the alarm a few minutes before. Lisa looked around at the four openmouthed law-enforcement officers.

"Dude," Junior finally said to Ben. "You tackled a pregnant lady."

"Trying to help," Ben said again, and sagged against the railing. "Besides, it's my baby."

Lisa moaned. "Oh, Ben!" Now she really was going to push him over the railing. Fortunately for him, two officers shook off their shock and leaped forward to support him.

Lisa gladly handed him over as she said, "Please take Mr. McAdams to the emergency room. You'll find the key to the elevator in the maintenance office downstairs. I've had enough excitement for one day. I'm going home, where I will doctor my own elbow. And, Sheriff Held, please remember to reset the alarm."

He opened his mouth but only a garbled

sound came out. He cleared his throat and said, "Certainly, Mayor Thomas."

Her face burning with anger and embarrassment, she ignored him and walked with as much dignity as she could back into the mayor's office, where she gathered up the papers she needed and grabbed her purse. By the time she locked the office and went down the stairs, the cops had Ben in the elevator.

She hurried to her car and rushed toward home, her mind furiously replaying everything that had happened. The secret she'd tried to keep was out now and would probably be all over town within minutes. She could have asked the sheriff and deputies to keep her secret, but she didn't want to ask for any special favors. Besides, her pregnancy was going to be quite obvious very soon. She could only hope that her news wouldn't make certain members of the city council even harder to deal with.

It was fully dark by the time she reached home, and Maureen came out to meet her as soon as she pulled into the carport.

"You're later than usual," Maureen said, fretting. "Are you okay? Did something happen?"

When she reached in to take the briefcase, Lisa waved her off. "I'm fine, Maureen. Nothing's wrong." But when she started to close the car door, she winced at the stinging pain in her elbow.

"There *is* something wrong. I can tell." Maureen stepped in front of her, looking her over to see what was wrong.

"I scraped my elbow, is all. I'll clean it and put a bandage on it." She started into the house, but Maureen was right on her heels.

"What happened?"

"It doesn't matter," Lisa said in desperation. "I'll take care of it."

"No, let me—"

"No." Lisa rushed to her room and closed the door. As she doctored her elbow, she met her gaze in the bathroom mirror and then looked away in shame. Just because she was angry with Ben didn't mean she should take it out on Maureen. Taking a deep breath, she returned to the kitchen.

"I'm sorry, Maureen. I shouldn't have snapped at you."

Her mother was taking a casserole from the oven. She set it on the stovetop and turned around. "I only want to take care of you."

"But I don't need you to. I thought you came here to get well, to recover from your illness."

"I'm much better. I almost feel back to normal. Being here, seeing you, seeing that this place isn't like I remember, has helped me get well. Besides, I can do both, can't I?" Maureen asked with a shrug. She opened the refrigerator and removed a salad along with a bottle of fresh homemade dressing. "Take care of myself and take care of you?"

"But I don't need... Oh, never mind." Lisa sat and watched her mother put dinner on the table. She was afraid Maureen wouldn't listen, so the best she could do was to try to smooth things over. "So, what did you do today?"

"Went into town. I needed a few things from the drugstore. Turned out that...they didn't have what I needed."

"Oh, that's too bad. But it's good that you got out. You've been holed up here since you came. I was afraid you were turning into a recluse. Did you...meet anyone you know?"

Maureen's quick glance told her she'd touched a nerve, but instead of answering, her mother changed the subject.

"When I got back, I went for a walk, started

a new book. I brought all the books with me that I haven't had time to read. It feels strange to not be working. I'll get a job soon, though, and get out of your hair."

"There's no rush, but…when you're out walking around the place every day, are you looking for something?" She gestured toward the open field beyond the house.

"Looking for something?" Maureen shook her head. "Not really. At first, I was walking to build up my strength, but now I guess I can't get used to seeing it empty, not full of hazards." She paused, as if trying to come up with the right word, and finally said, "Normal, like a place that a family cares about. You made it like that, Lisa, and I'm proud of you for it."

Lisa blinked and ducked her head in surprise. "Well, thank you." She watched Maureen for a minute, then decided this might be a good moment to bring up what was troubling her most. "Besides needing to get well, there has to be another reason you came back to Reston. I mean why now? Why after thirty-three years? You never wanted to come before. Not to stay."

Maureen didn't meet her eyes as she filled

a plate and handed it to her. Lisa didn't even bother reminding her that she was capable of filling her own plate. "It wasn't that I didn't want to. I couldn't. It was too hard. Being in this house…was too hard."

Lisa began eating the chicken and rice casserole, savoring the creamy sauce, the crunch of almonds and the tang of citrus. She didn't quite know how to respond to Maureen.

"There was another reason," Maureen admitted when she had taken a few bites of food. "As I told you the night I came here, I promised Aunt Violet."

"That you would come back here?"

"Yes. I didn't think it would be this soon. I didn't expect to get so sick. But I had promised her I would come and…get to know you."

"I talked to her a few months before she died. She didn't mention it then."

"She always wanted me to do it and finally made me promise. You know that's where I went when I…left, don't you?"

Lisa nodded and took another bite of the delicious casserole. She thought it was ironic that she was enjoying this food so much while having such a hard conversation with its cook.

"I stayed with her, took any job I could

find, finally got out on my own. I made a life for myself, made friends. I usually spent holidays working so that people with families could have the time off."

"You had a family."

"My cousins didn't really like me. They didn't approve of me, of what I'd done, so I didn't want to always go to Aunt Violet's and—"

"I meant me, and Grandma and Grandpa." Lisa heard a tapping noise, looked down and realized the hand holding her fork had begun to shake. She put it down and folded her hands in her lap.

Maureen gave her a desperate look. "I couldn't stay here. I just couldn't. It was smothering. I knew I'd never have any kind of a life if I stayed here."

"So you wanted a life of your own more than you wanted me."

"Lisa, honey, I was sixteen!" Tears spurted into Maureen's eyes. "I didn't know what else to do."

"I understand that you weren't ready to be a mother then, but later, why didn't you come back?" Now that she had opened the door on the subject, Lisa wanted to know all she could.

"I couldn't. I would have suffocated. It would have killed me. And…and I told myself that it would be too confusing for you if I showed up every once in a while, that it was better for you if I stayed away."

She pushed her plate away. "It wasn't that bad, was it? Living with them? Here?" She looked around the clean, uncluttered room, but then her face fell as if she was remembering what it had been like with nothing but a thin trail that gave access from the back door, and through the kitchen piled high with stacks of dusty old magazines and boxes of worthless junk that had teetered almost to the ceiling.

Her lips trembling, Lisa said, "I think it was probably as bad for me as it was for you."

Maureen covered her eyes. Tears leaked from between her fingers. "I'm sorry."

Lisa wiped away her own tears. For years she had dreamed of having this conversation with her mother, but she hadn't known how much it would hurt. However, she had come this far and there was more she wanted to know.

"That's…that's in the past now. I have to look ahead to the future. So do you. I've got to think about my own child now, about family medical histories, among other things."

Frowning in confusion, Maureen looked up. She wiped at her tears as she said, "What do you mean?"

"Maureen, who is my father? My birth certificate says John Jackson, and that he was from Ada, but who was John Jackson? I've looked at online directories and there are a ton of Jacksons in that area, but I don't know which one he could be."

"I don't, either," her mother admitted. "I'm not even sure that was his real name."

"What?"

Maureen grabbed a paper napkin and dabbed at her eyes. "He was only…someone I met. He was a few years older than me. I had a job in Toncaville, at the Burger Barn. He came in there a lot, said his name was John Jackson. He never actually said where he was from, but he mentioned Ada a couple of times, so when I had to put down his birthplace, I chose Ada. Picked it out of the air."

"You're kidding."

Maureen shook her head. "I was young, and stupid, and desperate. I believed everything he said, about how pretty I was, that he loved me the minute he saw me. Nobody had ever talked to me like that before, so I was flattered, overwhelmed, and since he wasn't from around here, he knew nothing about my family.

"Then he told me he was married, even had a little boy, but by then, it was too late. I was pregnant. I didn't tell my parents until I was six months along." She glanced up with tear-filled eyes. "They never really looked at me, so they hadn't noticed. When I told them, I was so ashamed."

Lisa covered her belly, cradling her child, trying to imagine what it would be like to be so young and scared even as she realized how lucky she was to have the benefit of age and the financial security she needed. She couldn't picture going off and leaving her baby, though, and she still didn't have a good answer about why Maureen had left her behind.

"Did he know about me?"

Maureen shook her head and her voice caught as she said, "No. He gave me a phone number, but when I tried to call, it was for a gas station out on Highway 6. They didn't know anyone named John Jackson."

"So, there's a chance I'll never know about hereditary illnesses or other issues."

"I'm afraid that's true." Maureen caught her lip under her teeth. "I didn't intend for it to happen. It just…"

When her words trailed off, Lisa pointed to her own belly and said, "I know that better than anyone. I'm the last person who would judge you for getting unexpectedly pregnant."

"I never wanted to stay here, in this house, in this town. I wanted something bigger and better. Even after you were born, I still had plans to get out of Reston. Have a good life, free of—"

"Me?"

Maureen didn't answer. With a shake of her head, she took her plate and utensils to the sink and fled to her room.

Lisa sat, staring at her uneaten food, forcing back tears. Maybe their situations weren't so different. She was having a child she hadn't planned to have and she had no idea what kind of mother she would be.

There were things she still wanted to know, more questions she wanted to ask. Now that they had broken the ice, as painful as it had been, maybe she could learn more. She decided to ask Maureen in the morning, see if they could clear the air, start fresh.

But in the morning Maureen was gone.

"WHERE DO YOU think she went?" Carly asked when a distraught Lisa arrived on her doorstep during breakfast. She hustled her inside and got her some herbal tea and toast, which Lisa ate while Carly scrambled some eggs. Luke was already out in their gardens and Dustin had left for school.

"I don't know. She just disappeared, because that's what she does best. She disappears."

"Did something happen?"

"Yes, she finally told me a little about why she left, why she stayed away, but not as much as I wanted to know." She told Carly everything she'd learned from Maureen.

Carly handed Lisa a plate of eggs and sat opposite her, cup of coffee in hand. "Wow," she said softly. "Just wow. She didn't even know if that was the guy's real name?"

"It was a big surprise, and not at all what I was expecting."

Carly sipped her coffee. "The biggest thing

you've always wondered about is why she left you behind, right?"

"Right."

"Honestly, I think you may have the only answer you're going to get. She just couldn't stay. She was young and scared and thought she'd never escape, so she took the only way out."

Lisa nodded. "I guess it's not the answer I wanted to hear."

"You want to hear her say she regrets it and to tell you why she didn't take you with her."

"Yes, I do."

"She probably couldn't. How did she get away?"

"I don't know. Maybe hitchhiked, rode a bus?"

"All the way from southeastern Oklahoma to Chicago, Illinois? That must have been tough enough on her own, much less with a baby." Carly smiled sympathetically and gave a little shrug. "At some point, you'll probably have to accept that you'll never know all the details and let it go."

Lisa thought about that as she finished eating. At last she said, "You're right. I guess I'll have to get used to that idea. I tried calling her cell this morning, but there was no answer. Maybe she'll be in touch someday. Soon, I hope, so I can ask her to forgive me. She seemed excited about the baby so maybe she'll want to see him or her."

"I hope so. In the meantime you've got to deal with as much information as you got from her and live with it, at least for now."

"You're right about that, too. I have so many other things to think about." She placed her elbow on the table and winced at the pain.

"What's wrong?"

Lisa rolled up the sleeve of her white silk blouse and showed her the bandage. "Besides giving me a baby, Ben McAdams has made another mark on my life. This and a bruised hip from hitting his bathroom sink." She told Carly about the happenings at city hall.

"I knew that building needed repair, but bats? Scary. It does explain the funky smell, though."

"I should have recognized it. We had bats in the barn when I was a kid." Lisa frowned. "I guess that's why I overreacted. I remember when I was little the bats would fly down and I thought they were after me."

"At least now, thanks to Ben, you don't

have to hide your pregnancy anymore. Might as well break out the big, puffy tops festooned with bows and ruffles."

Horrified, Lisa said, "I will *not*. There have to be some professional-looking maternity clothes I can buy."

"Well, of course there are. And I'm surprised you haven't already been shopping. You have to give up the five-inch heels, though—for a while." Carly pointed to the navy blue pumps that matched Lisa's slacks.

"I know."

Lisa finished her breakfast, hugged her friend and went to work, stopping by her real-estate office first. She quickly sorted through the mail, checked her email and then picked up her phone to call and check on Ben.

When he answered, he reported that the spasms were gone but his leg would be sore for a few days.

"I'm glad you'll be fine. I realize you were only trying to help last night, and thank you for that, but—"

"I'm sorry for what I let slip. Pain does that to me. One time I got sacked in a game against Denver and knocked out. I woke up calling for Nigel."

"Who was Nigel?"

"The coach's cocker spaniel."

Lisa snickered.

"And, speaking of being sacked, I'm sorry I tackled you and gave you a rug burn. How is that, by the way?"

"It'll heal. I'm wearing long sleeves to cover it up."

"I'm really sorry," Ben repeated. "I'm at Nathan's office. He wanted to have a look at my leg again today. You know, this is a historic moment for Reston."

"What do you mean?"

"The first time we've had a pregnant mayor. Has everyone in town stopped by to congratulate you?"

"Not yet. I haven't actually seen anyone yet. Sandy won't be in for a little while, so—" She broke off when she saw movement at the door and recognized the couple who were leaning closer to look in. "Oh, my goodness."

"What is it?"

"Ben, your parents are here."

"Oh, no. I forgot to call them, but somebody else obviously did. Blasted small-town gossips. Sorry. I'll be right there."

"That isn't necessary. I can handle—" But he had hung up and she was talking to the air.

Taking a deep breath, she hung up the phone, straightened her collar and smoothed her hair as she went to open the door. As she did, she tried to assess the looks on Ben's parents' faces.

Jim McAdams was a big man like his son, handsome with thick, graying hair. He walked with a slight limp from an injury several years ago, but worked every day at one or the other of his enterprises and probably always would.

Helen was tall, as well, a little overweight, but was very energetic in church and community activities. She almost always wore jeans or other casual clothes, but today she was in a dress printed with spring flowers. Lisa smiled to herself, hoping the dress was in celebration of learning of her first grandchild.

"Good morning, Mr. and Mrs. McAdams," she greeted them in a cheerful tone. "Please come in." She held the door open, wondering how quickly Ben would arrive. She led the way into her office and offered them seats on the small sofa, then sat opposite them. "How are you today?"

"I'd have to say surprised," Jim McAdams answered as he sat.

"Very surprised," Helen added.

"We came to find out if it's true." Ben's father leaned forward and fixed her with a steady stare. "That you're having Ben's baby."

Lisa calmly folded her hands in her lap, to forestall any trembling that might start. Seemed like this was her week for confrontations. "Yes, it is. But you could have asked Ben that."

Helen reached over and cuffed him on the arm. "I told you that. We should have called Ben, asked him if it's true."

Jim shot his wife a sideways look. "Well, yeah, maybe, but we need to apologize to Lisa first."

"True."

Lisa put a hand to her chest. "Apologize to me? Whatever for?"

Jim grimaced in self-consternation. "Because when you two were kids and old Sheriff Jepson took him to jail for popping Mrs. Crabtree in the behind—"

"And you broke him out of jail, Lisa."

"I remember."

"We forbade him from ever having anything else to do with you. That was wrong of us," Helen said.

"No," Lisa said, shaking her head. "It was an understandable reaction, given the circumstances."

"We knew he needed to learn a lesson about respecting others and we were afraid that having a friend like you, who was comfortable skirting the law...well, we were afraid you'd be a bad influence on him."

Lisa bit her tongue to keep from laughing or reminding Ben's parents that he was known as the Reston Rascal. "I *was* only twelve at the time, and maybe a little over-imaginative." She lifted her hands, palms up, to indicate her office. "I haven't pursued a life of crime."

"We know," Jim said. "And you've done very well for yourself."

Helen nodded. "But if we hadn't done that, dear, kept you two apart, you might have gotten together much sooner and we would already have several grandchildren."

Lisa stared at her. "What?"

At that moment the outer door swung open and Ben limped inside, hurrying across to her office.

"Good morning, Mom, Dad," he said, giving a quick, concerned glance at Lisa's stunned face.

Helen jumped up and ran over to give her son a hug. "Good morning, honey. We were just congratulating Lisa on the good news. So tell us the next piece of good news. When are you two getting married?"

CHAPTER EIGHT

"Married?" Lisa squeaked.

"Of course," Jim and Helen said in unison, and Jim added, "That's the next obvious step."

Ben held up both hands as if he was trying to stop a speeding train. "Mom. Dad. No."

"When is the baby due?" Helen asked excitedly, paying no attention to her son.

"September," Lisa answered faintly. She looked at Ben for an explanation, but he appeared to be as poleaxed as she was.

"Then we need to get busy planning." Ben's mom clasped her hands rapturously. "Wouldn't a Fourth of July wedding be delightful? We could have an entire patriotic theme going on. Sparklers and fireworks. Do you think Sunshine and Wolfchild Whitmire would let us use the pavilion out at their campground? It would make the perfect setting with star-spangled bunting draped from pillar to pillar.

"Lisa, dear, how do you feel about a white dress with a sweeping train, and a red, white and blue sash, and then red, white and blue bridesmaids' dresses?" Helen gestured as she spoke, her hands floating out as if to encompass a long dress. "Red-and-white-striped skirts, blue bodices? Oh, with stars on them! A little white top hat? Or maybe black?"

Lisa said the first thing that came to mind. "Gemma and Carly would kill me."

She tried to get a handle on this surreal situation even as visions of her best friends dressed as Uncle Sam floated through her head.

"Or perhaps we should have the wedding sooner, earlier this spring," Helen went on dreamily as Jim beamed at her. "A May Day wedding with the girls in soft pink with rows and rows of ruffles." She twirled her hand to indicate floor-length, puffy gowns. "Enormous bouquets and huge, floppy, straw hats." Her hands floated out in front of her and her fingers fluttered. "A carpet strewn with rose petals."

Lisa gulped. "Then they really would kill me. Gemma's a redhead. She looks awful in pink and…Carly isn't really a pink-and-fluffy kind of girl." She wondered in amazement why she was engaging in this crazy conversation.

"Sounds like *Gone With the Wind* live," Ben muttered. "I gotta get off this leg." He pulled a chair over and sat with his sore leg outstretched. "Mom, sit down and calm down, please."

Helen gave him a puzzled look but she retook her seat beside her husband.

"This is a side of you I've never seen before," Ben said. "I didn't know you were so interested in weddings."

"All women are." His mother sniffed. "And since I never had a daughter, and you've insisted until now that you never intended to get married—"

"Mom, I still am not—"

"Your dad and I got married at the county courthouse, no big white dress for me or tux for Jim. It wasn't my dream wedding."

"The courthouse was what we could afford at the time, and it accomplished what we wanted to accomplish," her husband reminded her. "Since we were trying to start our own business."

"Mom and Dad, you have to forget all this

talk about weddings," Ben said in a reasonable tone. "Lisa and I aren't a couple."

"You're having a baby together," Jim answered, his expression collapsing into a mighty frown. "How can you *not* be a couple?"

"Lisa will have the baby and raise it, and I'll provide child support." When he saw his mother's appalled look, he added, "*Generous* child support."

"I should hope so!" Helen said.

"But we're not getting married," Ben continued doggedly. "It's the decision we've made."

"This wasn't planned," Lisa put in. "It just happened."

Jim and Helen looked at each other then at Ben and Lisa. Everyone was silent for a second until Jim shook his head in that age-old way that fathers have of showing disappointment in their offspring. "Son, we didn't raise you to get a girl pregnant and not marry her."

"She's not really a girl, Dad. She's a woman with a career and—"

"I'm right here," Lisa pointed out, waving her hand.

"Well, she can give that up," Helen said. "I did when you were born."

"Mom, Lisa's got her own business and now she's acting mayor."

"Well, she can definitely give that up," Jim said with a dismissive sweep of his hand. "We've never had a woman mayor."

That statement snapped Lisa out of her stricken silence. No matter how much she respected Harley and his years of running the city, she wasn't going to let sexism go unchallenged.

"It's high time that Reston *did* have a woman mayor," she said testily. "And I'm not giving up either my real-estate business or my position as acting mayor."

"Well, dear, you can't do it all and be a good mother, too." Helen folded her arms and nodded her head as if that was the last word on the subject.

Lisa stared at her. What century did this woman live in?

"And another thing," Helen said. "Why didn't you tell us about this sooner, Benton James McAdams? I had to learn about it from June Rhodes, from the garden club. She called to congratulate me on finally becoming a grandmother, and I had to pretend like I knew what she was talking about."

"I'm sorry, Mom. I wasn't going to tell anyone until Lisa was ready."

"Well, it's your child, too. And we're your parents."

"Sorry, Mom, but you know now," Ben said, then added firmly, "We're not getting married. Mom, Dad, I never made a secret of the fact that I don't—" he cast a quick glance at Lisa "—*didn't* want children. I travel all the time. It wouldn't be fair to the kid."

"Then this will keep you at home, won't it?" Jim asked. "Sounds like a win-win to me."

"Or an April wedding," Helen said, sinking back into her daydream. "With dresses made of that shiny fabric that looks pink in one light, and then, in the right light, changes to a kind of bluish purple—like hydrangeas."

Lisa gagged but didn't bother to respond. Instead she announced to the room at large, "No wedding. No giving up of careers. If you want to be a part of your grandchild's life, we can work that out. I want him, or her, to have family."

"Since his father apparently won't be around," Jim said, giving his son a dark look, "we'd like that, too." The big man got to his feet. "Come on, Helen. We might as well go."

She blinked. "So, no wedding?"

"No wedding," Ben answered, standing to give his mother a hug.

She finally seemed to notice his leg and began fussing at him, asking what had happened, had he seen the doctor? She thought he hadn't showed up for dinner last night because he wasn't hungry. Why hadn't he called?

Murmuring reassurances and more apologies, Ben finessed them out the door. The three of them met Sandy, who was coming in with a huge grin and a fluffy teddy bear.

Sandy plopped the toy down on top of the desk and came to Lisa with her arms outstretched. "Congratulations on the baby. I've been waiting for you to tell me yourself, but I had to hear it from Raylene Prestridge over at the Gas 'n' Go, so I had to make another stop to buy the bear. That's why I'm late."

"Thank you. He's adorable." Lisa paused, admiring his goofy expression and the big red bow around his neck. "You knew I was pregnant?"

"Sure, honey. I'm the mother of three and

the aunt of seven. I know when a woman's going to have a baby. You've looked like death's favorite girlfriend around here for weeks, pale and sickly. 'Course, I didn't know that Ben is the father." She sighed. "Lucky you."

That wasn't the word Lisa would have used, but she smiled and picked up the teddy bear. She had a sudden vision of her child, a dark-haired little boy, dragging it by one foot down the hall as he came to find her and snuggle into her lap. The image caught at her heart and she paused, trying to remember if she had ever been held and cherished like that.

That made her think of Maureen. She hadn't meant to drive her mother away, and last night had doubtless been the worst time to have brought up the past. She had already been so distraught over her encounter with the bats, and Ben announcing she was pregnant, that she had overreacted to Maureen's hovering and caused deep hurt. She would certainly apologize to her mother, but it might be a while before Maureen would take her calls.

Lisa glanced up when Ben walked back into the outer office and greeted Sandy, who was settling in at her desk. When Sandy offered her congratulations, he murmured a thank-you that left Sandy staring after him. He closed Lisa's office door and sat once again, wincing as he propped his leg up on the coffee table.

"These past twenty-four hours just keep getting better and better," he said sardonically. "What's going to happen next?"

"I was just thinking about that, but I don't want to speculate. Life is already too crazy."

"You've got that right." He paused. "Listen, I'm sorry about my parents. I don't know where they got the idea we'd be getting married. They know how I feel about—"

"We all do, Ben," she said.

"Oh, sorry. I've wanted to keep this on a businesslike footing, so—"

"You don't get emotionally involved. We all know that, too."

He frowned at her. "What's wrong with you this morning? I'm trying to make sure the issue isn't clouded with unrealistic expectations about big weddings and…and fireworks."

Lisa turned her head so he wouldn't see her unbidden tears. There was no reason for her to feel so let down by him when he'd never made a secret of his feelings. Blinking quickly, she stood and said, "Yes, I know." She intended to find her copy of the financial spreadsheet of child-rearing costs when she felt a fluttering in her tummy.

"Oh," she said softly, her hands immediately going to cover the bump, trying to locate the precise spot.

Ben surged to his feet and, in spite of his hurt knee, was across the room in seconds. "What? What is it? Are you sick? Need something?"

"No." She looked up, tears forming in her eyes once again and her face filling with joy. "I think I just felt the baby kick for the first time. Gemma said that probably wouldn't happen for a week or two. Obviously, he's a prodigy."

With a soft laugh, Lisa reached out and scooped up his hand, spreading his fingers over her belly. "It was here, on the right. There! Can you feel it?"

Ben's face froze; his expression one she'd never seen before—disbelieving and concerned. "It's like little butterfly kicks."

"They'll get a lot stronger, or so I've read

in the four books I've received from Gemma and the million online articles from Carly."

Lisa released a laugh of pure delight. Until this moment the baby hadn't seemed quite real. His only manifestations had been nausea and frequent urges for the bathroom. Now she knew he was moving and growing.

She looked up into Ben's face, which was so full of emotions she couldn't sort them out, though none resembled happy. Looking down, she realized that she had his hand trapped against her, feeling the movements of a child he wanted little or nothing to do with. In her eagerness to share this moment with someone, she had let herself forget how he felt about the baby.

She stepped back. "I'm sorry, Ben. I was so surprised to feel it and know it's his first kick. It's like the first acknowledgment of him saying, 'Hey, I'm in here, and I'm a person.'"

Ben lifted his hand and covered his mouth for a minute, then dropped his arm and sucked in a deep breath as if he'd been keeping himself from breathing.

"Um, yes. That's a baby, all right. A person." He turned toward the door, lurching a little on his bad leg. "That's good," he said.

"That's good that it's so... Listen, I've got to go. Nathan insists on looking at my leg again. Can't keep the doctor—"

He didn't even bother to finish the cliché he'd been about to utter, simply disappeared out the door, didn't even acknowledge when Sandy told him goodbye. Her secretary gave Lisa a shocked glance, but she only shook her head and retreated into her office.

Lisa didn't know why she was surprised. He had made it clear time after time that he wanted nothing to do with the baby.

"That's okay, little one," she said, cradling her arms around the bump. "I'm happy about you."

Maureen tore down the highway, her thoughts scrambling frantically, picking apart the conversation she'd had with Lisa the night before. After packing her car as silently as possible, she had slipped away at dawn and left her daughter behind. Again.

Lisa had called, but Maureen let it go to voice mail. She wasn't ready to talk yet.

"I should have known I'd screw this up," she muttered, brushing tears from her eyes while trying to focus on her driving. "Should have known coming back was a bad idea."

Her encounter with Dorcas Poole the day before had unnerved her. Even though she knew how vicious the other woman could be, Maureen had been devastated by her words. They were the same things she thought about herself. Dorcas was only saying aloud what Maureen had been saying to herself all these years. She had some nerve coming back and expecting to have a relationship with Lisa.

She had let Violet extract a promise from her to see Lisa, but that had been a mistake. Maureen hated that she had tried to make up for thirty-three years of neglect in a few weeks. She'd ended up hovering over Lisa and annoying her.

Ever since she'd run away when Lisa was a baby, she'd had it in her mind that she would be able to go back and make things right, but it had never happened. She had to accept that. Although Lisa hadn't said so, she probably wanted nothing to do with the mother who had showed up and offered too little too late.

Maureen looked down at the gas gauge and was alarmed to see how low she was. A glance at the dashboard clock told her she her thoughts back to the business at hand. "Generous."

"Good." He stood. "But I'd feel better if you had an attorney look it over."

"I will, although I don't think you have any plans to cheat me, Ben, or our child."

"No, of course not. I only want to get things settled. I'm flying to Arizona tomorrow. I've got a board meeting in Phoenix for one of the charities I support and then I've got a golf tournament in Tucson. It would be good if we could get this signed as soon as I get back next week. I'll give you a call to set up a time."

Done and dusted, Lisa thought. Put a checkmark beside the line item that said Provide for Child, which, no doubt, was on the line right after Board Meeting and Golf Tournament.

She reached up to sweep unexpected tears away. "O…okay," she said.

"Hey, what's the matter?" Ben asked. "Are you in pain?"

"No. I'm fine. I was out at Reston Lake with the investment group who's considering building a resort, and I think I got too much sun. Now, if that's all, I'm sure you need to go and…pack your golf shoes or something."

"That's right. What good would having the recipe do you, since you don't cook?"

She had him there, and they both knew it. Clive wouldn't plan to keep her recipes and pass them on to his next cook. He was too honest for that. Anyway, given his past experience, he would never find another cook like her.

Maureen hadn't told him so yet, but she felt as if she would like to stick around for a while. To her surprise, she had discovered she liked Peachdale. She'd thought she'd had enough of small-town life after growing up in Reston, but it was different here. Peachdale was much smaller than Reston, and no one knew her. No one knew about her hoarder parents or the daughter she'd left behind. Twice now. No one judged her on anything other than her cooking—and she knew she was really good at that.

She had met many, maybe most, of the residents. The high-schoolers trouped in before school started, devouring mountains of pancakes and rafts of eggs and bacon. She knew they had food at home, or could get breakfast at school, but they liked the café. Clive didn't let them linger, though. The Marine shooed had been driving for two hours. Although she wanted to run as far and as fast as she could, she simply didn't have the money. She had enough for a few days, at most, but then she would have to get a job.

The next town she came to was one she'd never heard of before. Peachdale, Oklahoma, was typical of the small towns in the state. The highway ran through the middle, doubling as the main street. She slowed to the twenty-five-mile-per-hour speed limit and looked around.

Perhaps eight or ten side streets branched off from Main Street. There was a small grocery store, a Laundromat and a few other stores, and at the edge of the town, which couldn't have been more than a couple of miles square, she saw the school complex, redbrick buildings with neatly manicured lawns beginning to show their spring color. Across the street was a new-looking combination gas station, convenience store and café. Maureen pulled in, filled her tank and then went into the café, whose door held a hastily scrawled Help Wanted sign.

Although she wondered briefly what kind of help they wanted, she sat and ordered eggs, bacon and toast from a grumpy-looking man with a gray buzz cut and few words to offer.

To distract herself, she examined the café, which held about a dozen tables and four booths along a wall of windows. She was the only customer.

She'd been in more places like this than she cared to count. Worked in more places like this than she cared to remember. This one, the Peachdale Café, appeared to be a cut above the rest. The wooden tabletops gleamed, as did the floor, and the windows were adorned with crisp, red curtains tied back with white bows. Still-life watercolor paintings featuring fruits, vegetables and flowers graced the walls, giving the place a homelike, welcoming feel.

The waiter brought her a cup of coffee and the worst-looking breakfast she'd ever seen. The bacon and toast were the next closest thing to burned, and the scrambled eggs were hard enough to bounce on the floor.

Maureen gave him a you've-got-to-be-kidding-me look.

"The cook quit," he said. "And my regular waitress has a sick kid, so I've been filling in on both jobs."

Ah, that explained what kind of help was needed. "For how long?"

"A couple of weeks." He shrugged. "Lost all my best customers. But I never claimed to be a cook. I know how to run this place, and I'm good at a lot of things, but cooking isn't one of 'em."

Maureen observed him for a second. He appeared tough, probably ex-military, but he had a self-deprecating air she liked.

"My wife was the cook. When I got out of the Marines, we built this place. I ran that side of things—" he nodded toward the gas station and convenience store "—and Carol ran this place, did most of the cooking. Did the decorating..."

His voice trailed off as his gaze ran over the paintings. His tough face softened as he looked at them, and Maureen guessed his wife had also done the artwork. His obvious affection for Carol was touching. He had been almost silent when Maureen had walked into the café, but thinking about his wife had made him chatty.

"When did she die?" she asked quietly.

His gaze snapped to her and he was all business again. "Two years ago. Cancer."

"I'm sorry. It must have been very hard."

He nodded, his mouth firming into a hard line.

Maureen had the sudden, disturbing realization that there probably wasn't anyone who would mourn her if she were to die suddenly. Her mind veered away from that sad thought.

"I'm a cook," she said impulsively. "I've worked in kitchens all my life, as a short-order cook, sous chef, you name it, and I need a job."

He frowned. "Do you live around here?"

"I also need a place to live."

"There's a little apartment out back you can use, but I'll need some references."

"Of course, but in the meantime, why don't I fix us both a decent breakfast?"

"Okay." He picked up the plate of sad-looking food. "My name is Clive Forrest. Like I said, I own this place, along with the convenience store and gas station. Don't have any problems keeping good help over there. Just here. Only open from 6:00 a.m. till 2:00 p.m. and I still can't keep a cook."

Maureen introduced herself and followed him into the kitchen, which she was glad to see was as spotless as the dining room itself.

Of course, with few customers, there was too little cooking going on to create a mess.

Clive handed her a clean, starched apron, which she tied around her waist, then he pulled up a stool and watched her fix golden toast, crisp bacon and fluffy eggs.

"I watched Carol cook a million times, but I just don't have the touch."

Maureen liked this tough-looking, candid Marine. He seemed as if he would be an honest boss. With a flourish, she handed him a plate of food. "Try this and see if I've got the touch."

After a few bites he said, "You're hired. As soon as we're finished eating, I'll show you where the apartment is."

"Oh, okay. Thanks," she said, blinking in pleased surprise. She'd never landed a job so easily.

Clive was as good as his word, showing her where to park her car around back and then helping her carry her things inside. The apartment had a combination living room and kitchen, as well as a small bedroom and bath. The place was clean, with worn but serviceable furniture. It only needed a good airing out. She'd lived in worse.

"Can you be ready for work in about an hour?" Clive asked.

"Certainly. I just have to look at the menu, check the supplies and find everything I need in the kitchen."

"Good, because once I put out the sign, we'll have a lunch rush."

"The sign?"

"Yup."

Curious, she followed him outside and around to the side of the building. He pulled a canvas tarp off a wheeled marquee with an electrical cord looped over its top. He began pushing it toward the street side of the café. Snap-in letters read Hired A Cook!

TWO WEEKS AFTER Maureen's departure, Lisa stood by Reston Lake, enjoying the sparkle of light on the water, breathing deeply of the fresh air and then sitting gratefully on the tailgate of Roland Hall's truck, which he had thoughtfully backed up near the spot where the investors from Oklahoma City were holding a discussion.

The group had arrived that morning to walk the complete property for the first time and to get the particulars they'd need to go ahead with the development. They had brought along a survey crew and she had brought along Bunky and Roland.

To her delight, the two council members weren't arguing today. Instead they were ready to answer any of the investors' questions. The only problem was, they didn't know much about the project and continually ran back to her to find out what was needed.

"So the title is clean on the property the city is selling and what the Burleighs are selling, but not from the Masons, right?" Bunky asked, holding up a finger to indicate each parcel of land.

Lisa smiled at the investment group even as she tried to keep from gritting her teeth at Bunky. "Yes, I told you that, but it can easily be obtained. The Masons are eager to sell and are taking full responsibility for clearing up the title. They don't want any impediment to this deal any more than the rest of us do."

"Okay," he said. "Just making sure. You're the only one who knows this stuff since you're the only Realtor in town."

As he trotted away, Lisa's smile grew genuine and she shook her head. Bunky was only doing his job. The city council, the county supervisors, almost everyone in Reston County, in fact, was anxious to see this development happen. And it looked like it really would. Between the resort itself and its infusion of tourist dollars, the golf course, the fishing and the possibility of water sports in the future, the place would provide dozens of jobs.

Her smile faded when she considered Bunky's words. She was the only Realtor in town and that had been a good thing for her business, but wouldn't be for this deal. Since she was acting mayor, she couldn't also be the broker—that would certainly be a conflict of interest. However, she could be involved in every other way.

From what she'd seen of the investment group so far, they seemed sincere in their desire to create a quality development. And she liked them personally. The two women were the reason she was sitting on the tailgate of Roland's truck. When the ladies realized she was pregnant, they had been so horrified at the idea of her standing around on the hillside during endless discussions, they'd sent Roland scurrying to get his truck.

At last, the group seemed satisfied and

headed back to the city with assurances that she would be hearing from them soon.

Talking excitedly about the development, Bunky and Roland hurried to their vehicles.

Lisa climbed into hers and sat sipping water from an insulated bottle and rubbing her tummy. She'd been having odd twinges all morning. They had been coming and going for days. Gemma said they were perfectly normal for a mom who was well into her fourth month and for Lisa to stay off her feet when they started, but that simply hadn't been possible today. She made a mental note to put a folding chair into the trunk of her car for the next time she had to spend hours on a grassy hillside answering questions.

As she rested and prepared to return to town, she idly watched the surveyors and thought about all that had happened in the past week.

She had gone online and ordered some actual maternity slacks. It was as if her waistline had suddenly exploded. Gemma said that, too, was perfectly normal, but had scheduled Lisa for her first ultrasound at the hospital in Toncaville. Reston didn't have a sonographic machine yet.

Lisa was eager to have the exam and see the results, an actual picture of her baby, and so were Ben's parents. One or the other of them called every day to see how she was doing.

She hadn't heard a word from Ben since the day they had felt the baby move. What had been a delightful surprise for her had seemed like a terrible shock to him. She tried not to judge him too harshly because he'd never made a secret of his reluctance to be a father. Still, she couldn't help feeling disappointed in him.

That feeling warred with her disappointment in herself when she thought about how she had treated Maureen. She had called and left messages of apology, but there had been no reply except for a terse text message from Maureen saying she was okay and had found a job. Lisa knew she needed to let her mom go, at least for now, but it was hard to do so.

When her need for a bathroom became more urgent than her need to sit and stew over Ben, Lisa headed back to town. She had far too many things to think about. There was no time to worry over Ben or Maureen.

By the time she got home that evening, she

was too tired to make it past the living room sofa, where she lay down and propped up her feet, falling instantly asleep.

A knock on the door startled her awake and she jumped up to answer it. A moment of dizziness made her stagger as she swung the door open and she shook her head to clear it.

Ben waited on the porch with an envelope in his hand. He held it up, but froze in mid-air when he saw her face. "Are you okay?"

"Yes, of course." She put a hand to her head. "Why wouldn't I be?"

He stepped forward and grabbed her arm to support her. "Oh, I don't know. Maybe because you're white as a sheet."

"I...think I stood up too fast."

"Well, then, sit down." Ben didn't even wait for an invitation. He stepped inside, put a supporting arm around her and walked her to the sofa. Lisa leaned into him, resting on his strength, enjoying the comfort of depending on someone else, even for a moment.

He sat her down and looked at her with concern.

Ben straightened. "I'll get you some water."

He tossed the envelope onto the coffee table and hurried to the kitchen. She looked down at the envelope, which had her name written on the front and the return address of a law firm in Tulsa printed in the corner.

Ben walked back into the room with a glass of water, which he handed to her. Standing over her, he waited until she'd finished the glass before he sat.

Finally he said, "I went to a law firm, started making the arrangements to provide for the baby. Have your attorney look it over. If you think it's fair, we'll sign on the dotted line and it'll be a done deal."

Lisa looked the documents over and then glanced up. "You took that spreadsheet seriously, didn't you? This seems more than fair."

Even if the unthinkable happened and her career tanked, she would always be able to take care of her child. Her heart warmed as she looked at Ben. He sat, relaxed in a chair, looking around her living room as if unaware of the wonderful gift he'd given her.

When he felt her gaze on him, he smiled in a way that emphasized his dimples, and gave her a wink—reminding her of why he was called the Reston Rascal.

"More than fair," she repeated, corralling

her thoughts back to the business at hand. "Generous."

"Good." He stood. "But I'd feel better if you had an attorney look it over."

"I will, although I don't think you have any plans to cheat me, Ben, or our child."

"No, of course not. I only want to get things settled. I'm flying to Arizona tomorrow. I've got a board meeting in Phoenix for one of the charities I support and then I've got a golf tournament in Tucson. It would be good if we could get this signed as soon as I get back next week. I'll give you a call to set up a time."

Done and dusted, Lisa thought. Put a checkmark beside the line item that said Provide for Child, which, no doubt, was on the line right after Board Meeting and Golf Tournament.

She reached up to sweep unexpected tears away. "O…okay," she said.

"Hey, what's the matter?" Ben asked. "Are you in pain?"

"No. I'm fine. I was out at Reston Lake with the investment group who's considering building a resort, and I think I got too much sun. Now, if that's all, I'm sure you need to go and…pack your golf shoes or something."

She stood, ready to usher him out the door, but another wave of light-headedness had her reaching out to steady herself.

CHAPTER NINE

"LISA!" BEN LEAPED forward to grab her but she tried to shrug him off. "What's wrong?"

"It's nothing. Just need to catch my breath." She blinked at him and glanced around as if trying to remember something. "Shouldn't you be playing golf?"

"What?" Ben helped her to sit on the sofa. He should have known there was something wrong when she answered the door looking as pale as milk. When her face didn't take on any color within a minute or so, he bent over and gently urged her to lie down while he pulled off her shoes and stacked cushions beneath her feet. He watched her closely until her complexion appeared normal. "Golf isn't for a few days."

"What are you talking about?" she asked, frowning.

Realizing she was disoriented, he said, "Never mind. Are you in pain?"

"No, a little dizzy."

"Come on, I'm taking you to the emergency room."

"There's no reason for that. I can call Gemma—"

"Good. Then do it." He glanced around, spied her things on a table and grabbed her purse. "Here. Get your phone and call her. I'll wait."

She gave him an annoyed look, but he only stared her down until she punched the speed dial to call Gemma. In less than a minute she hung up and said, "She's coming right over. It isn't necessary for you to stay."

"Sure it is. She's a medical professional. I want to hear what she has to say. I'll stick around until I hear her diagnosis."

"I'm pregnant," Lisa said testily as color rose in her cheeks. "That's the diagnosis."

He grinned. Better to have her getting snippy with him than looking as though she was going to pass out.

"Do you mind if I stick around?" he asked, retaking an easy chair opposite the sofa.

"Of course I do, but it's not as though I can pick you up and throw you out, even if that *is* what I'd like to do."

"Instead of that, why don't you lie back, relax, close your eyes—"

"And imagine you disappearing."

"That's my girl," he said approvingly.

Gemma was there within a few minutes. Ben would have been okay staying in the living room while she conducted the examination, but both women had given him a no-nonsense look that sent him to find refuge in the kitchen.

He sat at the table, looked around at the ultra-neat room and compared it to his own shabby kitchen. He didn't have a big interest in living spaces, but it was obvious that Lisa did. He wondered if that was why she'd pursued a career in real estate. He was pretty sure it had something to do with the way she'd grown up.

She had made this house into a beautiful home. He was glad that his child would have a clean, safe environment like this one. His child. Lisa was right when she'd said it hadn't seemed like a real person until she'd felt the baby move. Until *he'd* felt it move. Before that point, the child was an obligation, a mistake he would own up to and for which he would take responsibility. Now it was a person.

"Ben." Gemma spoke from the doorway and he stood. "Thanks for making her call me. She's fine. It's like she said, she had too much sun and too much standing around today out at the lake." She glanced over her shoulder and raised her voice. "And she hasn't eaten nearly enough today so her blood sugar is low."

Ben followed Gemma into the living room, where Lisa reclined on the couch, her feet propped up. She wrinkled her nose at him and he grinned.

"Don't forget your ultrasound appointment tomorrow at eleven." Gemma said, leaning down to give Lisa a hug. "It probably won't show anything out of the ordinary, but you'll be able to find out the baby's sex if you want to."

"You know I want to," Lisa said, resting her hands on her belly.

"Call me if you feel sick or have *any* problems, and be sure to call me after your appointment."

"I will."

Ben saw Gemma out the door, then turned

back to Lisa. "So," he said, giving her an as-sessing look. "You're okay, then?"

"Obviously."

"Good." He paused, knowing she wanted him out of her hair, but not quite ready to go. "If you think you'll be all right, I'll leave that paper for you to look over and then I'll call you when I get back from Arizona."

"Fine." When he didn't immediately move to open the door, she asked, "Is something wrong?"

"Nah, but I'm wondering why you thought you had to be out at the lake with those developers. Couldn't somebody else handle that?"

"Yes, Bunky and Roland."

"Oh." He stepped away from the door, stuck his hands in his back pockets and took a turn around the room.

"Why do you ask?"

"I get that you feel obligated to be the act-ing mayor until Harley gets well, but don't you think you're doing too much?"

She raised an eyebrow at him. "You mean, for a woman, right?"

"For anyone, but especially for a pregnant woman." He frowned. "You know that song about the woman 'bringing home the bacon and frying it up in a pan' is a crock of bunk, don't you?"

Now she really stared at him. "That is a remarkably enlightened outlook."

He cleared his throat and looked away. "Well, my mom might have been lecturing me a little bit."

"Your mom, who thought I should give up my career and marry you?"

"That's the one."

"Hmm." Lisa turned onto her side and rested her chin on her hand thoughtfully. "Your mom didn't tell me she's been lecturing you."

"You talked to her?"

"I talk to either your mother or your father, or both of them, every day." Lisa smiled softly. "They're very excited about the baby."

"I know." Ben didn't know what to say to them. They had always wanted grandchildren, which he'd assured them he wouldn't provide. Now that one was coming, it felt awkward. What he saw as an obligation, they viewed with unbridled joy. "And their excitement grows every day," he added. "Nobody's ever had a happiness-induced stroke, have they?"

Lisa laughed. "I don't think so. And, by the way, you're under no obligation to pass your mom's lecture on to me. I know how much I can take on."

"I wonder."

"*I* wonder why this matters to you." She shifted on the couch and sat up a little, pushing a cushion down behind her back. "It's not as though I expect anything from you. Not as though we have any kind of relationship, other than one shared night, which was a mistake."

"In spite of that, I'm…I'm glad this has brought you back into my life," he said.

"You…you are?"

"Sure. When I saw you at the airport in Chicago, I couldn't believe it was someone from home, someone who knew me before football and fame. You seemed happy to see me, too."

"I was," she admitted with a smile that made him feel a soft glow in the pit of his stomach.

He couldn't recall ever experiencing that with her.

"I'd had an awful day," Lisa said. "Seeing you, having you rescue me in that storm…

well, it was…wonderful." She paused. "I admit that since I was embarrassed about that night, I thought the baby was a terrible mistake."

"You did?" Hearing her say it made him feel a little less like a jerk.

"I was beside myself, didn't know what to think, how to respond. Up until a couple of weeks ago, I couldn't seem to get my thoughts together, at least until I felt him move. Then everything seemed to clarify." She smiled. "Gemma tells me that's a common reaction."

Ben knew exactly what she meant, but her reality was different than his. He had obligations all around the world. He had spent years establishing his place in a network of charities that mattered to him, ones that involved people in education and sports. They were important, far-reaching and fun. But so was raising a child, if a person did it right.

Unwilling to give in to the circling thoughts that had consumed him for a week, he looked around. "Gemma said you're feeling faint because you haven't eaten enough today. Can I at least fry some bacon up in a pan for you?"

If Lisa was surprised at his change of subject, she didn't show it—probably because she didn't need for him to agree with her. "Don't think I have any, but check the refrigerator. There's plenty of other food."

She said it with a laugh in her voice, so he returned to the kitchen and pulled open the refrigerator. "Wow! Are you expecting a famine?"

"Look in the freezer."

He pulled that door open, too, and stood, open-mouthed at the neat stacks of filled containers, top to bottom, right to left, all labeled and dated. "You couldn't get so much as a business card in here."

"I know. Baby and I are well-stocked for the next six months. Help yourself. I'm not picky."

"You can be if you want. There's plenty of choices." From the fridge, Ben took out a container marked "mac and cheese" and one labeled "coleslaw."

"With all you do, how did you have time to prepare all this?"

"I didn't."

While he heated the mac and cheese in the microwave and prepared two plates, she told him about her mother's visit. "But she...felt like it was time to go, so she…went. Weeks ago."

There was an echo of sadness in her voice, along with something else that it took him a minute to pinpoint. Loneliness, maybe? She was certainly alone now. He didn't like the pinpricks of guilt that caused, so he finished the dinner preparations and set the table. Time for him to eat and run, he decided.

"Hmm. Home fries are just French fries with the spice kicked up. What is this?" Clive asked. "Chile? Garlic? Onion?"

Maureen smiled. "I'd think you'd be able to figure it out by now, Clive. That's your third plate of them. You do realize you're eating up all your own profits, right?"

"It's called quality control. I can't serve them to my customers if they're less than perfect." He squirted ketchup on his mound of fries. "And, besides, these are leftovers, and they *are* perfect."

"We aim to please." When he looked at her again she said, "And, no, I won't share my spice recipe. I keep all my recipes secret."

"Even though I'm paying for the ingredients?"

"That's right. What good would having the recipe do you, since you don't cook?"

She had him there, and they both knew it. Clive wouldn't plan to keep her recipes and pass them on to his next cook. He was too honest for that. Anyway, given his past experience, he would never find another cook like her.

Maureen hadn't told him so yet, but she felt as if she would like to stick around for a while. To her surprise, she had discovered she liked Peachdale. She'd thought she'd had enough of small-town life after growing up in Reston, but it was different here. Peachdale was much smaller than Reston, and no one knew her. No one knew about her hoarder parents or the daughter she'd left behind. Twice now. No one judged her on anything other than her cooking—and she knew she was really good at that.

She had met many, maybe most, of the residents. The high-schoolers trouped in before school started, devouring mountains of pancakes and rafts of eggs and bacon. She knew they had food at home, or could get breakfast at school, but they liked the café. Clive didn't let them linger, though. The Marine shooed them out in plenty of time to make their first class and he wasn't above calling the high school, in case the administration wanted to know why they were tardy, and giving the names of students who didn't move out at a double quick time.

The kids didn't argue with him. It was obvious they had respect for the Marine who employed several of them in after-school jobs.

She had learned right away that there was no such thing as an ex-Marine. "Once in the corps, always in the corps" was Clive's motto. She wondered if that was where he had learned his housekeeping skills or if he'd been schooled by his wife. He liked everything shipshape and sparkling clean.

Maureen still tired easily, so she was glad for the shorter work day. Fewer hours meant less pay, but Clive refused to charge her rent for her tiny apartment. He was so thrilled to have a competent cook.

Every afternoon she took a walk, receiving the same two-fingered wave so popular around Reston from every driver she met along the way. It always made her smile because it confirmed her feeling of being at home. It made her think she was fitting in.

She worked from six in the morning until two in the afternoon, stopping for a short lunch break whenever business slowed down. But slow-downs were rare. The café had a steady stream of customers and Clive was mostly happy to leave the running of the kitchen to her. He'd managed to hire two people to help her with food prep and cleanup, and someone to act as hostess and cashier. He told her he thought she had broken the jinx that had bedeviled the place since his wife's death. She was flattered.

Clive dropped by the kitchen several times a day, most often to see if she'd cooked up anything new and to try it out for himself. He had given up on keeping the menu updated and had installed an old-fashioned chalkboard he'd rescued from the elementary school garbage. On it, she wrote the day's offerings. She knew a number of customers came in specifically to see what new dish she created each day. They didn't have to know that every one of them was something she'd created years ago. They were new to Peachdale.

Now the café was closed and scrubbed spotless the way Carol had always kept it, according to her fond husband. Maureen was doing prep work for the next day and Clive was making sure none of the home fries suffered the indignity of remaining uneaten.

"If we'd had chow like this in the Marines, I never would have retired."

"You would also weigh six hundred pounds," Maureen pointed out drily. "Why did you and your wife decide to retire here?"

"Carol was from this area. The kids were grown and on their own. We planned to run this place, then hire a good manager or two and see the sights in the country we'd missed while I was in the corps. I thought she and I would have longer together."

"I guess that's the way it always is, when someone goes too soon." Maureen thought about all the people she'd lost over the years. The most painful was the one she'd walked away from. Her mind skittered away from thoughts of Lisa, whose calls she had yet to return. "Tell me about your kids."

"Todd and Blake. They're both cops in Tulsa. I see them about once a month. I go up there for the day when I've got someone to cover this place for me, or they come here with their wives and kids."

Clive told her about his three grandchildren,

which sparked longing in Maureen to see Lisa's child. She wanted to make things right, but she wasn't sure how. It would take time. For now, it was easier to focus on work, on her new home, on someone else's grandchildren—anything other than how she had failed her own daughter.

"Police work can be dangerous and under-appreciated. Do they like their jobs?"

"Yeah, mostly. Blake is a patrol officer and Todd made detective, works missing persons cases. Had one a couple of months ago, a man who disappeared. Turned out he had another entire family in Kansas that his Oklahoma family knew nothing about. He'd decided to stay with them permanently but hadn't bothered to let his Tulsa wife and kids know."

"How did your son track him down?"

"Social security number. You only get one, you know—at least a real one, and this guy wasn't a crook, just a philanderer. Amazing how he kept each family from finding out about the other." Clive savored a few more French fries before asking, "How about you, Maureen? Do you have a family?"

"No. I—" She broke off, thinking that she had ducked her responsibilities for so long, wallowed in the shame of having left her infant daughter in a home she could no longer live in, it had become second nature to her to hide the truth. And look where that had taken her—straight into an estrangement she'd never intended to have. Really, that didn't make her any different from the man with two families. He had ducked responsibility, and Maureen admitted that she had, too.

She couldn't face Lisa again yet, but she could make another change.

Her lips wobbled in a smile. "I have a daughter, although I haven't been a good mother by any means."

"Oh, why is that?"

"Long story. Let's just say, she grew up without me. I've been trying to make amends, but I went about it all wrong."

"So try something different," Clive suggested.

"What do you mean?"

"Do something you haven't tried before. You don't know what might work."

Maureen met his gaze. In the short time she'd known him, Clive had always been honest. At first, she had thought his taciturn nature meant he was withdrawn, but he was actually thoughtful, spending his time considering a problem before tackling it. Once he had a plan in mind, he was quite chatty.

Maureen knew she had avoided dealing with her abandonment of Lisa because it was simply too painful to face, a deeply ingrained habit she had yet to break. "I don't think I'm ready. I *know* I'm not ready."

Clive smiled. "An old Marine said, 'Being ready is not what matters. What matters is winning after you get there.'"

Maureen stared at him for a moment, then nodded and went back to chopping vegetables for the creamy vegetable soup she had planned for tomorrow. Clive finished his fries, washed his plate and utensils and left.

What was something different that she could offer her daughter? She had tried being there, taking care of her, but had ended up smothering her. She had shared the reasons why she'd left but the conversation had been too emotional for both of them. She hadn't showed Lisa the depth of her shame and sorrow for what she'd done. She'd never asked for forgiveness. Going back now, without something new to offer, might bring a rejection she couldn't face, something from which the two of them could never recover.

What else was there?

Maureen raised her knife onto its tip, slipped a celery stalk under the blade and brought the sharp edge down over and over until she had reduced the stalk into perfectly even little comma-shaped slices. She paused as she reached for the next stalk.

She could give Lisa answers about her father. It might not make any difference in their troubled relationship, but it was up to her to find him.

She glanced at the door through which Clive had disappeared. She'd never been involved with a man like him. A straight-up, honest man. She had never felt worthy of the few really good men who had come across her path, so she had kept to herself.

Maureen pressed her palms together as she stared anxiously around the kitchen. It was time for a change in that area, too. She didn't see Clive in a romantic light, but she did think they could be friends. There was something so completely bone-deep honest about him that she felt she could trust him, tell him about her shameful past, and he wouldn't come down with ironclad pronouncements.

Because of her shame and because she had been so young when she'd started working, Maureen never felt she could open up to people, tell them about herself. She felt she could talk to Clive, though, and maybe his son Todd was the same way. Perhaps he could give her advice on how to locate John Jackson, if that was his real name. Even if she didn't succeed in finding the man who had fathered Lisa, she would have proof that she had tried.

It was possible that was all Lisa wanted— a mother who tried.

LISA EMERGED FROM the mayor's office and hurried toward her car, but she was brought up short by the sight of Ben leaning up against it in his customary pose, legs stretched out in front of him, arms crossed over his chest.

She rocked to a stop and threw her hands into the air. "Ben, what are you doing here? Don't you have mustangs to feed or... I know." She snapped her fingers as she remembered. "I thought you had to go to Phoenix or somewhere for a big, important board meeting and then to a big, important golf tournament."

"Sweet of you to remember the details." He shrugged. "Yeah, I was supposed to go, but it can wait. I'm going to take you to your ultrasound appointment."

"Oh, I don't *think* so."

At her adamant tone he placed his hands on his hips and frowned at her. "I didn't like the way you looked yesterday. I'm making sure you're okay."

"That's the lamest excuse I've ever heard. You only want to… I don't even *know* what you want to do. Be in charge? Aren't you in charge at your charity board meetings? Don't you feel that's where you're needed?" She put her purse and laptop case in her backseat and slammed the door. "You heard Gemma say I'm fine. Why won't you believe her?"

"I do, but even she indicated you needed a second opinion. That's the reason for the ultrasound."

"No. The reason is to make sure the baby is developing normally, which I'm sure he is."

"Nevertheless, I'll drive you."

She treated him to a sickly sweet smile. "I'll

drive myself, thank you." She was annoyed that he'd showed up, expecting to take over.

"Then I'll ride along with you." He reached for the door handle.

She hit the lock button on her key fob. "No, you won't. I don't need you watching over me."

"Fine. I'll follow you in my truck."

"I can't stop you from using a public highway, but don't think you're coming into the examination room with me."

He only smiled and went to his own vehicle. At the end of her patience with people hovering and trying to do for her what she could do for herself, Lisa took a minute to breathe deeply and calm down. She had too much to do to let him get to her, too many details to handle.

As she pulled onto the street, her first inclination was to step on the gas, weave in and out of traffic and try to lose him, but she knew that would be stupid and dangerous. Besides, he knew exactly where she was going.

At the Toncaville hospital, she parked and went inside without waiting for him, but he soon caught up with her. She signed in at the desk, provided her insurance information, then sat to wait, her purse in her lap and her hands folded primly on top.

Ben lounged in a chair across from her, treating her to a devilish grin whenever she looked his way, smug that he had managed to do exactly what she hadn't wanted him to. A couple of people approached him, asking for an autograph or a selfie. All graciousness and affability, he happily complied.

There was no getting away from his celebrity. He seemed to enjoy it. She understood that he always encouraged it because it benefited his charities, which he usually mentioned in the most humble and charming way, but she knew she would get very tired of the attention if it was her. Simply having people calling on her regarding her mayoral duties was tiring.

When the technician called her in, she walked across the waiting room, quickly aware that Ben had jumped up and was striding along right behind her.

"You're not coming in with me," she whispered fiercely. "I told you that. Don't you listen?"

"Occasionally," he admitted. "I'll be quiet

as a mouse." His tone was breezy, sure he was going to get what he wanted. "You won't even know I'm there."

"I already know you're here, and so does everyone else." She stopped and gave him a defiant look, then nodded back over her shoulder where the entire waiting room of people watched as if they were enjoying an entertaining play.

Ben grinned at her and winked at their audience as he took her arm and gently urged her forward. "And I'm sure the acting mayor of Reston wouldn't want to make a scene in the waiting room, would she?"

"Actually, she would like to strangle a too-big-for-his-britches former football player."

"Honey, that sounds really exciting, but maybe later." He turned up the full wattage of his smile at the young technician, who blushed to the roots of her hair. "And this charming doctor won't mind if I come in and see the ultrasound of my kid, now will you?"

"No, of course I won't mind, but I'm not a doctor. I'm a technician." The girl fluttered her eyelashes. "I'm Brittany."

"Not a doctor? But another highly educated and hardworking member of the medical community. Excellent," he declared, holding the door for the two women and beaming down at them.

"That's right," Lisa muttered. "Break out those dimples."

He only treated her to a wink that made her roll her eyes.

Inside the small examination room, Ben took a seat against the wall where he had a good view of the display screen. Lisa gave him one more resentful look in case he'd missed the past hundred or so she'd thrown his way, and lay down on the bed. Following Brittany's instructions, she pulled her shirt up and eased her pants below her baby bump so the technician could squirt lubricant onto her skin.

Eagerly, she turned her head so she could see the screen, but couldn't quite distinguish what the blobs were. She could see movement, though, and was thrilled to match the tiny actions with the flutters she was feeling. This was her baby in real time.

"What am I looking at here?" she asked.

"Just a minute," the technician murmured. She slowly moved the wand into several different positions, then paused. "I need to get the doctor to check something," she said.

"Do you mean on the machine or on my baby?" Lisa asked, her heart rate speeding up.

Brittany didn't answer because she was hurrying from the room and calling out, "I'll be right back."

"Is something wrong?" Lisa asked after her, but the young woman was gone.

Ben stood and came to stand beside her. Reaching down, he took her hand and this time she didn't resist. "If she's not back within two minutes I'll go find her," he promised. "Along with the doctor."

Lisa gave him a fearful look, but he tightened his grip on her hand.

"What...what do you think is wrong?"

"Probably nothing. Let's wait and see."

Brittany returned quickly, a doctor with her. He was an older man whose white hair and smiling demeanor inspired confidence.

"Hello, Mr. and Mrs. Thomas. I'm Dr. Harber, and I just want to check something here."

Neither Lisa nor Ben corrected him on their names, but watched as he expertly moved the wand slowly across her belly.

After a minute he said, "You're probably

wondering what we're seeing here. It takes a little bit of practice to distinguish it exactly." He pointed to the screen. "Right here, we have a head. And over here is another head."

Lisa's voice squeaked as she squeezed Ben's hand and asked, "I'm having a *two-headed* baby?"

Dr. Harber chuckled. "No, of course not. There are also four arms, four legs and two bodies. You're having twins. Tentatively, from what I'm seeing on the screen, I'm going to say a boy and a girl."

CHAPTER TEN

"TWINS?" LISA SAID for at least the tenth time. "The surprises simply never end with this pregnancy."

"So it seems," Ben answered in a faint voice.

His face was as pale and shocked as she knew hers was. After Dr. Harber had delivered the news, assured them that everything seemed normal and hurried on to his next patient, Ben and Lisa had sat in stunned silence for long minutes after the ultrasound.

When they'd managed to make their brains instruct their limbs to move, Ben had insisted on buying her some lunch. Now they sat at Fins. The photograph was on the table between them. Every couple of minutes one or the other of them would pick it up, examine it and then put it down again.

Lisa indicated her cell phone, which she'd just placed on the table. "Gemma said she thought she'd heard two heartbeats, but wasn't positive. That's why she pushed up the date of the ultrasound." She gave the phone an annoyed look. "I don't know why she didn't tell me as soon as she suspected it."

"Because you would have been awake all night, fretting."

"Yeah, probably."

"This changes things," Ben said. Seeming to remember his food, he buttered a piece of bread and took a bite. He chewed slowly, while his eyes took on a faraway look. "I'll have to double the amount of child support."

Lisa stared at him. That was a fairly mundane issue to be thinking about right now. The very fact that she was expecting twins was a much bigger issue. In fact, it was world-shaking.

"I could picture myself taking care of one baby," she said. The shock of the doctor's news had made her forget her irritation with Ben. It seemed that she had no control over what was coming out of her mouth. "I had it all planned. I would set up a crib in my office, let him sleep while I took care of business. But two babies? There's not enough room in my office for two."

"I'm guessing that was before you became acting mayor, as well, right?"

"Well, yes. And before the lake resort went through. I got the call this morning. The investors are ready to go ahead with it."

"Congratulations. It will be a huge bonus to the local economy, but you realize you can't be involved in it, don't you?"

She held up her hand. "If you're thinking of the conflict of interest if I broker the deal, that's already been covered. I've contacted someone else to handle it."

"No. For cryin' out loud, Lisa. I'm thinking it's too much for you to take on. It's a project that, if started next week, will take a year or more to complete. I've been involved in a million projects like this for charities. There are always delays, unexpected occurrences, cost overruns. Are you planning to go check out the resort with one baby strapped to your front and one to your back? There's a limit, you know, to how much you can do."

"Are we back to 'frying up the bacon'?"

"I'm serious, Lisa."

"So am I. Ben, I don't know how I'm going to handle this yet, but I know that it will be my decision." She picked up her purse.

"Now, I'll pay our bill and you can take me back to my car." She stopped and stared at him. "And weren't you the one who made it clear he doesn't want to be involved with this baby, with *these* babies, other than fulfilling a financial obligation? Why are you worried about how much I'm doing?"

Lisa flagged down their waitress, asked for their bill and gave Ben a look that dared him to oppose her.

He held up his hands in surrender. "I'm only trying to prepare you for what else will happen. Once my parents learn it's twins, two grandchildren like they've always wanted, they will be a constant presence in your life. In the nicest, most loving way, they will attempt to provide you with everything you need now, or at any time in the future, or the afterlife. But they'll always be around, and probably some of my aunts and uncles and cousins, as well."

Lisa's face blanched. "I...I would welcome your family, but I can't have a house—a property—full of stuff, of belongings I have no space or use for." She gave him a pleading look. "I grew up in a house like that. You don't know what it's like. There's no place to walk or to breathe. I can't raise my kids like that."

Her voice was so fierce, so adamant, that he blinked, drew back and immediately took on a soothing tone. "Of course not. I'll talk them into reining it in, only buying what you ask for—if you ask for anything. It will be top-of-the-line, though, the best quality. Because that's what my mom believes in buying."

"I understand, as long as it's not too much." Lisa tried to push away a mental image of a baby's room decked out like the showroom at a Hollywood decorator's studio.

Lisa looked around. The restaurant was emptying of the lunch crowd. She and Ben were almost the only ones left because their discussion had gone on and on.

Lisa couldn't seem to understand what he was saying: that there was a limit to how little he could convince them to buy or how much. She was confused and overwhelmed. She tried to sort it out, but finally put her hand to her forehead and said, "Couldn't they simply start a college fund or something for the children?"

"They already have."

"Oh," Lisa responded in a helpless tone then looked up. "Is your mom still making wedding plans?"

"I don't think so, but I'm sure she's keeping her options open in case anything changes."

"Nothing's going to change. We're still set on our plans—individual plans, right? It doesn't make any difference that I'm having twins." She spoke firmly although her stomach quivered with uncertainty.

Two babies? she thought frantically. How was she going to do this? No matter how much she read, she would still be ignorant of what to do. Didn't a person need a good example to follow? A mother who had been there, laid a clear path to follow on what to do and not to do as a mom?

Ben must have seen the flash of panic in her eyes because he asked, "What's wrong? Do you feel okay?"

She gave a shaky smile. "I'm...I'm fine. Getting used to this news, is all."

He didn't look as if he quite believed her. "All of this is more than you can handle now, apart from your real-estate business, running the town, being involved in the lake resort development, trying to keep peace between

Bunky and Roland, the fact that there are two babies instead of one…is all too much for you. As far as I'm concerned, that's your only worry and everything else can go hang for a while."

"Well, how nice of you to tell me what my worries are." She shook her head. "No. Nothing can go hang for a while. There's too much to do, too many decisions that must be made right now."

"Which you can delegate. Wasn't that why Brenda asked you, begged you to take the mayor's job, because you can delegate and Harley can't and that's what caused his stress? No one wants that kind of stress for you, Lisa. And, frankly, I'd think you wouldn't want it, either."

Distress welled up in her. "I don't, but I also think I have enough to deal with right now, Ben. A quotation from Jacqueline Kennedy keeps running through my head."

"Jacqueline Kennedy?"

"She said something about nothing else mattering very much if you bungle raising your children."

"You're not going to bungle raising your kids."

She knew Ben was trying to be reassuring, but her head was swimming with worries and doubts. "I need to think about it... What it will mean to have two babies, not one. I need space and time." Her shoulders slumped. "And my two best friends. The one thing I don't need is pressure from you."

Regret filled his tone as he said, "I'm sorry, I should have realized I'm making it harder, trying to make order and organization when you're not ready and—"

"And when you've repeatedly said it's not your business, that your involvement will be limited."

BEN STARED AT her for a long minute. She was right. But his determination to fulfill his financial obligation without interfering with the child—now the children—was eroding by the day. He was also putting pressure on her that she didn't deserve. If he wasn't careful, everything he'd worked for over the years, all the sports programs and educational opportunities that were so important to him, would slip away, lose focus. When that happened they would die out. He'd seen it happen time and time again and he refused to let it happen to the charities where he'd pledged his involvement.

"All of this can be resolved later," Lisa said, standing and picking up her purse. "I've got to get back to work and you've got to…" She paused as if trying to recall. She waved her hand. "Go play golf."

"I do need to make that board meeting. I'll see if we can set up an online discussion. Golf can go hang."

She gave him a skeptical look, then reexamined the accuracy of their lunch tab.

She was obviously accustomed to paying her own way, taking care of details, being tightly wound. She had already made plans to take the baby to work with her, let him sleep while she worked. He didn't know that much about babies—okay, he didn't know anything, but he doubted they were that cooperative. She had already expressed her doubts about keeping two babies in her office while she worked, and Ben had to agree with her. As competent as she was, this was getting too complicated for even her to handle.

As for him, every time he thought he had his plans set in place, something changed. When he had called Phoenix last night to tell them he couldn't make the board meeting, then canceled out of the golf tournament, he had second-guessed himself most of the night. He'd feared looking like a fool when he showed up, insisting on taking Lisa to the ultrasound appointment, but the memory of her pale face had haunted him, urging him to stick around.

It was hard for someone as independent as she was to let him look after her. He didn't question the rightness of it, but the more he did for her and with her, the more committed he would become. He still couldn't see a way to be involved, to be the kind of father a child deserved. Wouldn't it be better to have an absent father who provided financially than one who bounced in and out of his child's life?

But now they knew there were two of them. It would be twice the financial obligation—although that didn't worry him. He would simply work harder, do more product endorsements than he'd done before, sell the property he'd bought in Oklahoma City years ago and invest wisely.

But how was Lisa going to handle this? She was convinced she could do anything and, from what he'd seen, she pretty much could. Being a single mom to twins, though, was all-new territory, even for someone like Lisa, who was willing to tackle anything. She had drive, determination and grit, but would they be enough to get her through what she would be facing?

AFTER LUNCH, NEITHER of them talked much on the short drive back to the hospital. When they got there, Lisa thanked him and hurried to her car, anxious to get back to work. Although he could see her casting him annoyed looks in her rearview mirror, he ignored them and followed her to Reston, then turned off and headed for home.

At Riverbend Ranch, he found a note from Zach Littletrees. Ben frowned as he tried to decipher his horse manager's chicken-scratch-inspired scrawl. He finally figured out that Zach was saying he'd gone to Ft. Smith, Arkansas, for the day, but would be back that night. Ben chuckled and shook his head. Maybe he had a hot date with one of those classic car ladies. Ft. Smith was a long drive from Fayetteville, but those ladies were obviously willing to follow Zach anywhere.

On the other side of Zach's note, he could

make out the name Carl Bodie and something about horses, some illegible words and an amount of money. Ben had no idea what that was about.

He tucked the note into his pocket and was headed for the house when he spotted a truck and horse trailer coming up his lane. He didn't recognize the rig, but he saw that the truck was old and the whine of the engine told him it wasn't well maintained. The engine knocked for a full fifteen seconds after the driver turned it off and stepped from the truck's cab. He was an older man with flowing white hair, a crooked nose and few teeth.

"Got hold of some bad gas," the driver said, gesturing toward his truck. "Gotta go get my tank flushed out." He held out his hand. "Hello. Name's Carl Bodie."

"Oh, yes." Ben took the note from his pocket. "My manager, Zach Littletrees, left me a note."

Carl went very still. "He did?"

"Something about some horses. Can't read it too well. There's a price here." Ben looked up. "Did you bring me some more mustangs? Is this the amount Zach agreed to pay you?"

"Yes." Carl's gaze shifted to the trailer and

then back to Ben. "That's exactly the price we agreed on. Why don't I unload them? If you've got cash, even better."

Ben looked down at the note, suddenly uneasy. "I'm not sure I've got that much cash on hand. Anyway, I'll need a receipt from you."

"Of course." Bodie flashed his sparse teeth in a grin. "Everything honest and aboveboard."

"I'll call Zach and make sure this is the correct amount."

"Now why do you want to do that? It's written down right there."

"Because he's the manager," Ben said, puzzled by the man's objections. "I'm only the guy who writes the checks."

"Well, all right. You want them in the pasture with the others?"

"Sure." Ben hit the speed dial button for Zach, but there was no answer. "Probably too involved with Cinnamon or Ginger," he muttered.

Ben opened the gate to the pasture and held it open for Bodie to pull the truck and trailer through, then hurried into the house to see if he had enough cash on hand to pay the man. As it happened, he did. He usually kept quite a bit in a safe in his office. Even though money transfers could be done almost instantly online, there were many old horse traders like Bodie who preferred doing business in cash.

When he got back, he saw that Bodie was starting to unload the horses, but Ben noticed that he continually craned his neck around to see what Ben was doing. When he saw Ben walking toward him with a well-stuffed envelope, he picked up the pace of his unloading.

This guy seemed a little shifty-eyed, but if Zach was willing to do business with him, Ben should trust him. The mustangs he was leading into the pasture were a sorry-looking lot, skinny and dull-eyed, with mangy coats. One was coughing.

"Are these horses sick?" Ben asked. "That one looks pretty bad." In fact, they all stood with their heads down, having barely moved five feet from where Bodie had unloaded them.

"I'm what you'd call a...broker," the other man said. "These ponies belonged to a guy who wasn't taking care of them. He's old and sick himself and didn't notice what bad shape they're in. I wanted to do the guy a favor, so I bought 'em to sell on to someone who can take better care of them. When I heard Zach Littletrees was working for you, and that you're building up a reputation as someone working to save these Choctaw mustangs, I knew this was the right outfit to take them to."

Ben nodded, feeling a spark of pride in his growing reputation as someone who cared about preserving the lineage. He quickly handed over the envelope, and Carl Bodie just as quickly counted it, stuck it in his pocket, then scribbled out an illegible receipt on the envelope, which he handed back to Ben. With a hurried goodbye, he hopped into his rig and drove away.

Ben closed the gate, although the additions to his herd showed no interest in trying to escape. In fact, they didn't show much interest in anything.

If ever there was a collection of horses that needed saving, these four were it. Zach had probably looked at them and decided the grass and water on the Riverbend would help them get well. Still, when the coughing horse lifted its head and Ben saw white matter around its nose, he decided to call Zach again.

This time Zach answered. Ben could hear voices, music and the rattle of dishes and cutlery, which told him Zach was in a restaurant.

"Zach, it's Ben. Did you get my message?" Ben shouted over the din.

"Nah. Didn't hear the phone. What's up?"

"That guy, Carl Bodie, stopped by with those horses he said you wanted."

"Wait a minute, Ben. I gotta go outside. I thought you said Carl Bodie stopped by with some horses."

"That *is* what I said." Ben was beginning to have a bad feeling about this.

"You didn't buy them, did you?"

"Um, well, yeah." Defensively he added, "If we're going to build up this herd, don't we need to be actually buying stock?"

"Oh, for cryin' out loud, Ben. I hadn't looked at them yet."

"You left me a note with his name and how much he was asking for the horses."

"Yeah, how much he was asking, not how much they were worth. I'd never heard of this guy before, so I was going to check him out. I should have called you instead of leaving you that note. How do the horses look?"

"Not good," Ben admitted. "They don't

seem to have much energy, standing with their heads down. One of them has moved over to the water trough, but one's coughing and has white matter coming from his nose."

"What?" Zach shrieked into the phone. "Call the vet. Tell him you just bought some horses that might have the strangles."

"Strangles?" Ben looked at his new horses in alarm. "That sounds bad."

"It is. Keep them away from the rest of the herd, and drain that trough so the water goes away from the pasture, then turn it upside down so the other horses will stay away from it. Strangles bacteria can survive for weeks. We've got to protect the rest of the herd. Call the vet. I'll be there as fast as I can."

Ben immediately called the veterinarian, who said he would have to travel nearly an hour to get there. Then he took the new arrivals out of the pasture and tied the docile animals to the porch posts. He wasn't sure why he bothered. They were so lethargic, they couldn't have run away if they'd wanted to.

As it turned out, the vet and Zach arrived at almost the same time. Both men, who had actual knowledge of horses, looked at the animals then at Ben with twin expressions that questioned his sanity.

"It's strangles, all right," Dr. Colvin said. "But they're not beyond saving. They'll have to stay quarantined from the rest of the herd until they're well."

"We can set up a temporary corral," Zach said. "I noticed all the pieces are out behind the barn. While you treat them, Ben and I will get it ready."

The vet nodded and set to work while Ben sheepishly followed Zach to the barn.

They silently pulled on gloves and set to work freeing the metal fence parts from years of impossibly tangled undergrowth while keeping an eye out for snakes. Ben had never been back here, but it was obvious that Zach had. In fact, he'd probably walked the entire property, doing his job of looking after the herd.

Zach didn't speak for a long time.

Finally, Ben said, "So, is this the Riverbend Ranch version of being taken to the woodshed?"

"It oughta be." Zach shook his head. "I don't get you, Ben. You hire me to manage your herd, but you don't wait to hear my advice? I was trying to find out some information on that Bodie character…"

"Was that before or after you took off for Ft. Smith?"

"That was personal business."

"I'll bet it was."

"Never mind that. If you'd waited for me to get back to you, this wouldn't have happened."

Ben couldn't argue with that. He knew he'd rushed into the purchase based on flimsy information and his own egotistical belief that he knew more than he did about buying and raising stock.

"Between the horses and the treatment, this is gonna cost you a small fortune, Ben."

"I'm beginning to realize that."

"So my question is, are you really interested in raising horses, preserving these mustangs, or do you only want to play at it?"

Zach picked up the first fence section they had freed, signaled for Ben to lift the other end, then led the way to an open area close to the house and Zach's Airstream.

"Raising these animals, training them to be cow ponies—or riding horses even, since they're the perfect size for little kids—is a huge commitment of time and money. If you don't get that, then maybe you shouldn't be in this business at all."

They didn't talk much during the construction. Stung by Zach's criticism, it took Ben a while to process it.

Ben had been on the receiving end of criticism before from reporters who had never actually played a down of football. He had received harsh bawling outs from coaches and had deserved them much of the time because he hadn't been keeping his head in the game.

This was different. As important as football had been to him, he'd always known his years in the game would be limited. That was simply the nature of the sport. Raising these horses was a much longer commitment, one that could affect generations of the mustangs.

Like raising kids, he thought, remembering the wisdom Lisa had quoted to him about nothing much mattering if you bungle raising your children.

Ben smiled, his heart warming at the thought. There was no way she would fail at raising their children. She was such a careful planner, so thoughtful and competent, she was certain to succeed.

CHAPTER ELEVEN

WITHIN MINUTES OF Lisa's arrival back at the mayor's office, Gemma and Carly had appeared with champagne glasses and sparkling grape juice.

"I'd hoped these glasses would come in handy," Carly said, proudly turning the crystal flutes to admire the play of light through them. "I bought them for my wedding, but figured I'd never use them again. It didn't occur to me that we'd have cause for another celebration so soon." She grinned at Lisa. "I hadn't counted on you having twins."

"That makes two of us." Lisa took a sip of juice and looked down at her growing belly. No wonder she had suddenly popped out of her clothes. "I'm going to keep this quiet for a while, although I'll have to swear Ben's parents to secrecy. They're pretty excited at the idea of one baby. They're going to explode when they learn there's two."

Gemma smiled. "It's nice to have someone so thrilled about it. Are you going to tell Maureen?"

"If she ever returns my phone calls. I've only received one text saying she's okay."

"Any idea where she is?"

"No. I have to give her time, have patience." She smiled. "Now that I know more about her, it's not so hard to do."

Gemma lifted her hand and made a gesture to encompass the mayor's office. "What are you going to do about all of this?"

"Keep at it as long as I can. The group building the resort will be ready to start soon. They want to open in the spring of next year. Trent Sanderson will be their liaison."

"Good. That will take one load off your shoulders," Carly said. "I'm handling the county-wide yard sale and it's going well. Frances Sanderson is a whirlwind of organization, influence, inspiration. I want to be exactly like her when I grow up."

Lisa laughed. "Sounds like a worthy goal."

Uncomfortably, she shifted as one, or both, of the babies began moving. She waited until they settled down again. "Then there's the issue of the Founder's Day street festival and parade. Bunky wants to be in charge, and it looks like the other council members will let him."

"All day and night dancing, right?" Gemma asked. "I wonder if I can talk Nate into going on a trip that weekend."

"Except with that much craziness going on, along with the end-of-July heat, we'll need every medical professional to be available. Plus, the hospital will probably want to do a health fair, check blood pressures and so forth."

"Ugh," Gemma said, resting her hand on her palm. "I'm going to have to spend the day in hiking boots to protect my toes from Bunky's two-step."

Carly grinned. "It's the price you pay for being such a great dancer. Too bad he isn't."

Lisa smiled even as her thoughts raced ahead to everything that needed to be done.

"Have you heard from Brenda about how Harley is doing?" Gemma asked. "The Sunshine Birthing Center is limping along with temporary reception help. I don't want to add any worry for her, but I'm hoping Brenda can return soon."

"Yes, I've talked to her. Harley insists he

can return to office. She's equally determined that he won't. I'll have the job until they make up their minds. That's another reason I'm keeping it quiet about having twins. If they know, they might feel forced into making a decision."

"That's hardly fair to you, Lisa," Carly pointed out.

"I'll be fine. I just need to stay organized."

Her friends exchanged a look and Gemma said, "You're not still thinking of running for mayor this fall, are you?"

"It's always at the back of my mind."

"Leave it there," Carly advised. "You'll have years and years to think about running for office."

Lisa shrugged. "Maybe."

"We'll help you all we can, but this is going to be harder than you think. How did Ben react to learning he's about to be the father of two instead of one?" Gemma asked.

"Twice as reluctant to do anything except send money. It was…disappointing. Also, he thinks I've taken on too much, as well. I told him I don't need pressure from him."

"You're right. You don't." Carly looked at

Gemma, who stood to begin gathering the glasses and juice bottle.

She packed them away in a canvas bag as she said, "We're available to help anytime, but right now we've both got to get back to work. And I think we have something else to take care of."

"Oh, what's that?" Lisa asked, but the phone rang, and as she answered it, her friends waved goodbye.

She took care of the phone call and then dug into the numerous other projects on her desk. She needed to get finished and over to the real-estate office by four o'clock so she could take a couple to see a house for sale. The advantage of being this busy was that she didn't have time to worry about how she was going to handle being the mother of twins.

By EARLY EVENING the horses had been doctored and isolated from the rest of the herd. Ben and Zach had taken care of all the other chores. Zach had disappeared into his Airstream and Ben sat on the porch staring out at his pasture.

He'd called the sheriff and reported Carl Bodie as someone who was selling sick and contagious horses, probably fully aware of their condition. Ben doubted the man would be caught.

Zach was annoyed with him, and Ben didn't blame him. This whole day had been one surprise after another. He didn't see how it could get any worse.

When a pair of headlights turned up his driveway, Ben wondered cynically if another grifter had heard what an easy target he was and come to sell him some more sick horses. But when he squinted into the darkness, he saw that it was the old Land Rover he'd seen Gemma Whitmire driving around town. She was behind the wheel, and Carly Joslin sat beside her.

The day just got worse.

When Gemma stopped the car, he stood, wondering what they wanted. He had no doubt it involved Lisa.

"Evening, ladies," he said, nodding as they stepped out of the vehicle and walked over to him. "I'm guessing this looks like a good time to tear a strip off me."

They looked at each other then at him. "Oh, we wouldn't go that far," Carly said. "We only want to make it clear, in the nicest possible way, that Lisa doesn't need any hassle from you."

"She's taking on too much, and you both know it."

"But it's her decision," Gemma added. "Ben, you can't have it both ways."

"What do you mean?"

"You can either be present in the lives of your children or you can be the absent father who sends a check every month."

"I can still have an opinion about how much Lisa takes on."

"No," Carly said. "You really can't. It's her decision."

That appeared to be their last word on the subject because they turned on their heels, returned to the Land Rover and drove away.

He would feel annoyed at their interference if he hadn't known them both all his life, and if he didn't know they had Lisa's best interests at heart.

Ready to be done with this day, he turned to the house as he pulled out his cell phone. It was time to call his parents and tell them they were going to be grandparents of twins. In spite of the day's surprises and his own stupid mistake, he was looking forward to his parents' excitement.

MAUREEN SAT IN her car staring at a building, much as she had on her first day back in Reston. Only this wasn't her daughter's real-estate office. It was Jackson Iron Works in Muskogee. The front of the establishment was fenced with wrought iron beautifully decorated with leaves and vines. The small yard was crowded with metal and wood park benches, whimsical animals, enormous flowers painted bright colors and a horse at least eight feet tall. The entire display was overwhelming while also being artistic.

"Are you sure you want to do this?" Clive asked from the passenger seat. He'd offered to drive her but she'd wanted to be in complete charge of this trip. It was her way of proving to Lisa that she was doing all she could to locate John Jackson. In truth, Lisa probably couldn't have cared less about Maureen and Clive's travel arrangements.

A few days ago she had worked up her courage to return Lisa's calls. It had been awkward, but joyful, too, when she had learned her daughter was having twins. Hearing that had strengthened her resolve to find Lisa's father. She and Lisa couldn't move forward until every effort had been made to find him. When that happened, she was sure she would have a better shot at developing a more normal relationship with her daughter.

"I do want to do it if your son...if Todd thinks this is truly Lisa's father."

"It's the only lead that's panned out and if he's sure, I'm sure. You've spent every spare minute for weeks tracking this guy down and Todd has put in a lot of time, too. There's every reason to think it's the right guy."

Maureen looked over at him and nodded, giving him a shaky smile. "Thank you for coming with me. I'm so used to doing everything myself, it never occurred to me to ask for help until you mentioned Todd's job. I'm glad you didn't mind the time I spent on this search."

Clive shrugged. "Your work didn't suffer, and I've got to keep my cook happy."

And she *was* happy. Instead of trying to remain unnoticed as she'd done for years in almost every previous job, she had begun making friends in Peachdale. Rather than wallowing in self-pity, she had focused on her plan to find Lisa's birth father.

When she had told Clive the truth about herself, about how she had abandoned her daughter to a fate she couldn't face herself, he hadn't been judgmental. Instead he'd called Todd and asked for his help. Although his son couldn't use the resources of his police department for a private search, he had given her many tips and spent his own time helping her out.

They had begun the search in April and had followed numerous leads, false starts and wrong turns over the past several weeks. She had actually gone to take a surreptitious look at two of them, but neither man fit the memory she carried in her head, even after she had accounted for all the years in between.

"Do you want me to come in with you? I can pretend to be interested in that giant horse."

"Where would you put it?" Maureen asked with a chuckle.

"On top of the café. It would be quite an attention-getter."

"It sure would." She paused, knowing he

was waiting for an answer to his question. "No. I need to do this on my own."

Clive leaned the seat back as far as it would go. "Call me, or come and get me if you need me. I'll just take a little nap while I wait. Thanks for parking in the shade." He crossed his arms over his chest and closed his eyes.

Maureen paused. "Clive, when I told you about my daughter and how…I'd left her, you didn't judge me. Why was that?"

He turned his head to look at her as he shrugged. "Why would I? I'm not perfect, done some things I'm not proud of. In the Marines, you learn everybody has a story, a background they might want to forget, so you do forget in order to focus on the job that needs to be done. Besides, you'd already spent thirty-three years beating yourself up over it. No need for me to add any more blows."

"You're a really good man, Clive Forrest. I'm lucky to know you."

Clive grinned as he closed his eyes. "That's what they all say. I've got my phone right here. Call me if you need me."

"Okay."

Maureen stepped out and smoothed the front of the blue camp shirt she wore with crisp jeans and polished boots. The May sunshine felt good on her back, though she knew it was a promise of the summer heat and humidity that was to come.

She opened the gate and crossed the yard, pushing open the front door before she could lose her nerve. An old-fashioned bell over the door announced her arrival. She found herself in a large room full of shelves and tables of all sorts of wrought-iron art objects.

Beneath a display table, a family of coyotes marched across the floor, accompanied by one of quail, all of them watched over by a hungry-looking coyote. Some of the items were painted bright colors and some were in shades of rusty brown.

"Hello," a voice called out from the other end of the room. "Welcome to Jackson's. Let me know if I can help you find anything."

Maureen looked up to see a young woman arranging candlesticks on a table. She was a short, chubby girl with a cheerful smile who appeared to be in her late teens or early twenties.

"Thank you. There are so many interesting and unusual things here, it's hard to choose."

The girl grinned. "I know what you mean.

If you're looking for a gift for someone, though, you can't go wrong with the quail. People love them."

"They're very cute. Do you order these from somewhere else or are they made locally?"

"My dad makes them, mostly from reclaimed iron. He's got a shop out back. Are you interested in a special order?"

"Your dad is John Jackson?"

"That's right," the girl said proudly. "And I'm Zoe."

"Nice to meet you." Maureen turned away, pretending interest in a parrot in a cage that swung from a wall hook. Somehow, in all of her searching, she hadn't counted on John having other children, ones who were younger than Lisa, and might be hurt to find out about her. Back then, he'd told her he'd had a son, who would be in his late thirties now. Old enough to handle finding out his father was a philanderer. But this girl appeared to be barely out of her teens. How would she accept such news?

On the other hand, this might not even be the John Jackson she sought. And if it was, it was his decision to share the news about Lisa.

She was trying to think of a way to ask after him when the girl handed it to her.

"Are you interested in a custom-made piece? Dad gets lots of orders for those." Zoe grinned. "One lady wanted new front gates for her house made in the shape of angel wings. They turned out great."

"That sounds interesting. Yes, I might want to discuss something like that with him."

"Outstanding," Zoe said. "I can't leave the front right now, but you're welcome to go on out the back door. The workshop is across the courtyard."

"Thanks." Maureen followed the sound of metal striking metal outside.

The doors and windows of the workshop were open, which made it possible for her to look inside.

A man was pounding the end of a metal rod. After several blows with a mallet, he picked it up, examined the end and then laid it next to a row of similar rods. He set the mallet down and took a minute to twist his hips, stretching his back.

When he turned his head, Maureen knew she'd found the man she'd been looking for. He was older, of course, chunkier, with the massive arms of a man who worked with iron. His hair was thinning and going gray, but it was certainly the man she remembered.

Memories flooded back, of what it had been like to have his full attention, to have him tell her how pretty she was.

She stepped inside. "Hello," she said.

He turned around. "Oh, hello. Sorry, I didn't hear you come in. What can I do for you?"

Her palms were sweating, and she rubbed them on her jeans as she cleared her throat. "You're John Jackson, right?"

He tilted his head in a little sideways dip she remembered. "Yeah, the last I heard. You looking to order a custom-made piece?"

"I'm sure you don't remember me, John, but I'm Maureen Thomas."

He stepped closer to get a better look at her. "Hello, Maureen. I'm afraid you'll have to remind me where we met."

"You seriously don't remember?"

"No, sorry."

He shrugged as if it wasn't that important, so her voice was testy when she said, "At the Burger Barn in Toncaville, right here in Oklahoma, almost thirty-four years ago."

He peered closely at her, then felt in his shirt pocket for a pair of glasses, which he put on to look at her even more closely.

She lifted an eyebrow at him as she waited.

He frowned. "Toncaville, I don't—" His eyes widened. "Oh, yes, Maureen. I...I do remember you." He licked his lips nervously. "How are you? How did you find me, after all these years?"

"Determination."

His gaze darted guiltily to the open windows and door. That told her he definitely remembered her.

"Do you have an office or somewhere we can talk?" She pointed a thumb over her shoulder. "What I have to say probably isn't something you want your daughter to hear."

"Yes, okay. Over here." He pointed to a room at the back of the shop and Maureen preceded him inside.

John gave a quick look around the shop before he shut the door. He moved a stack of mail and newspapers off a chair, gave it a dust-off with his bare hand and said, "Here, sit down."

He took a seat on the other side of a scarred and dented metal desk. Clasping his hands together on top of a pile of papers, he asked, "So, what can I do for you?"

"You can agree to meet your daughter."

He frowned and pointed toward the store at the front of the property. "My daughter is—"

"Not that one. Zoe seems like a very sweet girl, and I'm sure you don't want her hurt."

"No, of course not. You can't come in here threatening—"

"I'm not making threats. I'm talking about your older daughter. *My* daughter. Her name is Lisa."

"Lisa?"

"That's right." As she spoke, her confidence grew. "I came to tell you about her because I've decided there's no point in holding back any information about her, or about me."

Maureen told him everything that had happened since he had made love to her and abandoned her, concluding with her recent visit to Lisa, who was herself expecting twins now.

"You lied to me. You got me pregnant. I'm surprised to discover the name you gave me was real. You said you worked at a garage outside town, but when I called, they'd never heard of you."

"Uh, well, I didn't really have a job. I didn't want you to think I was a deadbeat."

"Well, guess what? You were, and now you owe me. You owe Lisa."

John made a strangled sound. His hands moved back and forth across the cluttered desk as if he was searching for something without looking down. "You want money? All I've got is this business and my house. I can't give you my retirement fund. Sheesh," he muttered. "My wife will kill me."

"I don't want money. I told you, all I want is for you to meet Lisa. She deserves to know her father, and her siblings."

He frowned in confusion. "There's just the one. Zoe."

"But you said you were married and had a little boy."

He shifted in his chair. "Ah, yeah, about that. I lied about having a wife and kid, too," he admitted, shamefaced. "It was what I always told the girls I dated."

"Good grief! There's more? Do you have kids scattered all over the state?"

"Nah. At least, I don't think so. You're the first one who's showed up. I said what I said because I didn't want you thinking there was a chance I'd marry you."

"What you did was against the law, John. I was sixteen. A minor."

"I know. I know. I'm sorry." He leaned forward, propped his elbows on the desk and dropped his face into his hands.

Maureen waited in silence until he seemed to have control of himself.

His hands fell onto the desktop. "What do you want from me?"

"Only for you to do the right thing." Reaching into her purse, she took out Lisa's card. "She's a successful Realtor in Reston, and currently she's acting mayor. She's very accomplished and...and brilliant."

He took the card, which looked delicate in his work-roughened hand. "A Realtor and mayor, huh? You must be proud of her."

"I am."

"It sounds like she's really made something of herself." He placed the card on top of the assorted papers and mess on the desk.

"She has and it's all her own doing. I...I'm ashamed to admit I wasn't there for her, but I'm going to be now, and that starts with telling her I found you and that you want to meet her."

Looking up he said, "I can't, Maureen. I'm sorry for what I did. I'm sorry for what I put you through. It…it sounds like you made hard choices and I'm sorry for that, too, but I can't meet her, be part of her life. I've got to think of my family. My wife will be furious and Zoe will—"

"Find out about your past."

He lifted his hand as if to ward off a blow. "I told you, I'm not proud of it. I was screwed up for a long time, took advantage of everyone I met, had no consideration, no conscience. It changed when I moved here, learned to do iron work, met my wife, had my daughter." His eyes were pleading. "I've got a good life here, Maureen. I can't mess that up."

She knew she shouldn't have expected anything more. She didn't really know him, and she'd been too young and naive to see what kind of man he was when she was sixteen. Now he was concerned for the welfare of his family, as she was for hers. She couldn't fault him for that even though it hurt. Still, she had some information for Lisa, proof that she had found him.

She stood and hooked her purse over her shoulder. "If you change your mind, my phone number is on the back of Lisa's card. I know she would be happy to meet you."

He didn't stand to see her out, only sat and stared at the card.

To her relief, she saw that she wouldn't have to walk back through the main store to return to her car. There was a gate, no doubt more of John's ironwork, that opened to a side street.

Maureen hurried to her car and fell into the front seat.

Clive, who had been napping, woke with a start, rubbed his hands over his face and said, "How'd it go?"

"Not well," she answered and burst into tears.

Clive sat straight and reached out to give her an awkward pat on the back. That made her cry even harder. Fumbling around, he found a package of tissues and pulled out several, which he used to dab at her face.

"There now," he said. "I'm sorry it was so bad. Do you want me to go in and talk to the guy?"

She took the tissues and said, "No. I came

on too strong, too accusatory. I don't blame him for feeling defensive." She paused to catch her breath. "I can't make him see her if he doesn't want to."

"Did he say he wouldn't see her?"

Maureen nodded and related the entire conversation to him, including the full extent of the lies John had told her. "I was so young and stupid."

"And he took advantage of that."

"He said he's sorry, but he doesn't want to ruin the life he's got now."

Clive whistled between his teeth. "Irresponsible jerk."

"He swears he's changed. I hope he has. He won't agree to see Lisa."

"No, but now it's not your choice. You told him all about her, right?" Clive continued to pat her on the back.

"Yeh…hes."

"Then it's out of your hands. You hope he's changed, but you don't know what kind of man he is now. He was a rat in his earlier years, but now he might be the kind who'll do the right thing."

Maureen nodded and mopped up her tears. "He does seem to care about his family."

"Then he has changed." Clive opened his door. "Why don't we switch places? You're not really in any condition to drive."

Willingly, Maureen traded sides with him.

As they headed toward Peachdale, she leaned back in her seat and turned to face him. "Thank you, Clive. The day I walked into the Peachdale Café, I had no idea how my life would change for the better."

"Me, neither."

The grin he gave her spread a warm, sweet feeling through her. She took a deep breath and released it slowly, feeling the tension flow out of her. Clive was right. She had done all she could. Now it was up to John.

She had come far since last winter when she'd been so deathly ill. At her lowest point, she'd hung on to the promise she had made to Violet that she would make amends with Lisa. She and her daughter might never have a normal mother/daughter relationship, but they were making steps.

Her thoughts drifted to where she was now.

She had lost everything in Chicago, everything she had worked toward for so long. She'd left there barely hanging on to her health, with a car that was past its prime and with all her possessions packed in boxes in the backseat and trunk.

Now she was well. She had a job, a place to live and a new town. Best of all, there was someone who had her back.

"Clive?" Her voice was hesitant because she didn't know what kind of answer she was going to get to her next question.

"Yes?"

"Why are you doing all of this for me? I'm just the cook in your café. You don't really owe me anything."

"Marines."

"What?"

"We never let a man go into battle alone, and we never leave a man behind. Or a woman."

"You'd better be careful, Clive Forrest. You're going to make me fall in love with you."

This time, he laughed out loud as he gave her a wink. "*That's* the plan."

CHAPTER TWELVE

"I GET THAT I might not be your favorite person right now," Ben said from the door of her real-estate office. It was now July, and she had barely seen him since April, although he had checked in frequently to see how she was doing.

He had one hand behind his back and his cowboy hat in the other, clutched over his heart. He wore a white shirt with the sleeves rolled up over his sinewy forearms, faded jeans and old, dirt-kicking boots.

"You're so perceptive." She sat back in her chair and resisted the urge to rub her spine where she had developed a mighty ache. Her children were apparently engaged in a lively game of Who Can Kick Mommy the Hardest. She didn't want Ben to know she was uncomfortable. She still had eight weeks to go, at which point she expected to deliver a couple of full-size elephants.

"But hear me out." He stepped inside and pulled a big bouquet of flowers from behind his back. They were multicolored roses and freesias, her favorites. She wondered who he'd been talking to. A glance through the doorway at her smiling secretary told her.

"All right, Ben. Come on in." She accepted the flowers from him and laid them on her desk, where the sweet aroma teased her nose. Her sense of smell was more acute with pregnancy, which Gemma said wasn't unusual, but Lisa found it disturbing that she could also smell a subtle hint of Ben's cologne— something of which she certainly didn't want to be aware.

He had been mostly out of town during the early summer, and she'd been busy with real estate and city issues. Now he was running the football camp Harley Morton had requested, including one for girls. Gemma said she'd been out to her parents' old campground and had seen all the activity.

Ben had seemed to be in his element, running the kids through exercises, drills and games in the muggy heat and following each session with a swim in the Whitmires' private lake with him acting as lifeguard.

He even ran an evening session for kids who worked at daytime summer jobs. The whole thing was a huge success. Any parent or child in Reston County who hadn't already been in love with Ben had fallen hard now.

She had been doing absolutely fine without him, but for some reason she felt a burst of joy at seeing him now. "You don't have football camp today?"

"Founder's Day weekend. Gave the kids the day off. You know it's a city holiday, right? You can take holidays off. It's allowed."

"And I would, too," she answered sweetly, "if the parade and street festival weren't tomorrow."

He nodded and held up his hand. "I get it. You're in charge. I've got something to ask you, though, and I'm not here for myself or to pressure you into giving up all you're doing."

"Wise choice."

"I'm here to ask you to come with me out to my mom and dad's place."

"Why? They can't possibly need to check up on me. I still talk to them every day, or one of them stops in. I'm convinced your mom is going to whip out a blood pressure cuff one of these times."

Ben grinned as he took a seat in front of her desk. "I'm sure that's in her plan. She's been practicing on my dad."

Lisa laughed and shook her head, but it warmed her heart that they were so concerned about her welfare and that of her babies. She knew they considered this their only chance to get grandchildren.

Against her better judgment, she was glad to see Ben. When he wasn't trying to tell her his opinions on how she should take care of herself, she actually enjoyed his company.

And, darn it, she had missed him. Completely of its own will, her heart skipped a beat and her mouth curved into a happy smile. Even her babies seemed to be excited, apparently breaking into a happy dance because their father was near. She put her hands on her belly to soothe them.

"It's not that they want to check up on you," Ben went on. "They want you to see the room they've fixed up for the babies."

She stared at him. "A room? You mean a nursery?"

"For when you let them sleep over. Mind you, they know this won't happen for several years, but they believe in being prepared."

"I guess so." Lisa stared down at the flowers, trying to take this in. "They've made a room for the babies?"

"Yup. My old room and, from what I understand, it's pretty spectacular. They haven't let me see it yet. They've installed an air-filtering system, a new smoke alarm and a carbon monoxide alarm."

"Wow." She didn't have anything nearly that elaborate in mind. So far, she'd only cleared out a guest room. Nathan Smith and Luke Sanderson had done all the heavy lifting. She had installed two new cribs and two beautiful antique dressers that Carly had refurbished. Her friend was also refinishing a changing table she'd recovered. Gemma and Carly were planning a baby shower for next month, and refused to let her buy anything else for the babies.

"That's…that's really nice of them."

"Don't say that until you've seen it," he advised. "How about it? Wanna go for a drive to the McAdamses' homestead?"

"Sure. I can't believe they haven't mentioned it before." When she stood, Ben's gaze went to her belly then up to her face.

"It's a surprise," he said, smiling.

"Okay." Self-consciously, she tugged her shirt down over her belly, even though there was no hiding it. He looked away, as if feeling guilty that she'd caught him staring, and she surreptitiously rubbed the pain in her back.

"And I'll take care of those flowers," Sandy volunteered, appearing in the doorway. "We don't want to let such beautiful blooms wilt in this heat." She beamed at Ben, who responded with a wink.

Lisa rolled her eyes at the two of them, bringing a chuckle from Ben.

Before they stepped out the door, Sandy said, "By the way, Lisa, where is the paperwork for the contract on the Fredricks' property?"

"I gave it to you this morning."

"No. I haven't seen it."

Lisa frowned, trying to remember. "I was sure I—"

"Never mind," Sandy said brightly. "I'll find it."

Out of the corner of her eye, Lisa saw Ben exchange a look with Sandy, but when she glanced back, her secretary gave her a cheery wave and bustled off to find a vase.

Ben hurried ahead to open the door for her

and she headed outside to his truck, making a conscious effort to walk normally and avoid the waddle she was convinced was taking over her gait. The Oklahoma July heat and humidity hit her with full force, breaking sweat out on her brow and upper lip and reminding her how far off the cool days of autumn were.

Ben boosted her into the seat and then dashed around to get the engine started and the air-conditioning running.

As they drove through town, the few people on the street waved and she waved back. By now, everyone knew she was pregnant and that the baby was Ben's. Also, they probably knew she was having twins. She couldn't stop the gossip, so she simply went with it.

Lisa's thoughts circled back to the Fredericks' paperwork. She bit her bottom lip, thinking hard, trying to recall what she'd done with it. She was sure she'd put it where it belonged. If not, what had she done with it?

"How are things going in the mayor's office?" Ben asked, breaking into her train of thought. "Any sign of Harley returning?"

"You probably heard he's home and recovering well. Brenda's back at work for Gemma, so he's at the house, bored out of his skull and chomping at the bit to get back to the mayor's office. He calls me or one of the council members, or the county supervisors, or the water meter readers, or somebody else, every five minutes. He's frustrated because he can't be involved in the city or the resort development or anything. The doctor won't release him yet, and Brenda is fighting him all the way, so I don't know what's going to happen."

"Well, the stress can't be good," Ben said. "And I can't believe it's good for—"

"Don't say it," she warned, leaning forward a little and turning her head to give him a steady look. "I know my limitations."

He cleared his throat and said, "Right."

At the McAdamses' place, Ben slowed to almost a crawl. When she gave him a questioning glance he said, "My mom doesn't like anyone to drive in too fast. It stirs up the red dust and it coats her roses. She's very particular about her roses."

Lisa smiled, then her eyes widened when she spied the rose garden. "I can see why. The roses you brought me—did they come from here?"

"Yes."

"Amazing," she whispered, taking in the dramatic arrangement of bushes planted in a huge round bed in the center of the circular drive. Red roses filled the middle, then every shade of pink, peach, yellow and, finally, white blooms spiraled around. A yellow-brick walkway ran between the rows. Every bush was bursting with blossoms.

"Follow the yellow brick road," Ben commented. "My mom is a big fan of *The Wizard of Oz*."

"It's the most beautiful rose garden I've ever seen."

"Tell her that. She'll be your slave for life. Actually, she already is since you're providing her with grandchildren."

She smiled. While she knew the McAdamses were excited about the babies, she hadn't expected them to prepare a full nursery. She took it as another sign that they were committed to being fully involved grandparents.

Ben parked by the front porch and came around to help her out. She stepped down from the truck carefully, aware of how her center of gravity had changed. Ben had a firm grip on her arm, and slipped his arm around her shoulders when he appeared to think she might stumble. She looked up to give him a grateful smile. When he grinned down at her, warmth sifted through her and her heart fluttered. One of her babies brought her back to reality with a mighty kick. Lisa started and moved out of the circle of Ben's arm.

"Thank you," she said.

The front door flew open and Jim and Helen rushed from the house.

"Thank you so much for coming," Helen said. "We're so excited that you're here. How are you feeling? The ride out here wasn't too much, was it? What about your ankles? You said the swelling has been bothering you. Mine were so swollen when I was carrying Ben, I looked like I was walking around on a couple of tree trunks."

"Now, Helen, don't give the girl the third degree," Jim chided. He turned to Lisa, his thick brows drawn together in concern. "What are your cravings like today, dear? As I told you, Helen ate cream cheese and green bean sandwiches for months before Ben came. I've been reading up on natural cures for that heartburn you've been having and they won't hurt the babies. If you need anything, I've got all the information you could ever want."

Ben glanced down. "Her ankles are perfect, Dad."

"I'm fine today, thanks, Jim." The babies didn't have a whole lot of spare time to create heartburn just now. One was crowding her lungs and the other was bouncing on her bladder.

"Excellent," Helen said, smiling at her with such joy that Lisa felt tears prickling her eyes.

"Come on in, come on in. See this room. Helen designed it and I did all the work."

His wife cuffed him on the arm. "Not all the work. I helped with the painting and I made the curtains."

Jim held the door for everyone to troop inside as he continued talking to Lisa. "Now, we don't want to be pushy here, only want to have a comfortable room for the kids when you feel like you need a break."

"And we're available to babysit anytime," Helen added. "But we don't want to be pushy."

"I understand," Lisa said, smiling at these two people who were so desperately happy about the babies. They made the same statement every time she talked to them.

"It's this way," Ben said, and gave his mother a teasing look. "And I'm not even going to mention that I had the same pale blue paint and wallpaper from infancy to adulthood."

"Oh, for goodness' sake," Helen said, flapping a hand at him. "If you'd wanted to change it, we would have, but interior design was never an interest of yours."

"True," Ben answered with a shrug.

Lisa thought of that ramshackle house he was living in now. She doubted he'd done a thing to fix it up since she'd been there in the winter.

"Okay," Helen said, her hand on the knob of a door that was securely shut. "Close your eyes. We want you to get the full effect."

Obediently, Lisa did so. She heard the door open and felt a rush of air, no doubt from the new air purifier, she thought with amusement.

"Okay, you can look," Helen said.

Lisa opened her eyes and her smile froze when she came face-to-face with a life-size poster of Ben McAdams in full football gear, all six foot, four inches of him. From shoulder pads to cleats, he was fully decked out, his helmet under his arm, his smile full of good humor and confidence.

"Sheesh, Mom," Ben grumbled. "Are you trying to scare them to death?"

"Don't be ridiculous," she answered in a snippy tone. "This is the perfect poster to have in here." She pointed to a ruler that marched up the edge. "See? We had it printed so we can measure their heights as they grow."

To see if they measure up to their father, Lisa thought with a sinking heart. Overwhelmed, she looked away, taking in the fact that one side of the room was done up in a pink-and-purple, princess, ruffles theme, and the other in blue-and-brown football gear. The window beside the poster was exactly in the center of the room, and they'd used it as the dividing line. One curtain panel was purple with pink ruffles and the other was printed with bunny rabbits and raccoons playing football. There were two cribs, each matching its gender theme, a changing table, a dresser and a rocker. It was so wildly jarring that she couldn't think of a thing to say.

Jim cleared his throat. "So, Lisa, what do you think?"

She looked at Ben, who seemed as taken aback as she was. His gaze went from the poster to the ruffles to the football-and-goalpost-printed crib sheet, and back again.

"It's…simply… There are no words—" When she caught sight of the McAdamses' frozen expressions, she said, "Stunning. Absolutely breathtaking. I…can't imagine anything more girlish." She pointed to the feminine side. "And more boyish." Her hand swung to the football side. "Completely amazing."

"See, Jim," Helen said, all but hugging herself in her joy. "I told you she'd love it."

"And you were right, as usual," Jim agreed. "Now, young lady, you've been on your feet long enough. Let's go into the living room where you can relax. We'll get you something to drink. How do you feel about lemonade? And maybe something to eat? Are you getting enough protein? The articles we've been reading say you need one hundred and twenty grams a day. Would you like a roast-beef sandwich?"

"And maybe a paper bag to hyperventilate into," Ben muttered from behind her.

"What was that, son?" Jim asked.

"Nothing, Dad. Nothing. You and Mom did

an amazing job on the room. I've never seen anything like it."

"I'd love some lemonade," Lisa said as Jim settled her into a chair and then lifted her feet onto an ottoman. "But I had a big lunch, so I'm not really hungry."

Lisa looked around at the living room, conventionally decorated in warm earth tones. She couldn't quite imagine where they had come up with the decorating scheme for the nursery, but after thinking about it for a minute, realized they were living their own dream.

Helen had never had the big white wedding, and she didn't have a little girl whose room she could make into a princess haven. She was living out her fantasies, and throwing in Jim's football glory days for good measure.

She simply couldn't burst their bubble by letting them think it was anything less than perfect.

Their enthusiasm was touching, and brave, she decided, because they knew their son wouldn't be involved with his own children, but they were more than willing to take on the role of grandparents. They were part of her support system, people who would love her twins, spend time with them and teach them valuable life lessons. They seemed completely prepared to overcome any awkwardness that ensued. Lisa wondered how long it would be before her children realized the giant man on the wall was actually their father.

Ben was a grown man who made his own decisions in spite of what she might think and what his parents had taught him about responsibility. It would be years before her children questioned her about why they never saw him. She had been five and in kindergarten before she'd understood and questioned why other kids had a mom and dad and she only had grandparents.

Helen brought in a tray of lemonade in frosty glasses. Lisa thanked her, took a sip and looked at Ben over the rim. He was holding his glass and gazing at her with a brooding expression, as if he trying to decipher what she was thinking.

She wasn't going to let him know. Turning to his parents, she complimented the rose garden and they discussed flower food and watering schedules for several minutes.

Finally, Jim and Helen exchanged a glance

and Helen stood. "We've got something we hope you'll like." She went into her bedroom and came back with a large gift bag, which she handed to Lisa with a nervous smile. Then she sat on the arm of Jim's chair to watch her. "I could have brought it to the baby shower Carly and Gemma are planning, but we thought you might like to have it ahead of time."

"What is it, Mom?" Ben asked, sitting forward, but Helen didn't answer.

"Oh, thank you," Lisa said, setting her glass on a coaster and reaching into the bag to pull out two baby blankets. One was hand-knit, cream-colored and soft from many washings. The other was quilted in shades of yellow and green, with a mother duck and her ducklings marching importantly across the topside. It, too, was soft and faded from loving use.

"They were Ben's," Helen said, her gaze shifting to her son and back.

Tears started in Lisa's eyes and she blinked them back. "They're perfect. Thank you so much. I...I really appreciate you thinking of me with these heirlooms. I don't have much from my childhood."

Since her grandparents had never gotten rid

of anything, there had been boxes of mouse-chewed baby clothes in the overstuffed barn. The only intact item had been a blackened bulbous object with a handle that turned out to be a silver baby's rattle. She had saved the rattle and cleaned it up, and it now sat on top of a dresser in her babies' room, waiting for the unsure grip of their little hands.

"We're glad you can use them," Jim said gruffly, exchanging a smile with his wife, who was as teary-eyed as Lisa.

"They've been packed away in acid-free paper and freshly laundered," Helen added.

Lisa gazed at these two people, whom she'd barely known but who were going to be such a big part of her life from now on. They looked back at her, and it was as if the three of them had formed a pact, cementing the bond they would share.

With absolute certainty she knew she could depend on these people as she had never been able to depend on anyone in her own family. The overdone decorations in the nursery didn't matter. Her children would have another two people to love and care for them, who would have their welfare and best interests at heart. She was overwhelmed with gratitude.

"Thank you," she said again, and the McAdamses seemed to know her thanks was for more than the blankets.

"That's nice, Mom," Ben said.

Lisa started, as did his parents. They had forgotten he was there.

Ben frowned, his attention going back and forth between.

"I'd better get back to town," Lisa said. "I've got a lot of work to do this afternoon." When she started to her feet, Ben hurried to help her up, his hand firmly under her arm. She glanced up and saw his father give him an approving smile.

Lisa felt tempted to tell Jim not to read anything into it, but instead she picked up the gift bag, thanked them again for the blankets and preceded Ben to the truck.

He helped her climb inside and as she fastened her seat belt, settled the gift bag by her feet. "I don't even remember those blankets."

"Obviously your mom did, and they're important to her."

He didn't answer and was quiet on the ride back to town. He assisted Lisa from the truck and watched until she opened her office door. She waved goodbye as he left.

Inside her office, she showed the blankets to Sandy, who admired them and then said, "About the Fredricks' contract, I can't find it anywhere. Do you think you may have left it in the mayor's office? I know we've got the electronic copy, but we need the one with Mr. Fredricks' signature."

"Yes, of course, but I don't understand it. I really don't." She was a fiend for organizing her paperwork. "Maybe it's in my briefcase, which is—"

"Over in the mayor's office," Sandy supplied.

"I'll go get it." Before Sandy could say anything, Lisa raised her hand and said, "And, yes, I'll use the elevator."

She picked up her purse and returned to the heat and humidity. She sat in her car and let the air-conditioning run cold before she drove the few blocks to city hall.

In the mayor's office she found her briefcase and the papers she needed inside it. She called to tell Sandy, then sat to rest, frustrated by her physical limitations and her sudden disorganization and forgetfulness.

Swamped with exhaustion, she put her head back and fell instantly asleep. She wasn't aware of how long she slept, but was startled awake by a perfunctory knock on the door.

"Sorry, Lisa," Trent Sanderson said, walking quickly to the desk and bending to look at her. "Are you okay?"

"Yes." She sat up, blinking and trying to clear the fog from her brain. "I'm fine. Did you need something?"

Trent stared at her for another second before he answered. "I'm afraid we've run into a problem."

He nodded to the group of men in the doorway. As they entered, Lisa recognized one of them as Isaac Rojas, the construction supervisor on the resort project. He laid a map of the Reston Lake area in front of her and pointed to a line penciled in from a distant point to the edge of the lake.

"This is an old petroleum fuel line leading to an underground storage tank."

"What?" She pulled the paper toward her. "That's impossible. It would have been disclosed." She ran her finger along the line. "This is on the property the Mason family sold. They wouldn't have kept that a secret."

"Mason said he put it in the paperwork he gave you," Trent said. "There's a regular disclosure form, right? He said he filled it out."

Lisa felt herself go cold and Trent hurried around the desk in alarm to offer her a glass of water. She shook her head. "I...I missed it. I...can't believe... I'm so careful with paperwork."

Stunned, Lisa studied the map, vaguely recalling mention of the watersports that had once taken place on the lake. "I should have checked this," she said, shaken. "I should have known. People were depending on me."

"Mayor Thomas," Trent said, "everyone makes mistakes."

"I'm responsible." Sick disappointment filled her. "I've been the one pushing this project."

"These things happen," Trent said. "Remember last year when Carly's gardens were almost ruined by water polluted by an old landfill everyone had forgotten about?"

"Yes, of course."

"This is the same sort of thing. People had forgotten about this and we might run into these situations again as we continue with construction projects, renovations, and city and county improvements."

"I should have checked and rechecked the paperwork."

Another of the construction crew spoke up. "We can't move ahead until both the old fuel line and the storage tank have been inspected. If they're safe, maybe they can be used for future watercraft. If they're not, they'll have to be removed."

"How long will that take?"

Rojas grimaced. "What with permits and governmental bureaucracy, it could take months."

"Months?" she asked in a small voice. "That means the entire project will be delayed." She looked up, horrified. "And you and your crew will be out of work until then."

"That's right," he answered. "It's the nature of the construction business."

He started to pick up the map but she placed her hand on top of it. "Do you mind if I keep this? There has to be a way—"

"I wish there was," he said. He motioned to his crew, who followed him from the office, closing the door behind them.

"Trent, what can we do?" She stared at the map in distress. "I should have seen this, should have done something. My mistake is costing time and money, not to mention jobs."

Trent was as distressed as she was. He spread his hands wide, palms up. "Other people missed it, too. Surveyors, construction professionals—all of us. There's nothing we can do. It's out of our hands. The contractor will take it from here."

"They can't be blamed. They were going with the information I provided," Lisa said.

It was almost impossible for her to accept that, to acknowledge that she could do nothing to correct her own error. Misplacing the Fredricks' contract was a minor glitch, but this was huge. She only hoped the investment group would want to go ahead with the resort once the fuel line and storage tank issues were resolved, but she wouldn't blame them if they backed out. She would call the head of the group. They probably felt as if they couldn't depend on the city of Reston. On her.

"In the meantime—" Trent started to say, but then broke off when the door flew open once again. "Roland and Bunky are here."

The two older men rushed into the room, both talking at once. With a sigh, Lisa reached into her desk drawer and pulled out the insulated bottle of water she kept there.

RESTLESS IN THE HOUSE, Ben wandered out to the pasture fence and climbed up to sit on the top rail. On the rare nights that Zach didn't have a date with one of his girlfriends, he played chess with Ben, but his manager was gone tonight. Ben could still smell the cologne Zach was convinced drove the women wild.

As for his part, Ben hadn't had a date or even looked at a woman since the night he'd spent with Lisa. He'd thought about it for months—his surprise when he'd looked up from his phone where he had been making arrangements for what must have been the last hotel room near Chicago's Midway Airport and seen someone from his hometown. Lisa had looked exhausted, vulnerable and devastated, but she'd smiled when she'd seen him, those deep blue eyes of hers lighting up in delight.

The truth was, he'd been touched that she was glad to see him, and flattered. His desire to comfort her when she'd told him about her aunt's passing, one of her few remaining relatives, had gone too far and he'd taken advantage of her need. He'd felt guilty about it ever since, which was why he now felt compelled to check up on her and stick his nose in to a degree he knew irritated her.

He gazed out at his peaceful herd, grateful that all the sick horses had recovered and the strangles bacteria hadn't spread. He'd felt like a fool for buying the horses from that crook, whom they'd never managed to locate. He had notified the sheriff, who had let the state know the man was selling sick horses, but there had been no trace of him. Zach said the guy was probably long gone to pull the scam on someone else.

Ben had taken Zach's lecture to heart and was studiously learning all he could about the horses before his planned departure for India in a few weeks. Zach had agreed to stay on for a year to select and train the cow ponies and those who would be strictly for riding. After that, Zach planned to move on and Ben would find a new manager.

Zach had asked why he was even interested in these mustangs and Ben had given that question a great deal of thought.

He liked them because they had a connection to the land, the same land where he'd been born and raised. They were unusual, smart, wild and beautiful.

He envied their freedom, the way they would suddenly take off running across the fields, their manes and tails flying. He loved how they would run in a circle and stop to graze. He liked that they were part of a herd but had no problem wandering off by themselves when they wanted.

Although he was excited about starting the American-style football league in India, he couldn't keep his thoughts away from what would be happening here while he was gone.

Lisa would become a mother. To his children.

He had already set up automatic child support payments. His financial obligation was fulfilled. He had been shaken to the core when he'd felt the baby move all those weeks ago, and even more so when they had found out that twins were coming. He felt good about the amount of money he was providing for them.

Still, he couldn't stop thinking about how uncomfortable Lisa had looked today, and how she had shared his flabbergasted amazement at the nursery his parents had decorated, and how sweet she had been about receiving his old baby blankets. Because he didn't hold attachments to very many physical things, it hadn't occurred to him that his mom still had his blankets. It made sense, though. He was her only child and, in spite of his repeated statements that he never intended to have children, she'd had hope.

Ben ran a hand over his face. That poster was too much. His parents had probably had it made from one of his old team pictures.

They seemed to have given up their certainty that he and Lisa should marry. They never mentioned it anymore and the bridal and wedding magazines had disappeared from their house.

Today he had realized that something else had taken its place. Lisa and his parents seemed to be united, with his mom and dad determined to be the best grandparents possible, and Lisa just as set on being an outstanding single mother. He had no doubt she would succeed. She would have the help and support she needed, and he wouldn't get in her way.

The work he did was important, too. He knew that, and he hoped she did. He vetted the charities he supported very carefully, getting deeply involved in helping people, especially kids, through sports and academic achievement. That really mattered. He would never give it up.

He jumped down from the fence, took a turn around the yard and then went into his house for his keys and wallet. It wouldn't hurt to go into town, drive by city hall and make sure Lisa had gone home and was taking care of herself, he told himself, but as he strode toward his truck he muttered, "Great. Now I've turned into a stalker."

When he got to city hall, he saw that the only light in the place was shining from the mayor's office, and there were four cars out front, including Junior Fedder's cruiser.

CHAPTER THIRTEEN

"Lisa! Lisa, wake up," Carly's voice drifted into Lisa's sleep.

"Don't wanna," she answered. She was perfectly comfortable in this chair, with her feet propped on a box she had placed under the desk.

A hand gently tapped her cheeks and Gemma's voice said, "Lisa, I'm going to check your blood pressure, but I need you to wake up. I want to check your pupils."

"I'm tired, not concussed," Lisa insisted, but she managed to pry her eyes open.

Luke Sanderson was there, too, along with Junior in his deputy uniform. The two grim-faced men were standing on the other side of the desk, arms crossed over their chests.

"Trent called," Luke said. "He told us about the snag at the resort site."

"It was a stupid mistake I should have caught," Lisa answered. The lengthy discussion with Bunky and Roland had drained her and she had fallen back to sleep the minute Trent had ushered them out. It was frustrating that she had been unable to accomplish anything today.

"You have to let it go, honey," Carly said gently.

"Easier said than done," Lisa answered. She looked around. "What are all of you doing here?"

"Luke and I were on our way to pick Dustin up at his grandmother's, but we stopped by here first with the posters for the county-wide yard sale. You were so deeply asleep, I couldn't wake you up," Carly said. "I called Gemma, then Junior came, too."

"Well, since medical people are on site, I'll go," Junior said. "Just stopped by on my regular rounds because your light was still on. I'll send somebody over to make sure the door is shut and the alarm is reset. I've got to go supervise the setup for the parade and street fair. Call if you need me." With a wave, he left.

"I need you to get on your feet, Lisa," Gemma said. "And move over to the sofa so I can examine you."

Luke stepped forward to help her up. He was easing her onto the sofa when they heard the sound of steps pounding up the stairs before Ben rushed through the door.

"What's going on?" he asked, his gazing sweeping the crowd in the room.

"Absolutely nothing," Lisa answered. "Except my friends are worrying too much, so I'm going home."

"I'm checking your vitals first," Gemma said in a tone that brooked no argument. She lifted a black bag and waggled it in front of her. "Got everything I need right here."

Gemma checked Lisa over while Carly and Luke moved to the other side of the room to spread the posters on the table. Ben stood nearby, watching her with brooding eyes.

Finally, Gemma said, "Everything seems okay, but I want you to come into the Sunshine tomorrow before the parade for a more thorough checkup. If there's even a hint of distress, you're skipping the Founder's Day festival and going straight to bed."

Lisa glanced at Ben and saw his grim expression. She didn't want to hear his opinion, so she said, "Whatever you say."

Gemma sighed. "I wish."

"I know you all have to help with the festival setup," Lisa said. "So if all of you will clear out of the mayor's office, I'll go home and make everyone happy."

"I'll drive you," Ben offered, picking up her briefcase and laptop case.

Lisa marched over and took both items from him. "Not necessary. I'll drive myself."

Ben shook his head. "Of course you will, but I'll follow you home, make sure you make it okay."

"As I've said before, I can't stop you from driving on public roads."

"Oh, Lisa," Carly said on a sigh. "He only wants to help."

Lisa stared at her with an expression that questioned whose side she was on, but Carly only smiled at her.

Even though she was annoyed with her friends, Lisa cheered up when she took a look at the posters that would go up soon to advertise the county-wide yard sale in the fall. They were eye-catching with a bright background and all the pertinent information printed in clear black. She gave her approval as Luke and Carly gathered them up.

Her friends headed off to set up for the next

day's festivities and Lisa fought the urge to go and make sure everything was done correctly. She had to trust those who had been appointed to handle the parade and street fair.

She drove home, Ben following along. When she reached her driveway, Ben gave her a wave, made a U-turn in the road and headed back to town.

As she stepped from her car, Lisa wondered how much longer he would be around. She knew his trip to India was coming up, but she didn't know when. It was a good thing she hadn't come to depend on him.

"This needs to be your last day out in the heat, Lisa," Gemma told her as she stretched a tape measure over her belly and recorded the number on the computer. She frowned as she compared the numbers on the chart. "In fact, you're to the point where you need to spend a lot more time sitting with your feet up, or even lying down."

"But I can keep working, right?" Lisa asked anxiously. "With the glitch in the resort plans, there's so much that needs to be done."

Gemma gave her a hopeless look. "I know, so I'm simply going to say that anything you can do from a prone position, go ahead and do it." Reaching out a hand, she helped Lisa sit up.

"Lisa, honey, what's really going on?"

The door opened and Carly whirled inside carrying several canvas bags stuffed with other canvas bags. "I'm stopping by to see how you're doing. What's up?" She placed the bags on the floor and looked at her friends expectantly.

"Lisa was about to explain why she's being so bone-headed about working and taking on so much."

"I have to," Lisa answered, standing and slipping her feet into the flat shoes that had replaced her beloved pumps. The only fashionable thing she could see about her current footwear was that they were bright red.

"Don't you understand?" she went on. "I feel so guilty about the failure of the resort project."

"How on earth is that your fault?" Carly asked.

"I should have caught it. People are out of work because of that mistake, oversight, bungling ineptitude, whatever you want to call it."

"Wow," Gemma said. "Letting you be acting mayor was a big mistake. No offense, but your shoulders are awfully small to carry the weight of the world, or even the city."

"I'm just trying to figure this all out," Lisa said. "So much has happened in the past few months."

"But you're not responsible for everything," Carly said.

"I have to be both mother and father to these kids. I've got to have financial stability beyond what Ben will be providing, a place in the community, people who'll look after them if something happens to me. I know I can always depend on you, but I have to be sure they can depend on me."

Carly and Gemma exchanged a look that Lisa read as "She's kidding, right?"

"Oh, honey," Carly said. "Everyone depends on you, but that's got to stop. I'm glad you're able to delegate, but people have to quit looking to you to handle everything. And that won't happen until you make it happen."

Lisa nodded. "I know you're probably right, but for now I've got to go check the preparations for today. The parade starts in twenty minutes."

"Fine," Gemma said. "I'm coming with you."

"Me, too," Carly added. "I've got Upcycle bags to hand out." She held up one of the tan shopping bags with the name and logo of her shop printed on the front.

"It's not necessary for you to come with me," Lisa said after admiring the bags.

"Maybe not, but we're doing it, anyway." Gemma took out her keys. "As soon as I lock up the Sunshine, we'll be on our way. Then, as soon as the parade is over, we're going to have a talk about what happens next."

Lisa looked from one to the other of them. "Why? What's wrong?"

"Not a thing right now. We'll know more after the parade passes by."

"I hate it when you're cryptic," Lisa grumbled.

With Gemma on one side and Carly on the other, Lisa left the Sunshine Birthing Center and walked over to Main Street. She found there was nothing for her to do. The preparations were complete, so she sat in a chair Bunky provided in a spot out of the late-July heat. Soon enough, the parade started and she watched the best of her hometown pass by.

As Scout troops, local clubs and the high

school marching band moved past, the people of Reston waved flags, clapped, whistled and sang along to the patriotic songs. Lisa saw Ben in the crowd, cheering and singing along with everyone else.

Lisa felt a fierce pride in Reston and in the way they could pull together. Even Roland and Bunky were on their best behavior.

After the parade, everyone in the crowd milled around, enjoying the games and food in the festival booths.

When Lisa started to follow, Gemma pulled her back. "Nuh-uh, Mayor Thomas. You're done."

"What are you talking about?"

Gemma nodded toward city hall across the street. "You're getting out of the heat and into the air-conditioning. Your Founder's Day celebration is over." Looking at Carly, she said, "Can you call Nathan and Luke and ask them to meet us at the mayor's office?"

"Absolutely."

Carly whipped out her phone and called as she kept a firm grip on Lisa's arm and helped propel her across the blocked-off street.

"If you want me to get out of the sun, I can go to my office—"

"No need," Gemma said in a breezy tone. "We're here. Where's the key?"

Lisa dug the city hall keys from her purse, unlocked the door and walked over to disable the alarm. Carly waited by the door for Luke and Nathan. They arrived within minutes, Nathan carrying both his medical bag and Gemma's.

"Hey, what's going on?" Lisa asked, giving them a worried look.

Through the glass doors, she saw Ben leave the group he was with and hurry across the street. He rushed up the city hall steps as Carly was getting ready to close the door. He gave Lisa a look that asked what was happening, but she could only shrug.

Once they were all upstairs in the mayor's office, Lisa balked. "All right, I've been cooperative long enough. What's going on?"

"Nathan's going to examine you," Gemma said.

"You just did."

"Second opinion."

Before Lisa could say anything else, Luke and Carly stepped forward, each taking one of Ben's arms and turning him back toward the hallway as Carly said, "Lisa is going to be examined right now. Let's step outside."

Ben craned his head around to see what was happening, but they whisked him out and shut the door.

Alarmed, Lisa looked at her friends, who were both opening medical bags and pulling out stethoscopes. Gemma also held a tape measure in her hand. "What's wrong?"

"Have you been having backaches today?" Nathan asked.

"Well, yes, for a couple of days. Isn't that normal?"

"Yes," Gemma said, pulling up Lisa's top and tugging her slacks down below her belly. "But you're also bigger than you were when I examined you a few days ago."

"Lisa, we're pretty sure you have polyhydramnios, too much amniotic fluid," Nathan added, putting his hands on her belly and gently pressing it here and there. The twins responded by kicking back, which made him chuckle.

"What he's saying is you've got six pounds of babies and about twenty pounds of amniotic fluid right now," Gemma said.

"Is that dangerous?"

"It can be, but since we caught it early, the danger isn't as great. Too much fluid pressing on the cervix can cause premature labor. With this condition, the risk of your water breaking spontaneously is simply too great. That amount of amniotic fluid gushing out suddenly is very forceful and could cause the cords to come out, too, creating cord prolapse."

"That sounds bad."

"It's an immediate emergency C-section, but we're going to do everything possible to avoid that."

Lisa looked from Nathan to Gemma. "How long have you known about this?"

"Only since yesterday, but Nathan wasn't available to examine you until this morning, and I knew you felt like you had to be here for the festivities."

"But not at the risk to my babies."

"That's the attitude I was hoping to hear." Gemma gave her a bright smile as she pulled up the front of Lisa's slacks and smoothed her top. "Sooo, that means the Founder's Day parade was your last hurrah. You ought to go on complete bed rest for the remainder of your pregnancy."

"That's eight weeks," Lisa said. "That's a long time."

"But it's necessary to ensure the safety of your babies," Nathan said.

"Of course I will, but my business—"

"Can be handled online and by phone. Sandy will be glad to take care of it." Gemma grinned. "You might have to give her a raise. Also, Luke will help out at your office."

"Luke? How?"

"He was in the real-estate business in Dallas, remember?"

"Oh, yes." Lisa and Gemma shared a smile over the memory of the day they'd dressed in their best and gone to tell him to be careful in how he dealt with Carly.

"I heard about that," Nathan said. "Did you two really—"

"Any threat to his good health was purely implied," his wife assured him.

He grinned and shook his head.

Lisa went back to fretting. "I...I guess that will work, but the mayor's job—"

"Will have to go back to Harley."

"But his heart?"

"Is much better," Nathan said. "I think

he's learned his lesson about doing too much, which is something you need to learn."

"And it's only for four months, until the election."

"I know. I was thinking about running for mayor, for a full four-year term."

Gemma stared at her. "Are you kidding? I thought you'd given up that idea."

"With two infants?" Nathan asked.

"Gemma, you know I've always wanted to do it, but I guess it was only a dream," Lisa admitted, glancing away. "There are so many things I want to do for the town, so many improvements that could be made." Her gaze was snagged by the map on her desk. "Although I may not be as great at it as I thought."

"You've done an outstanding job," Nathan said.

"And there will be plenty of time later for you to run for mayor. Right now, you've got other priorities." Gemma smiled at her. "Brenda and I have talked about this endlessly. Harley has promised to finish out his term."

Gemma and Nathan fell silent as Lisa thought over what they had said. "It's not even a choice, is it? I can wait until this amniotic fluid thing gets really bad, or I can avoid it altogether by staying in bed for the rest of my pregnancy."

Gemma smiled. "That's right."

"Then bed rest it is," Lisa responded with a firm nod. "The babies' health comes first."

"Atta girl," Gemma said as she walked over and opened the door. She motioned for Carly to come in. Luke and Ben followed, with Ben skirting the others and coming right over to crouch beside the sofa.

"Are you okay?" He looked her over carefully. "I saw you at the parade and you didn't look too good."

"Gee, thanks."

Lisa told everyone what was going on.

"So now we have to decide who is going to take care of you, Lisa," Carly said. "I know it didn't work out when your mother was there, but would you want her to come back?"

Lisa shook her head. "No. She's happy where she is. She and I talk every couple of days. Our relationship is better than it was, but we've got a long way to go. I can't expect her to give up her new life and come running back." Her smile flickered. "Besides, I think she's got a boyfriend."

"Okay, then," Carly said. "We'll have to take turns."

"There's enough of us that it should work," Luke agreed.

"No need," Ben said, standing. "I'll do it."

"Do what?" Lisa asked in alarm.

"I'll move in and take care of you."

"Move *in*? Not in this lifetime."

"Someone needs to be on hand because you never know when you might need help."

"I'm not going to put my babies at risk. Besides, aren't you going off to China or someplace?"

"India. But not for a few weeks."

"This is a terrible idea." Lisa started to sit up but had to wait for help. It annoyed her that Ben was the one to give it, supporting her while she sat and then lifting her to her feet as if she wasn't as big as a beached whale.

"I'm the obvious choice," Ben said. "I can arrange my time more so than most people."

"At least until you leave," she pointed out.

Lisa became aware that her friends were watching this exchange closely, their attention shifting back and forth as if they were at a tennis match.

"And I'm these babies' father."

He was obviously averse to being put off by her reluctance and downright hostility.

"At least until you leave," she repeated.

Unwillingness to go along with the plan dragged at her. Ben had always been up front about not wanting to be part of the babies' lives, and she understood that now he wanted to offer temporary help, but she wondered why. Did he want to impress his parents or his adoring public? She was too tired and confused to figure it out right now.

"I think it's the best option for now," Carly agreed, and Lisa gave her a betrayed glare.

"I agree," Luke said. "By the time Ben leaves, we can figure out a more permanent solution until the babies arrive."

Everyone else murmured assent. Seeing no way out, Lisa walked over to the desk. She picked up the map of Reston Lake and put a sticky note with Isaac Rojas's name on the front so it could be returned to him. "Fine, then. It looks like I have no choice."

"So glad you're being reasonable," Ben said sardonically while she wrinkled her nose at him, making him grin. "I'll go home and get my things, and be at your house in a couple of hours."

"Gemma and I will walk down with you and tell you what you need to know to take care of her," Nathan offered.

Gemma hurried over and gave Lisa a hug. "We'll see you at your house in a little while." She smiled at her friend. "I'm proud of you. Choosing bed rest is the best thing to do."

Lisa nodded, but she couldn't imagine what she would do with herself while she was lying around all day. She had been working since she was sixteen, had been completely self-sufficient since she was eighteen. Now she had to depend on someone else to take care of her. And not just anyone—Ben McAdams.

The three of them left.

"I'll drive you home," Carly said. "Luke will check on Dustin then drive your car over to your house. And don't forget that I'm your Lamaze partner. Gemma and I will be over to practice what you're going to need to know to deliver these babies safely."

Lisa wanted to remind her that she was still in possession of her faculties, but knew it was pointless. She saw the worried look in her friend's eyes and recalled that Carly had lost a baby years ago, and the threat to Lisa's pregnancy must be a hard thing to handle. Without another word of objection, she handed Luke her car keys.

Everyone else walked out to the hallway while Lisa picked up her briefcase and stood looking around the mayor's office. She knew it would be a long time before she saw it again, and even longer before she could fulfill her dream of being mayor. It might seem silly, but she had nurtured the thought for years and it was hard to make herself believe that the day might never come. Finally she turned off the lights and locked the door before joining the others outside.

CHAPTER FOURTEEN

"So, LISA, YOUR choices for dinner are spaghetti, meatballs in some kind of mushroom sauce and—" Ben examined the contents of another covered container. "More spaghetti."

Almost all the food Lisa's mother had left neatly portioned and labeled was gone. At least he knew she'd been eating well, but it was time to restock the pantry.

"I don't care," Lisa called from the bedroom.

"You're not sulking, are you?"

"Certainly not," she answered.

He grinned at the resentful tone of her voice. "That's good. My mom and dad will be over as soon as they get back from my aunt Marie's house in Tulsa and I'd hate for them to see you in a bad mood."

When there was no answer, he set the meatball container on the counter and walked into her room.

Lisa was propped up in bed, wearing a

baggy pink T-shirt and shorts. She sat cross-legged, with her laptop propped up on a couple of pillows, probably so she could see over her belly.

"Are you working?" he asked, leaning against the door frame and crossing his arms over his chest.

"I'm allowed to run my own business," she answered in a snippy tone. "And I'm only answering emails right now, anyway." She looked up. "Surely that won't overtax my system."

"Let's hope not. I'd hate to get another visit from Gemma and Carly."

"What? When did that happen?"

"Back in May. Told me to leave you alone and let you make your own decisions. Now, I guess they'd tell me *not* to leave you alone, and *not* to let you make your own decisions."

As if she couldn't help it, Lisa grinned. "The Stiletto Mafia strikes again."

"The what?"

Lisa explained about the time she and Gemma had gone to see Luke at his office in Dallas. She told him they weren't sure how much it had helped, but they'd known they had to stand up for Carly, who had already been badly hurt by Luke years before.

Ben watched her face as she talked, noting the outrage at the idea that Carly would ever be hurt again.

"Luke gave us the nickname 'Stiletto Mafia.'"

"Well, if the shoe fits…" Ben said, causing Lisa to groan at his pun.

Ben looked down at the floor then at her. "I'm glad you made the decision to stay in bed."

Lisa's eyes narrowed, but when he grinned at her, her expression cleared. "Me, too, although—" she looked at her laptop "—it's going to be hard."

"As my grandmother used to say, 'It's only worthwhile if it's hard to do.' She had a strong work ethic." He smiled. "You do, too, Lisa. I don't think we have to worry about our kids being lazy."

Her answering smile was slow to form and sweet to see. Warmth spread through him as he let his gaze rove over her, noting that her face was flushed and her hair was a little messy, not smoothed into its usual soft curve. He liked her in her baggy T-shirt and shorts, so different from the chic perfection of her usual attire.

He admired the way she always appeared professional, how hard she worked and the way she gave her all for their town, even while maintaining her friendships and professional relationships. He liked her sassiness and determination to do what was right. In fact, if he was ever to settle down with someone, get married, it would be with someone like Lisa.

Or Lisa herself.

Surprised by that thought, he shifted and broke his gaze away from hers.

"Speaking of businesses, what about yours? Your Oklahoma Heritage Horse operation, aren't you needed there?"

"I'll go over and check on things. The truth is, Zach can run the whole operation just fine without me. In fact, I probably get in his way. I've been learning from him, though. If this is going to be successful, I need to know what to do. He might drop by here, bring me some paperwork to handle."

Ben didn't want Zach, with his charm and roving eye, to stop in at all. As he watched, Lisa turned on her side and lay back against the pillows. Her chocolate-brown hair spread across the pillow in a fan and her blue eyes regarded him with interest, as if she really wanted to hear all about Zach and the wild mustangs.

No, she was too appealing, Ben decided. There was no way he was letting Zach near her.

"And your football camp?"

"I talked to the coach at the high school. He and his football team will handle it for the next few days. Last day is Friday."

"Sounds like you and my friends have this all wrapped up," Lisa said around a delicate yawn. "I'm completely out of a job."

"I'd think the one job you've got going would be enough," he said, pointing to her belly.

"I know, but until the babies arrive, I'm going to be bored."

"Do you know how to play chess? Checkers? Poker?"

"No, no and no."

"I'll teach you. Dinner will be ready in a few minutes. I can't cook, but I can punch a mean microwave button." He turned toward the kitchen and then glanced back. "By the way, what do you want me to do with that box of books under the bed in the guest room?"

That snapped her eyes open. Lisa propped herself up on her elbow and shook her head. "What box? There shouldn't be anything under that bed. I don't keep boxes of things around that I don't use."

"It was definitely a box of books. I bumped into it when I was stowing my gear in there. I'll get it."

He went into the room next to Lisa's, scooped up the box and carried it back. "The flaps were open like that so I saw it was books."

"They must be Maureen's," Lisa said, peering inside. "I didn't notice it when I changed the sheets."

"The toe of my boot hit it. My feet are much bigger than yours, which is probably why I ran into it and you didn't." He started for the kitchen. "Maybe you can find a good book to read."

Ben heated up the meatballs and tried to make a meal that covered all the food groups while also sticking to all the restrictions of the pregnancy diet Lisa had clipped to the refrigerator door. He looked at the list of do's and don'ts and knew he would have to ask his mom about some of it, but he knew exactly how to measure grams of protein and Lisa needed to be packing away enough for three people.

His mom and dad desperately wanted to be involved in doing whatever was best for Lisa and the babies. His mom was a great cook and would probably love to come over and cook up meals for him to freeze. Also, they could stay with Lisa when he had to run out to Riverbend or take care of other errands. They would see it as part of their "grandparental" duties.

Even after he left for India, he knew he could count on them to look after things. He paused in his efforts to slice celery for the salad.

Maybe he should be looking at this the other way. His parents wouldn't be the ones on temporary duty, taking over to help out while he was gone. They would be on permanent duty with him striding in and out of his children's lives, passing through on his way to a charity event, a new project or business opportunity.

His dad had been making noises about retiring full-time. It wasn't until this moment that Ben understood it was so that he could help Lisa and be with his wife and grandkids.

That was a huge change from the workaholic life Jim McAdams had pursued so far.

But that was his dad's choice, Ben thought, and he was grateful for it. He would be free to pursue the important things he had to do all around the world. That was what he wanted. Wasn't it?

Ben tapped the flat of the knife against the cutting board. After his football career had ended, he had built his entire working life on his determination to not let work rule his life the way it had ruled his dad's. And, by extension, affected his mom and him. He could remember endless numbers of dinners where he and his mother had eaten without Jim. Retirement would be a complete one-eighty for him, but he must have thought it was worth it.

Returning to the task at hand, Ben thought about his reasons for the path he'd chosen. Impatience with his father's quest for more and more deals, more and more money, had been one reason he'd been driven to the charity work and projects he pursued. He might be just as busy as his father, but what he was doing was good, worthwhile. There were too many people and organizations depending on him. Plans were set, wheels in motion. He couldn't quit now.

Again Lisa's voice echoed in his head with that quote from Jackie Kennedy about nothing else mattering if you bungle raising your children.

With an annoyed growl, he shoved all those thoughts out of his mind and finished making dinner. He placed two filled plates on a tray, added napkins and cutlery and carried everything into Lisa's room. He intended to eat every meal he possibly could with her and refused to let her relegate him to the kitchen table.

With a flourish, he swept in the door and found Lisa sitting up in bed weeping and shaking, the contents of the box spread out around her.

"LISA, WHAT'S WRONG?" Ben asked as he deposited a loaded tray on top of the dresser and came to sit beside her on the bed. "Are you in pain? Why didn't you call me? I'll get Gemma—"

"No." She held up her hand. "I'm fine."

He grabbed her hand and then took her into

his arms. Frantic, with distress, she tried to pull away, but he wouldn't let her go.

"Ah, Lisa, honey, don't cry," he said against her hair. "It kills me when you cry. And...and it's probably bad for the babies. You have to look out for the babies, you know, they're—"

"Oo-ooh," she moaned. He had opened the floodgates once again.

Ben turned to grab the tissue dispenser from the bedside table. Doing so dislodged a pile of the books she'd taken from the box he'd found.

He handed her some tissues as he said, "I'll gather up these books and get rid of them. They're in the way and—"

"No!" Lisa hiccupped and repeated, "No. I want to read them. They're Maureen's journals, my mom's diaries."

"Wow. Really?"

Lisa picked up a slip of paper. "She left me a note saying I could read these if I wanted to, that they would explain some things." Sick with anguish, she crumpled the paper. "But I've talked to her so many times since she left. She never mentioned these."

"Maybe she didn't know how to bring it

up since you two barely have the start of any kind of relationship."

"That could be it. She might have been embarrassed about them, might have wanted to leave it up to chance that I would find them. I'm not sure, since I still don't know her well."

He didn't release his comforting hold on her, but he looked more closely at the books. Some were ordinary spiral-bound notebooks, others were cloth-covered or had brightly printed paper-stock covers. "I didn't even know people still kept diaries anymore." He stared at them curiously. "Anything I need to remember goes in my phone."

Lisa gave him a tremulous smile as she leaned into his comforting arms. "These start from when I was a baby. No one had cell phones then, and I'm sure she didn't have a computer."

"So…these are about you, aren't they? That's why you were crying."

She nodded and picked up a spiral-bound one. "The later ones mostly talk about her friends in Chicago, the restaurants where she worked, recipes. But the early ones are very different. Look."

He opened it to the first page.

"Read it out loud," Lisa said, gesturing to the yellowed pages.

Even though he gave her an unsure look, he started reading.

I've got a job washing dishes in a café. The pay is lousy, but Aunt Violet says I can stay with her until I get on my feet. That will take years. It's winter. I've never been so cold.

 I wonder if Lisa is cold at home. I left my baby! I left my little girl! My mom and dad are raising her in that house where no little kid should live. I can't go back and face the shame of leaving her. I can't. I miss her every minute of every day. I wake up in the night hurting for her. My arms are empty and I can imagine I hear her crying for me. I see her blue eyes looking at me, trusting me, even though I was someone she can't trust, can't depend on because I left her. I couldn't stay. I was trapped. Leaving her with Mom and Dad is better. Right? At least they've got money to take care of her. I don't have anything and I can't support her by working at the Burger

Barn. But leaving her hurt so bad. It's like a knife in my heart, twisting, every day, twisting. I wonder if it hurts very much to die. Who am I kidding? I'm too much of a coward to kill myself.

"Wow," Ben said, closing the notebook. "That's horrible, unbelievable. I thought she left you because she didn't want a baby, but—"

"That's what I thought." Lisa dabbed at her tears and blew her nose. "All my life I thought she didn't love me, that I was so ugly or repulsive or…messy, that she couldn't stand me."

"No, Lisa. How could you think that? You're beautiful, and kind, and…and sweet." He kissed her forehead with each word, which brought another flood of tears. She needed the comfort, so she clung to him while she wept.

"It…it wasn't until she showed up here in February that I was able to start understanding a little about why she left, but this explains so much more." Lisa shifted away from him and looked around for her phone. "I need to call her."

"Not now," Ben said, releasing her and

standing. Apparently he'd been sitting on her phone, and knew it, because he reached down and snagged it before she could get it. "You need to eat dinner and you need some rest. It can't be good for you, or the babies, to be getting upset like this."

"But I want to tell her I'm sorry." Lisa held out her hand. "That's my personal property," she reminded him.

"I get that, but now that you've started reading *her* personal property, don't you think it would be a good idea to go ahead and finish? Get a complete picture of everything she's been through since she left?" He shrugged. "It might help you understand her even better."

Lisa blinked. "When did the big-time football player get so sensitive and touchy-feely?"

He rolled his eyes. "Since I slaved over dinner and I don't want it to get cold. Punching those microwave buttons can really take it out of a guy." He returned to the tray and picked it up. "Come on. Time to eat. You can read more journals later, but if I see even a sign of too much stress—"

"Yeah, yeah, you're calling Carly and Gemma." Lisa picked up her fork. "Maybe if you're lucky, they'll make you an honorary member of the Stiletto Mafia."

Ben took his own plate from the tray and sat in the bedside chair. "They should be so lucky."

Lisa laughed and began eating. In spite of the emotional upheavals she'd experienced today, she was famished, and ate everything Ben had prepared. The food her mother had left for her was almost gone. Lisa wondered what Ben would make to replace it.

Her mother. Ben was right about needing to read all of Maureen's journals before she called her. She finally had the answer she'd been looking for, the one piece of the puzzle that had eluded her, even after she and Maureen had talked. Somehow, spoken words of how unhappy Maureen had been didn't express the true depth of her anguish as well as her written words did.

Finally she understood that she wasn't at fault for Maureen's departure. It had been excruciating for her to leave her baby behind.

"I guess I always knew it wasn't about me," she said slowly. "It was about this place."

"What do you mean?" Ben asked.

"She was desperate to get away from the

overpowering, overwhelming mess she lived in. That we all lived in. I can understand that. It's why I moved out and got my own place at eighteen." Lisa paused. "But she couldn't do what I did because she had a baby at sixteen. Now I think I understand her need to escape."

"Is she the reason you cleaned this place up, stayed here, didn't sell the whole mess and move on?"

"Well, I...I don't—" She broke off and stared at him. Her fingers went slack and the fork clattered to the plate.

"What's wrong?" Ben started forward in concern.

She held up a hand to stop him as thoughts raced through her mind. "I never made the connection before," she said. "That must have always been in the back of my mind, cleaning the place up meant my mother might come back. And she did." She grimaced. "And I was horrible to her."

"Never too late to fix that."

Ben gestured for her to finish her food, which she did quickly so she could get back to reading Maureen's journals.

"Is that why you're so...fixated on this

town, too? On improving things and being mayor, and everything else you do?"

"Maybe." She shrugged. "Probably. And I didn't want to be one of the unambitious, weird Thomases. Really, I was raised more by Gemma's and Carly's parents than by my grandparents. They taught me what it was like to have goals and plans, to be people who mattered. Doing all I can for Reston is a way of paying them back, paying the community back."

Ben nodded, considering. "I never gave any thought to what it was like to have any kind of parents other than my own," he admitted.

"You had a happy childhood. Your parents are awesome." She paused when she heard a vehicle pull up outside. "And they're here."

Ben scooped up their plates. "I'll let them in and then I'll clean up the kitchen, or I'll hear about it from my mother."

Lisa smiled and began organizing the journals by date so she could read them in order.

"YOU'VE BECOME WAY too good at this," Ben grumbled, staring at the checkerboard.

"I believe in doing well at whatever I attempt." Lisa was lying on her side on the sofa.

The board was on top of the coffee table and Ben sat opposite, leaning forward with his forearms on his knees.

"It's working for you." He studied the board again. His eyes lit up and he said, "Aha," and moved his checker to a new position.

"You're making this way too simple for me," she said, and easily defeated him.

"Why do I never see that coming?"

"Because you think one move ahead instead of several." Lisa raised an arm over her head to work out a stitch in her side. "Which is surprising because you would have had to carry football plays in your head all the time."

"Smug much?" he asked. "Maybe I'm out of practice. Another game?"

"No. I'm tired."

He gathered up everything and put it away in the box, then sat across from her.

Lisa laid back and tried to relax, though she was heartily sick of lying around. She knew Ben was doing his best to distract her because company was coming today—someone she never thought she'd meet.

"Are you nervous?" Ben asked. "About meeting your father?"

"Yes, but it will help that Maureen and Clive will be here, too."

After she had read all Maureen's journals, she had called her mother and they'd had a long talk, with tears, apologies and the beginning of forgiveness on both sides. Since then, Lisa had come to understand where she'd gotten her own need for independence.

Maureen had brought Clive to meet her. It was the first time spending time together had been easy and natural. Ben and Clive had hit it off and if the Marine had thought it odd that Ben would soon be heading to India, he hadn't let on.

"I'm grateful that Maureen found John and convinced him to come meet me." Lisa clasped her hands nervously. "I don't know what to expect."

"That's understandable." Ben wandered around the room, peeked out toward the road, then sat again. "Do you want me to call Gemma and Carly for backup?"

She smiled. "No need. You'll do."

It had been a few weeks since he had moved in. Although he would go to Riverbend Ranch for a while each day, he spent every night at her house, did much of the cooking—with assistance from his mother—and most of the cleaning. If she needed anything while he was gone, she only had to call. He answered right away or got back to her in a hurry if she left a message.

When he was due home, she found herself sitting straighter, craning her neck to catch sight of him pulling into the driveway or listening for the sound of his truck. When she heard it, or the closing of the door, she smiled. Most of the time she didn't even question the joy that filled her. She was simply happy he was there.

Luke and Sandy handled things at the realty office, and Ben frequently picked up papers or other things she needed to see.

He helped her to the bathroom and back to bed, had learned how to take her blood pressure and check her blood oxygen level, and portion out her prenatal vitamins. He drove her to her doctor's appointments. If anyone had thought their arrangement was odd, no one said anything. After all, he was still the local sports hero.

Lisa recalled the doubts she'd had when she had agreed to this arrangement, her worries that he wanted to impress his parents and his fans.

That thought made her squirm. She had known from the very beginning that she couldn't depend on him long-term for anything except child support, but that was hard to remember lately.

He talked often about his trip to India, which was coming up. For days he'd had papers and schedules, player profiles and information spread out all over the dining room table. He'd asked if it was okay and she had put aside her reluctance because she felt like she owed it to him for the care he was taking of her and the babies.

As it turned out, she hadn't minded the mess because she had loved watching him study the player statistics and the demographics of the cities where it was most likely a football team would gain supportive fans.

He had talked through issues with her, and she had enjoyed listening to him and offering suggestions. It made her happy to have him share his dreams with her.

Ben walked over to the dining table and once again became absorbed in his football project. "I'll clean all of this up in a minute," he said.

She only smiled.

He read silently, then said, in an absent voice, "It's different when you're working with kids who have played football since middle school. They know the rules, the plays, the positions."

"But with these players, you'll be starting with guys who know little or nothing about American-style football," she said.

"That's right. And they're smaller than American boys, so that's another factor." He picked up a chart, absorbed in what he was reading.

Lisa watched his face, saw how his eyes scanned the page and the way he smiled with satisfaction when he found the piece of information he needed. His dimples curved into his cheeks.

She hoped one or both of her babies had those dimples. In fact, she wanted them to have his approach to life—achieve your dreams, but enjoy the journey.

Since he had moved in to look after her, she had discovered more and more things she liked about him. He was involved in more charities than she could have imagined, and served on the boards of several. He was generous and had a big heart, things she had come to admire about him.

Watching him writing careful notes, she frowned as her mind clicked through all the time they had spent together in the past eight months, the conversations, conflicts and resolutions they'd had.

Ben's phone rang. He glanced at it, then answered. "Hey, Dan, how's it going?" He laughed at the response, his deep chuckle sending a wave of delight through Lisa.

Oh, my gosh, she thought as a chill ran through her. *I'm in love with him. I've been falling in love with him for weeks.*

She must have sucked in a breath because Ben looked up quickly, his expression one of concern. She grabbed a magazine and opened it, staring unseeing at a page of advertisements.

She couldn't quite wrap her mind around what she had only now realized. It had been coming on for weeks, sneaking up on her with every kind thing he did, every generous gesture, each time he'd teased her and shown concern for her.

She wanted to tell him how she felt, but she wouldn't. From the beginning he'd made it clear that he didn't intend to be a family man. She didn't want him to stay out of obligation or duty or because she told him she loved him. Besides, if she told him she loved him, she would want him to love her back. That wouldn't happen with Ben.

Because of her strange upbringing, she had never seen what devoted love was in her own family. She had seen it in the Whitmires and the Joslins, though, and had witnessed what it was like for two people to work hard on their partnership.

Lisa had long understood she might never have that kind of partnership, so she had begun making her own decisions, planning her life and working toward her goals at the age of sixteen. Because she'd been careful to cover every possible glitch, her missteps had been rare.

She had thrown caution to the wind in a major way exactly twice—both times with Ben McAdams. Once when she had slept with him and now that she had fallen in love with him. Those two decisions would have lasting consequences throughout the remainder of her life.

She shifted uncomfortably and laid a hand over her belly, cradling the children who would know their father only as a full-size poster.

"Are you okay? Do you need anything?" he asked as he ended the call, his gaze noting the protective placement of her hand and then watching her face. "Should I check your blood pressure?"

Lisa shook her head. "I'm sure it's fine. Between you and your mother, I'm going on record as the most well-monitored pregnant woman in history."

"She and I are in competition." His face grew grave. "But if anything happening today is too much, I'm clearing the place out and you're going back to bed."

"Bossy."

"Darned straight."

Two cars slowed out front and pulled into her driveway.

"They're here," she said.

"I'll get the door."

OVER THE NEXT two hours Lisa met her father, who turned out to be a decent man with a regrettable past he'd overcome. She also got to know his wife, Beth, and her own half sister. Although Zoe looked like she was in her teens, she was twenty-five, finishing college with a degree in education and had a fresh, funny, outgoing personality.

Maureen had brought along mountains of food. She acted as hostess, with Clive proudly watching from the sidelines, and Ben acting as host, passing out lemonade and iced tea.

Lisa stayed on the sofa, feeling like a giant lead balloon with legs, but experiencing happiness and a sense of family connectedness she'd only ever felt during rare visits with her great-aunt Violet.

She admitted that a lot of it had to do with Ben, who used his natural charm and good humor to put people at ease. It made her love him even more and she desperately wondered how much longer she would be able to hide it.

It was early evening when everyone was ready to leave and Lisa exchanged phone numbers with Zoe, Beth and John.

Before she left, Maureen gave Lisa a hug and gripped her hands in a warm clasp. "I'll come back whenever you need me. Before the babies come. After. Whenever. I've trained someone to take over the kitchen at the café, and as long as Clive doesn't eat up all the profits, we should be fine." She threw him a teasing glance over her shoulder.

Touched that she now had a mother she knew she could depend on, Lisa said, "Thanks, Mom. I love you."

Maureen's lips trembled as she kissed her on the cheek and whispered, "I love you, too."

When the house emptied, Ben helped Lisa to bed and then said he'd clean the house. In spite of a backache that had been bothering her for a while, she fell asleep, but woke to the sound of his footsteps going up and down the hallway. Turning over, she flipped on the bedside light and called his name.

He immediately stepped inside, dropped a packed duffel bag onto the floor and came over to the bed.

"What's going on?"

"I've got to go. Something major has come up with the project in India that only the board members can handle." He looked at the bedside clock. "I managed to book a flight from Tulsa to New York. It leaves in a few hours, so I've got time to get over to Riverbend and get the rest of what I need. From New York, I'll have to scramble for a flight to New Delhi."

"Oh." She shook her head, trying to clear it, thinking she was still in a dream. "When will you be back?"

Ben pulled up the bedside chair and sat. His usually charming, smiling, teasing expression was gone. "I won't be back for months. Once I'm there, I'll stay. If I— If we don't take care of this emergency, the entire project will fall apart. People have been depending on this for employment and many others have invested in it. You understand, right?"

She nodded. After her experience with the Reston Lake development, Lisa certainly knew, but she could feel her face freezing into an expression of disbelief. She couldn't seem to stop it, but she managed to say, "Yes, of course."

"You knew about this, Lisa. I never tried to keep it a secret. I've been honest and up front with you from the very beginning."

"I know. I know," she said, holding up her hand to stave off a reminder. "You never wanted children, a family. I get it." How foolish of her to have harbored a secret dream that he would change his mind.

"So, you do understand. That's…that's good." He stood and moved the chair back where it belonged. "I've called Gemma and she's on her way over. I'll wait till she gets here—"

"No need," Lisa said brightly. "I'll be perfectly fine staying right here until she comes."

Ben stood with his hands on his hips, ran his palms down his thighs as if to dry them, then said, "If you think that's best, I'll be going, then."

"Yes. No need for you to hang around. Thanks for all your help these past weeks. I…I know it wasn't enjoyable for you, but I appreciate that you stayed with me."

"Not enjoyable?" he said, obviously trying to follow what she was saying. "Why would you think that?"

"Oh, come on, Ben. You were only here out of a sense of duty and…and because you didn't want grief from your parents or to spoil your image among your adoring public."

"What? That's not true. I was glad to help."

"Fine. And now you've helped and you're ready to go. No surprises there." She could feel her frozen expression beginning to thaw as the words poured out. She wanted him to go before she melted into tears. "Leave the door unlocked so Gemma can get in, okay?"

"Well, I—" He looked toward the hallway then at her. "Maybe I can wait until she—"

"No need." She lifted her arm and waved her fingers at him in goodbye. She was quite proud of the steadiness of her hand because she was beginning to shake inside.

He frowned as he bent to scoop up his duffel bag. "Fine, but I'll see you—"

"No," she sang out again. "I completely understand the arrangements we've made."

"So all you need is my money."

"It's all you're willing to give," she reminded him.

Ben's dark gray eyes stared at her with irritation. Finally he said, "Right."

He turned, hitched his duffel over his shoulder and strode out the door. She could hear his boots ringing on the hardwood and she held her breath until the back door closed with a firm thud, leaving her alone.

She held it together until the truck's engine rumbled and he pulled out of her driveway— and out of her life.

Then the tears came in huge, gut-wrenching waves that stole her breath and sent her back into spasms. She'd been crazy to fall in love with him. She would have been better off sticking to a business arrangement and not letting emotions get involved.

Gemma and Nathan rushed in a few minutes later. Gemma climbed straight onto the bed to gather Lisa into her arms.

"Oh, honey, I'm so sorry," Gemma said.

"I'm sorry about this, about…everything, and—" She broke off as another back pain hit her. "Ooo," she moaned.

Gemma sat back, took a good look at her, then eased her fully onto her side as she nodded at Nathan, who immediately came over to help.

"How long have you been having those pains?" she asked.

"Several hours. I thought it was a regular backache or Braxton Hicks contractions."

Gemma smiled. "Lisa, it's been a tough evening for you, and it's about to get worse. I think those *are* contractions. You're probably in labor."

"I can't be," she argued, struggling to sit up. "I've still got a month."

"Multiples often come early," Nathan reminded her. "We're going to examine you and see where we're at."

They had a verdict a few minutes later.

"You're already dilated to six centimeters," Gemma said. "Congratulations. These babies are going to be born in the next few hours."

Frantically, Lisa looked at them. "But I'm not ready."

"Doesn't matter, honey. They are."

Nathan spoke up. "If you're okay with it, Gemma, I think we'd better take her straight to the hospital."

"I agree. We will almost certainly need more resources than what are available here or at the Sunshine."

"I'll call for transport."

After that, it was out of Lisa's control. At this moment, it didn't matter if Ben was gone, if he would never be part of his children's lives. She had hard work to do for the remainder of this night and she wasn't going to think of Ben flying away.

BEN HAD HIS bags packed and had talked to Zach, glad to leave such a responsible ranch manager in charge. He had called his aunt Marie and asked if he could leave his truck parked at her house for an extended period, then phoned his parents and told them he would be in touch. They had greeted the news of his departure with coldness but had wished him safe travels.

As he pulled onto the highway and headed north toward Tulsa, his mind clicked over everything he needed to do in the next several hours. He hoped to sleep on the plane because it might be a while before he could get a flight to New Delhi.

He would be traveling almost nine thousand miles from home. Home. Ben's thoughts ground to a halt as he considered that word. Other than the house where he'd grown up, he'd never really had a home, only places where he'd parked his things and lived out of boxes. Even at Riverbend, he was basically camping out.

Now the word *home* immediately brought up a picture of Lisa's house, the comfortable place she had wrestled from the stifling chaos of her young life. She had created a haven for herself, by herself, after everyone had abandoned her. Her mother had left, she hadn't known her father until today, her grandparents had been physically present but emotionally absent. As a kid, he'd never understood what her life had been like.

The memory of the day she'd broken him

out of jail surfaced. He had never really understood why she'd done it. They had been friends, but not best friends. A whole gang of them had hung out together.

And then a blinding flash of understanding hit and he eased his foot off the gas pedal. All these years later he finally understood. Lisa had broken him out of jail because she couldn't stand the thought of anyone being imprisoned like she was. She'd mentioned something about an uncle being in jail and how it had ruined his life, but he doubted she had even known that uncle.

Ben spotted a gas station up ahead. He drove into the parking lot and pulled into a dark corner to think. Lisa had made a successful life for herself in spite of all the setbacks she'd had. And then he had handed her the biggest setback of all: getting her pregnant and insisting that his obligation ended with a signature on a check. He'd been so fixated on all the things he thought he needed to accomplish, all the people and charities he wanted to help, that he'd forgotten that charity begins at home.

He placed his forearms on top of the steering wheel, leaned forward and dropped his forehead onto them as deep shame rolled through him.

"McAdams," he muttered, "you're a flaming fool."

He was in love with Lisa, had been for months, maybe since Chicago, but he'd been too bone-headed and self-involved to see it. That was why he'd pestered her, stuck around, insisted she needed to take better care of herself. The weeks with her had been the best of his adult life. If he hadn't completely screwed this up, maybe she would forgive him, marry him, make a life with him, show him how to be as good a father as she would be a mother.

Straightening, he checked his mirrors and reversed out of the parking space. Swinging onto the highway, he headed in the opposite direction, back toward Lisa. And home.

LISA WOKE UP in the Reston County Hospital to the sight of a shirtless Ben McAdams seated beside her, a diaper-and-beanie-clad baby on each shoulder.

"Hey," she whispered through a dry throat. "What are you doing here?"

He looked up and grinned. "Skin-to-skin

contact is supposed to help bonding with a newborn."

"I know, but why are you doing it? I thought you were on your way to India."

"Someone who didn't just become a father can handle India." He stood, careful to cradle the babies' bodies and heads against his chest. He laid the sleeping infants, side by side, in the bassinet.

Lisa's mouth dropped open. "How did you learn to do that?"

He shrugged as he filled a glass of water for her, placed a straw in it and held it so she could drink. "Basically the same as carrying a football. Best to hold it close, tight against your chest. They're not a whole lot bigger than a football, but heavier, a little less than five pounds a piece."

"I know. I was there."

He grimaced as he set the glass down on the bed table and wheeled it out of the way. "And I wasn't. I'm sorry. I got a few miles out of town and realized I was a first-class fool. I turned around and went back to your house, but you were gone. Scared me to death until I called Gemma who told me that you were here and too busy to talk."

Ben snagged his shirt off the back of a chair and pulled it on, doing up the buttons as he stood beside the bed. "And I'm here, holding my son and daughter because I've been a complete idiot. I love them, and I love you, Lisa. I've been falling in love with you for weeks, but I was too stubborn and fixated on my own concerns and projects to understand what was happening. Can you forgive me?"

She looked up at him, then over at the twins, then around the room before meeting his eyes again. "I know I didn't have strong pain meds, but I think I'm hallucinating. Did you ask me to forgive you?"

"Yes." He gave her a rueful smile, his dimples pocking his cheeks. "Even living with you—looking after you these past few weeks, finding out what your life had been like growing up—my focus was still on my projects, my own concerns. I didn't take this as seriously as I should have—this business of becoming a father. I was focused on everything I thought was so important, things I wanted, wanted to do, instead of what was truly important—these babies, and you and how much I love you."

"I never thought I would hear you say that." Her lips trembled. "I love you, too."

He chuckled, put down the railing on the side of the bed and leaned over to gingerly gather her into his arms. When he kissed her, warm, sweet happiness spread through her. "I've never said it before. I love you, Lisa, and I admire you for everything you've accomplished, everything you've overcome."

"I love you, too, Ben. My feelings for you have been growing for months, but I didn't realize until yesterday just how much I love you."

Ben kissed her again, then sat beside her and took her hand in his. "I know this might not be the most romantic moment to ask this, but will you marry me? Make a life with me and our kids? Are you willing to marry a man who'll probably be underfoot a lot, make mistakes, annoy you to pieces, but who'll love you and our kids forever?"

Lisa gave him a teasing grin. "That depends. Do you think you can be married to a woman who still wants to be mayor someday? Someone who takes on too many projects and does too much?"

"I'm willing to take the chance if you are."

"Well, then, yes. I'll marry you."

He kissed her again and let her go reluctantly when the door opened to admit Gemma and Carly.

"The entire population of Reston is in the waiting room," Carly announced, marching straight over to the bassinet to admire the babies.

"If I don't take these two so they can be seen through the nursery window by their legions of fans, we're going to have a riot on our hands," Gemma added.

"Go ahead," Ben said. "My fiancée and I would like a little time alone."

"All right," Carly said, giving Gemma a high five. "Our husbands owe us a weekend away. Lisa, we told them Ben was in love with you."

"You were right," Lisa agreed. "And I'm in love with him."

EPILOGUE

"ARE YOU READY?" Big Jim McAdams asked, looking down at Lisa and smiling. "I never thought I'd have a daughter to give away in marriage."

"I'm glad you're willing to do it. And thanks again for convincing Helen to tone down the wedding preparations." Lisa looked at her two best friends, whose bridesmaids' dresses were a shade of deep blue that complemented both their skin tones and hair color. The design was simple, with just enough fullness to accommodate their growing waistlines. They were both expecting to give birth in the spring.

The church sanctuary wasn't swathed in the miles of bunting that Helen had wanted, but baskets of flowers were affixed to every pew along the aisle, and standing baskets of her late-blooming roses marched up the steps to the podium.

Ben waited, with Nathan and Luke beside him, all three of them dressed in tuxedos.

Helen was holding three-month-old Gabriel James and Maureen cradled his sister, Rose Heleen.

Lisa couldn't imagine a more perfect day and a more perfect setting to marry the man she loved.

The past year had been hard in so many ways. Her life had changed, and her goals, even her way of thinking. She had new goals now, new people to love and a new future.

She couldn't wait to get started.

Lisa took a deep breath, looked up at Jim with shining eyes and said, "I'm ready."

* * * * *

*If you loved this book, look for
more in Patricia Forsythe's*
OKLAHOMA GIRLS *miniseries:*

*AT ODDS WITH THE MIDWIFE
THE HUSBAND SHE CAN'T FORGET*

Available now at Harlequin.com!